# Grace Along the Way

# Grace Along the Way

## Jeanne Drouillard

# Grace Along the Way

© Jeanne Drouillard 2012

Published by
Lighthouse Christian Publishing
SAN 257-4330
5531 Dufferin Drive
Savage, Minnesota, 55378
United States of America

www.lighthousechristianpublishing.com

DEDICATED TO:

The One Who Writes All The Books

And

Creates All The Stories

**SPECIAL THANKS:**

*To my daughter, Elena, who taught me what this book is all about. And, thanks to her two sons, Dominic 5, and Jaysonn (known as JJ) 3, who continue my education.*

*Also, thanks to my mom and dad who started me on my journey and are always around me; I'm beginning to recognize you.*

# CHAPTER I

Jeffrey Barnes desperately struggled to keep his attention in history class. He kept brooding about Sunday--another show-and-tell session at the Cambridge Home for Boys. Open houses were humiliating, he thought. He didn't enjoy feeling like a give-away kid. His nerves were always edgy when people looked him over for their own personal reasons. Just thinking of previous times made him shiver with dread.

Being formally presented to everyone had to be the toughest part, and it happened every time. The headmaster gathered all of the children together in front of a group of prospective couples and walked down the line introducing each one separately. He put his hand on your shoulder, probably for a soothing effect, as he told your age and something extremely personal about your life. Sometimes Jeff felt he'd puke at this point. God, he hated that part. Later he had to talk to strangers, not his personal forte. Even as he grew older, he felt awkward. He remembered one painful time when, at a young age, some potential parents approached him, and his shy personality took a strong hold on him and wouldn't let go.

"Hi, we're the Baileys. I'm Janice, and this is my husband, John."

"Hi," he said forcing a smile, but couldn't quite raise his head. What else was he supposed to say? He suddenly felt unimportant.

"You're Jeffrey Barnes, right?"

"Yes," was all he could think of saying.

"And you're seven years old?"

"Yes, I'm seven." He knew his part of the conversation was clumsy. Still, he wondered how was he supposed to talk to these people. He didn't know them. He wanted to make a good impression. He wanted to be adopted. But his mind always froze.

"What do you like to do?"

"I play baseball and basketball," he said shakily, then added, "I ... I do like ... school." Did that seem okay, he wondered? He couldn't quite look them in the eye.

"Well, that's nice. And you do have a nice smile, Jeffrey."

"Thanks." Another short answer.

"We'll see you later, okay?"

They both smiled as they walked away. They hadn't talked long, but then no one did. He wanted to yell for them to come back and talk some more. He'd like them to know he really was a fun and interesting kid when you got to know him. Instead, a crushed feeling took over as he watched them walk away. He suddenly felt depressed.

A loud noise startled him back to the present. Several heads suddenly turned in his direction. John Talbot, who sat directly behind him, dropped his book on the floor. Jeff almost forgot where he was. And Grade 6 at St. Mary's Catholic Boys' School happened to be his current stepping-stone.

He looked around swiftly. Apparently, no one noticed his wandering attention. He didn't even know how long he'd been daydreaming. He looked up and saw Sister Margaret working at her desk in front of the classroom. She would cleverly peer from behind her glasses that were purposely positioned part way down her nose. Most of the other students thought she was engrossed in her paperwork and unable to keep a roving eye.

Jeff knew better. Although her head was at a downward angle, he knew she could see them all trying to defy the rules of good behavior. He was sure Sister always had them in her sight.

Nervously awaiting his turn, he hoped he'd know the answer to whatever question she threw at him. He had studied. He always studied. Yet, he still felt anxious. Knowing he must perform well kept him tense. But he knew succeeding academically was his escape--his path to a solid future. His hands started to sweat, and his body took on a predictable tenseness as he waited. His turn had to come soon.

"Okay, Jeffrey, you get the next question." He concealed his annoyance at being called Jeffrey. He liked Jeff much better.

"Yes, Sister Margaret Mary," he answered anxiously. He jumped up from his seat so fast he banged his knee on the side of his desk. Darn, he knew his face showed pain.

"Here now, just a moment. Let's see what question I have for you today."

Jeff often wondered if Sister purposely paused to create tension. She seemed to do that to everyone. Didn't she know what question she'd ask next? He saw her trying to rearrange her notes, but then, she always seemed to be doing that. Jeff's mind was racing back to his study time and the answers he'd memorized. He hoped she'd pick a question he knew. Come on, Sister, he thought, let's get this over.

"Okay, Jeffrey, can you name the third President of the United States and give us a little detail about him?"

Jeff cleared his throat, giving himself a moment to think. "Yes, that would be President Thomas Jefferson," he answered, luckily remembering some facts. He continued, "He studied many languages, law, mathematics, and philosophy. He was an architect and an inventor--I think he invented the American system of money and, he was a good musician." Almost as an afterthought, he added, "And he bought the Louisiana Territory."

Jeff had been in his own world of thoughts during his response. It was only after he'd finished he even looked at Sister. She seemed to be smiling. Did that mean he did okay? He loved history and had spent many hours reading stories about the presidents. And lucky for him, Sister had picked a question on his favorite president.

"That's right and very good, Jeffrey. You may sit down." Jeff let out a big sigh of relief. He did okay. At least today, he did okay.

As he sat, he heard several eager boys behind him make comments. They were teasing him, but also slightly irritated at his good and ready answer that he threw out easily and effortlessly.

"Gees, Jeff, did you memorize the entire presidential history of our country or was that a lucky guess?" said one of the students cynically.

"Probably a little bit of both, but I do like Thomas Jefferson. He's one of my favorites."

"Oh, my God, he's got a crush on a president," chorused a few boys.

Several of the boys involuntarily giggled aloud, catching the attention of Sister Margaret. Usually one glare from her small blue-green eyes that could look cold and threatening when needed, halted most further remarks. But Jeff was surprised as a few more comments made it through.

Another student remembered, "Don't forget, Jeff likes classical music, too, so it figures."

"I like rock and roll, and even some jazz," Jeff said defensively. "But I happen to like President Jefferson."

These guys could be so funny, he thought. Jeff's snicker was involuntary, but he wondered how long Sister would remain silent. Yet the discussion wasn't over.

"Somewhat of a nerd, if you ask me," muttered one student.

And another grumbled, "Maybe just a little suck up going on today."

Sister cleared her throat signaling to keep the conversation decent and refrain from unpleasant remarks.

"Hey, give him a break. He does study a lot." That was Frank Anderson, one of his friends.

"Any other presidents that you like?"

"Well, I'm happy President Clinton got elected for a second term."

"Yeah, but that's present day. Maybe I could just study your history notes, or better yet, we could eat lunch together before a test, and it would be just like studying."

Jeff stated. "We do have group sessions now. You could join us anytime. We'd all welcome the extra help. How about it?"

Jeff would have liked his regular study group to expand. After all, the semester wasn't even half over, and he didn't know how he'd do tomorrow or next week. A good academic record meant everything to him at this point in his life. He was desperate for it.

"Don't think I'm in your league, Jeff, but if I ever decide to run for Congress someday, I may call on you." Several students reacted silly to that remark. But he saw a few look at him with approval.

"Okay, now, settle down," said Sister seriously. "This'll be it for today. The bell will ring in about fifteen minutes, and I want to remind you we have a test on Chapter 2 of your history book next Thursday. There's a practice test at the end of the chapter, so if you can answer those questions, you'll do well on the test. Also, pay special attention to pages twenty-two through thirty. Now, you can use the last few minutes for study. Don't forget to stop in my office tomorrow to discuss your biweekly progress."

Jeff was certain Sister would now walk back to her desk and proceed to write notes on today's class. And she did. Sister Margaret seemed to write notes every day at the end of class. He figured she must have a total record on him as well as every other kid in this room. But he liked her. She was fun and liked to joke around sometimes, but also took time to help anyone who wanted it. He was glad she was one nun who was good at teaching boys. Some of the others, he'd heard, had to teach girls since they were considered easier. Some adults had remarked Sister was a little off center at times, but Jeff figured that must be a good thing.

* * *

Waiting his turn outside Sister Margaret's office, Jeffrey sat on the rather uncomfortable simulated park bench provided. He looked up and down the corridor trying to amuse himself. Time passed slowly. All was quiet. He felt somewhat isolated. Most children had already been picked up. But he was sure Sister would get him out in time to make the bus.

As the door opened and his friend Frank Anderson walked out smiling, Jeffrey got up from his seat and walked into Sister's office. She always seemed to have a bunch of papers on her desk and a rather large collection of folders, some of which Jeffrey knew were the other students' files.

"Sit down, Jeffrey. I'll be with you in a moment," she said as she finished her busy routine, which never seemed to end.

He sat comfortably in the large brown leather chair on the other side of her crowded table. Her office wasn't very large really, although it did have room for two other chairs, which were situated on either side of his chair. Jeff was quite certain the other two chairs were probably for parents when Sister had a meeting with them and their child. He'd never had one of those meetings; he didn't have any parents.

Looking around, he noticed there were only a few religious pictures on the wall, one of which was Jesus after the Resurrection. He wasn't surprised Sister had this picture of Jesus since she always looked at the positive side of life. It wasn't that Sister ignored the suffering aspect; he just figured she didn't concentrate on it very much. Jeffrey liked that; he liked that a lot.

"Well now," Sister said pleasantly as she put away the other file, "you sure do know a lot about Thomas Jefferson. That was an excellent answer you gave in class."

Jeff felt proud. "Thanks. I do like him. I think he was a good president. In fact, the history books say he was a 'great' or 'near great' president."

"Yes, he was, Jeffrey, and he made some good decisions for our country. I think you're progressing nicely in both my history and religion class. How are your other classes? Any problems?"

"No, not really. Math is hard, especially the algebra part, but if I keep at it, I understand it. Mr. Larson told us the other day no one is flunking his class. He said we're all moving ahead nicely. That's good. English is fine, and I'm okay in Science. I think I'm okay right now."

"That's good," said Sister thoughtfully as he saw her check his folder. "Your record here shows you're doing good work in all your classes. But then, you do apply yourself, and your study habits have greatly improved. Now, maybe you could lighten up, just a little. Good study habits do help, don't they?"

He knew Sister thought he was too serious. But he was alone in the world. Didn't she get it? He had to stay aware so he could always do his best.

"Good study habits mean everything," Jeff admitted agreeably as he shifted in the big chair, trying to find a comfortable position. "When we first talked, honestly, I didn't get it. But now, I know how important it is to keep up with my classes and not get behind. Other kids might get more help at home than I do, but at the orphanage some of the kids tease me. They think schoolwork is dumb. But I don't, and I'm glad I can use the study hall here sometimes when I need to."

"Jeffrey, that's one of the reasons you were chosen to attend this school. Others had their chance, but some didn't want to work. They were put back into public school. Now, there isn't anything wrong with public school, and if they work and study, they'll get a good education. But our school will give you more exacting work and better prepare you for high school and college if you show an interest--and you've done that."

"I'm already eleven, you know; I probably won't get adopted now. Hey, I'm not being negative, Sister," he added as he saw the uncertain look on her face. "I'm stating a fact. A lot of older kids don't get adopted. That's true. I've got to be able to face that. And that'll mean I won't have anyone to help me later, if I should need it. I want to study hard and do good so I'll be okay ... know what I mean?"

Just then Jeff noticed a familiar expression cross Sister's face and added, "I know you say I think too much, but I have to. I must prepare myself, you know?"

"I do understand and that's pretty neat. But you're such a serious thinker. Some older children get adopted sometimes, right? I know you've had a few foster home placements that didn't work out, but don't give up, okay?"

"I'm not giving up, honest, I'm not. Sure, I know it could happen, but I must be prepared if it doesn't. If I'm supposed to be alone, that's okay. But I've got to be ready."

"Isn't there an open house at the orphanage this Sunday?"

"Yeah, there is," answered Jeff as he heard his tone of voice head downward. He didn't want to think about that. That subject made him moody and sometimes gave him a stomachache. So he looked down at the floor, then at his well-polished black shoes that still didn't quite reach the floor from the chair he was sitting on. The stiff collar on his white shirt suddenly became uncomfortable. He fidgeted as his thoughts raced to think of something more pleasant.

He knew Sister must have noticed his nervous reaction to her question. Still he had to wonder how she'd react to being presented at an open house. She didn't know how upsetting it could be. No one knew, except the other kids.

Sister continued. "Well, Sunday could be a good day for you. You could get chosen again, but even if you don't, they usually have good food and fun games, right?"

"Yes, that's true and everyone is on their best behavior," Jeff answered easily. "That's usually fun to watch. But what I don't like," said Jeff, continuing in a softer tone, to himself mostly, "is the fact that I feel like I'm on display, you know? People come and look at you and they smile nice, especially if they're looking for an older boy. Then maybe they see a boy they think looks better than you and off they go. That hurts."

For a moment Jeff didn't talk. What more was there to say? Life was just the way it was. This topic was depressing, so he tried to think about something else. Then Sister changed the subject with a question.

"Remember what I taught you in religion class a few weeks ago? I know it's a new thought and will take time to understand, but do you remember what I said?"

"Yeah, sure. You said we should cooperate with the graces we are given.

"That's right. So you at least remembered what I said."

"But I don't think I understand it." He searched Sister's face for a possible clue.

"That's okay, Jeffrey. I'm just starting to present some new thoughts for you to analyze. Many adults wouldn't know what that meant either. So again, it's the fact that God loves all of his children, not just some of them. And he gives different graces to each of us. If we fight these graces, we don't get the benefit from them. But if we cooperate with them, then life can change in a good way for us, understand?"

"Sort of," answered Jeffrey aloud, but inside he felt confused.

"Well, God has no favorites; He loves us all the same." And Sister ended the discussion.

But Jeff continued. "Do you mean God loves me as much as Frank Anderson? Frank has a mother, father, sister, his own dog and lives in a nice house. His mother is always there with him in the morning before class, and his family goes on vacations and they do fun things. Are you saying God loves me as much as Frank, because right now, it don't seem to me that He does."

"Yes, He does love you as much. Everyone's life is different, Jeffrey, and for someone who'd been so alone, now you've got some friends, and you're doing great in school. You don't know what'll happen in your life tomorrow or Sunday, for that matter." Sister paused for a moment, and Jeff saw her give him a reassuring look. "Everyone's life isn't going to be the same, and that's just the way it is."

"Yeah, I know," Jeff answered thoughtfully. "And a few times I got to go to a sleepover at Frank's house, and his mom and dad are always nice to me. That's something I didn't have a few years ago. Frank's mom and dad said they like me a lot. They really said that to me."

"I know, You've told me about the fun you've had at the Anderson home. I'm sure his parents like you; you're a nice boy."

Feeling immediate embarrassment, he continued at once to change the tone of Sister's last remark.

"Maybe you're saying that I cooperated with some of God's graces then."

"Maybe you did," said Sister, and Jeff noticed she was laughing.

"That means then I can be cooperating with grace without knowing it when good things happen."

"Well, that's certainly part of it, of course, but not everything happens immediately. I think your bus will be coming soon, so that'll be all for now. Think about what I've said and stay positive about Sunday, okay? Just have a good time. And--"

"I know, I know. Cooperate with the graces I'm given."

"That's right, and don't forget to have a good time, too." Sister smiled at him as she completed the session.

"Yeah, I will."

# CHAPTER II

Jeff sat alone on the bus ride back to the orphanage. He preferred sitting by himself with his elbow on the window frame looking out the dirty pane of glass. He could dream whatever he wanted about his present and future life. No one could tell him his dreams were impossible because Jeff didn't share his dreams with anyone. Somehow though, at odd times, he felt someone was paying attention. It was a strange feeling he got every now and then, but he always knew someone out there was listening to him.

Back at the Cambridge Home for Boys, Jeff immediately went to his room and changed from his uniform into his play clothes. He only had two white shirts and two pairs of black pants, one for winter and one for summer. His shiny black shoes were also part of the dress inspection, so he'd change into his running shoes. He felt he must stay on good report and that meant keeping his clothes in good shape. Until now, he'd held his own on his personal hygiene and clothes inspections, and he planned to continue. In his eleven-year-old mind, he thought his best chance at life was doing well in school and staying friends with Sister Margaret.

A loud bang against his bedroom door startled Jeff. As he rushed to see what was happening, he heard silly voices.

"See what you made me do, Tim? Now you've got Jeff upset," said Nick, one of the other boys who lived on his floor. Turning to Jeff he added, "Tim pushed me, and I slipped against your door. Sorry. But, as you can see, I'm the one carrying most of the stuff."

Jeff was laughing. "That's okay. You two just keep me awake, that's all. What's going on?"

"Steve's not around, is he?" asked Tim with a nervous tone to his voice as he peeked a little inside Jeff's bedroom. Tim and Nick were both somewhat hesitant around his roommate.

"No, he's not back from school yet." Jeff knew this would calm Tim considerably. "So what's happening?"

"We're heading down to the baseball field. Come on down if you want, okay?"

"I just might. Are we having a game today or just practice?"

"Not sure, but if Tim here stays as clubfooted as he's been, we'll probably lose anyway. Come on down, we need a level-headed player like you, okay?"

"I might come later," Jeff said thoughtfully as he watched them go laughing down the hall, clumsily hitting each other along the way.

Jeff's thoughts returned to what Sister had said about cooperating with grace along the way. That phrase was totally beyond him. He didn't get it. He certainly knew what the word cooperate meant. It was like don't fight something, but go along with it and along the way was referring to as you grow and live and mature in your daily life. But the word grace was the most confusing to him. What was a grace anyway? Sister said grace could be like a kick in the pants since it got the intellect moving in the right direction. Or it could be a nagging voice to remind you of things. Jeff wondered if he was supposed to understand this piece of confusion, because he didn't. Maybe in the future he'd figure out what it meant. He'd be a lot smarter then.

* * *

After changing clothes Jeff was about to wander downstairs when his roommate Steve Johnson came in.

"Hey, Jeff, how's it going, little buddy?"

Steve was usually cheerful and somewhat flippant.

"Not bad, Steve, how about with you?"

"Good. Real good. Yep, I did pretty good today."

Steve actually sang his comments as Jeff watched him prance around the room for increasing visual effect.

Jeff laughed. "Does that mean you passed your math test?" he asked, feeling hopeful as he searched Steve's striking blue eyes for a clue. He didn't get any, which prolonged the suspense.

Steve had grown to a respectable height for fourteen years old; Jeff envied that. He liked his sense of humor and light-spirited personality, when he chose to show it. He usually didn't let too many things bother him, at least not that anyone could tell. Jeff was the only one who knew that sometimes in the dark, uncertain night, Steve wasn't always so casual about his life.

"You know, Jeff, I think I just may have passed it," he finally said smugly. "I'd have to be really dumb to flunk it with all the help you gave me."

Steve sent a big satisfied smile toward him. He'd already flunked one grade and got discouraged easily. But then Jeff knew no one had ever helped him.

"Yep, we may beat the odds together and get me through this math stuff yet. And you'll also be happy to know we've had a rather dull week at school."

"No kidding. No problems at all?"

Steve went to a different school that got regular visits from the police for drugs, smoking, fighting, etc. Steve seemed to relish the excitement.

Steve added proudly, "That's right. It was rather boring. Nothing happened."

"Well, I'm glad about that," Jeff said laughingly. "It's been about two weeks, right? That's pretty good for Roosevelt."

"Yeah, that's about right. But Roosevelt's a big school. Shit--normal for them is at least once a week."

"True, and sometimes it's serious. Remember last year, you told me about that kid who got beat up pretty bad? Did he ever make it back to school?" Jeff noticed Steve was rather serious about that incident.

"Yeah, he's back this year. I remember seeing him, but he's still limping. His leg was broken in a bunch of places. What a bunch of retards."

"Are those other boys still there?" asked Jeff.

"No, no, no. One was expelled, but the instigator landed in jail. Not sure for how long."

"Doesn't seem worth it," Jeff said quietly.

"No, it's not. But those kids are into peer stuff. Get it? If someone insults you, you have to save your reputation. At least that's what I heard it was about."

"I'm sure I'd walk away," Jeff said adding a casual hand gesture.

"Yeah, but Jeff, you don't think like those kids. They have to be first, you know? Numero uno. If anyone tries to bring them down, well, shit, they get even. That's their rules."

Jeff thought Steve seemed to know a lot about these kids. Yet, he didn't appear to be one of them.

"You don't think like that." Jeff's comment was almost a question.

"Number one, number ten, no difference to me. It's really all crap. But I do understand where they're coming from. They're gang groupies, you know, and they have this gang mentality. But it's just a few at the school. Most of the kids are okay."

Jeff remembered living alone without a roommate for almost six months. He felt alone at night when he had to be in his room with lights out, especially when sleep wouldn't come. Then Steve was moved into his room, and the atmosphere changed drastically.

"I'm going to play ball. Got to work off that hard brain work from the math test," Steve said jokingly. "You coming?"

"No, I'd better not. I've got some notes to check."

"Hey, you can't always study. Come on, play some ball."

Jeff thought for a moment, then answered, "Maybe later. I need to correct a few things."

As he watched Steve change for the game, Jeff began to believe their friendship had a chance to pass the test of time, even though their goals were different. Jeff wanted to go to college and get a degree as a way to secure his future. Steve had no college ambition and thought he'd wait and see what life would throw at him.

\* \* \*

Later, while getting ready for dinner, the conversation turned to the open house. Steve wasn't eligible for adoption at this time, but he was considered for foster homes. Jeff knew Steve tried to hide his apprehension.

"How are you feeling about Sunday, Jeff? Any worries?"

"I never like it, and I'm always nervous. That's normal for me. Don't think much will happen anyway. People always pick someone else. But I've had two trials already, and it's hard when it doesn't work out, you know? I think I'm okay here." Jeff knew he didn't fool Steve. He wanted to be adopted, but was tired of being rejected. "What about you? Are you hoping for a foster home or not?"

"I'm not sure. There are real advantages, as long as I don't become too attached. And a foster home set-up can last for years. Oh, crap, I'm a lot like you; I don't want to get my hopes up either. Life sucks for kids like you and me, doesn't it? Other kids only worry about keeping good grades, and what cool kids are doing, or maybe getting a speed bike or something normal. You and I get to wonder where we'll be living and for how long. Life just sucks, that's all."

Over the more than nine months they'd been roommates, Jeff was surprised how Steve shared his true feelings here in the privacy of their bedroom. No one outside this room suspected Steve had hurt feelings inside and a pain that didn't seem to go away. Heck, Jeff knew Steve didn't trust people and would never show his true feelings, but then, he didn't either.

Yet Jeff tried to keep optimism in his doubt. Steve had decided life was mostly ugly and crappy, yet he played the role of a happy-go-lucky kid who loved to play jokes on people. He never let his guard down, except with Jeff. But even Jeff had learned never to cross a certain line. He could seldom mention religion, no cute little hopeful remarks, and only a slight optimism was ever allowed. Jeff hoped Steve would mellow in time and become more satisfied with his life, as well as hopeful about his future. And he was expanding somewhat, but very slowly.

"Let's forget Sunday, okay? Crap, it's so damn depressing," Steve said grumpily. "What are you doing tonight? We might go to that baseball game if we get enough escorts. You want to go?"

"No, I'd better not. I've got to study my history and math. Two big tests next week. And not much time to study this weekend."

"Study again. Gees. You can't always study, and you're doing great. Take a break and go to the game."

"Maybe next time, but I need to do well on these tests."

Just then the dinner bell rang, and they went downstairs to the dining room. They were allowed more free time on Friday evenings, so later many watched TV or played indoor or outdoor games. It wasn't often they got to go somewhere away from the orphanage, especially the younger children. Much of the time they were a family within themselves and offered each other companionship and activities. Tonight the older boys had opted for a ball game, and Saturday night would be a late movie because it had special low rates. Steve and other teenagers would be allowed to go.

\* \* \*

Back in his room, Jeff attempted to study as he straddled his bed with mountains of paperwork and books. Tests gave him butterflies and, although he felt pleased with his progress, he wasn't comfortable enough to avoid any extra study time. Before Sister Margaret helped him develop better study habits, he nearly flunked math, religion, and biology. But not history; Jeff always did well in history. Having any extra time at all meant he could review, and that helped him relax more when taking tests.

However, tonight anxiety was consuming him, and he couldn't relax enough to study. Parades of uncontrolled thoughts quickly crossed his mind. He didn't even know what was bothering him. Dark shadows were trying to overtake his enthusiasm and alarm him. He felt quite alone. That's the one tough part of being an orphan, he thought. No one really cares about me. They take care of me, feed me and make sure I'm okay, but they don't really love me. It'd be nice to have a mother and father who loved me and cared whether I passed an exam. It would be great for someone to wonder if I were feverish and sick and want me to be well.

Frank Anderson's mom had been worried about him when she dropped him off at school on Tuesday. She had felt his forehead and spoke to one of the teachers, saying if he got any worse to call her and she'd come and take him home. I wonder what that would feel like, he thought, I don't know. If I get sick, the orphanage is concerned about me, but in a different way. Sometimes he felt frustrated that he couldn't even put his feelings into logical thoughts.

Since he couldn't study, and his thinking process wasn't producing what he'd hoped for, Jeff decided to put his books away. He could clean his room and get some sleep. No sense wasting time. Tomorrow he'd try again with a clear, rested mind. Staring at the ceiling, he tried to relax, but tension crept throughout his body and more frightening impressions crossed his mind. He managed to fall asleep quickly, but repeatedly woke up. His broken cycle of interrupted sleep brought sweat beads to his forehead, as something from his dream world came forward almost to consciousness, then backed off in irritating withdrawal.

What's bothering me? Jeff wondered. He realized he sometimes got vague reminders of his earlier years that teased and worried him. What had happened to him so scary that it still created dark gloomy memories? Some nights he almost remembered an important feeling, but then it was gone so quickly he couldn't even remember the thought.

He recalled certain things in his young life; some memories made sense but many didn't. He half recalled at five years old living with his father in a trailer park. He could still remember a few details of the fateful night that changed his life.

Coming out from the bathroom, Jeff looked for his father in the kitchen. He wasn't there. Then he noticed him lying on the floor in the living room. He thought his dad was playing a game with him.

"Daddy, daddy, get up--play with me." He waited, but there was no response.

"Daddy, daddy, play with me. Okay?" Again, no response.

Jeff walked up to his dad, who lay motionless on the floor. He thought he'd fallen asleep. He touched him on the shoulder, but there was no response.

"Daddy, you scare me. Talk with me." Jeff felt something was wrong, and he was close to tears. His dad wouldn't wake up. Usually his dad was cooking dinner about now, but he couldn't smell anything good.

For a while, Jeff sat there waiting for him to wake up. He began rocking his body back and forth, as he anchored his arms around his knees. He remembered singing to himself, just a little. He was scared. He couldn't help crying aloud. His daddy looked funny.

"What's wrong, daddy?" he asked. No answer. His dad always played with him, and always talked to him. But now he didn't.

Jeff didn't know what to do. He needed someone, but he was never allowed to play outside alone. He couldn't visit any of the other people in the trailer park unless his dad was with him. What should he do? The blue trailer across the way was off limits for him and so was the other silver one. But he had to find someone. He sat there crying, wondering what to do.

Just then, there was a knock on the door. He'd been told never to answer the door. So at first, he didn't. He continued to cry. Then he heard a familiar voice.

"Jeff, Jeff, it's Mr. Allen from the blue trailer across the road. Are you all right? I can hear you crying."

He ran to the door with red eyes and tears coming down his face.

"Daddy's on the floor, and he won't get up. He's sleeping, but he won't get up. Can you get him up, Mr. Allen? Can you?"

"Open the door, Jeff, and I'll try and help."

Mr. Allen rushed in and held his dad for a moment. Then he turned and Jeff heard him say, "I'm going to get your dad some help, okay? You come with me while I make a phone call, okay?" Jeff didn't know if he should leave his dad. And he wasn't allowed to go to the blue trailer alone. But Mr. Allen took his hand and led him to the blue trailer across the way.

Soon the police came, then the ambulance. They took his dad away. Jeff stayed with the neighbors. He didn't know them very well. They told him the hospital was taking care of his dad. He remembered being scared sleeping in a bed inside the blue trailer, especially because his dad wasn't there.

A few days later, the entire trailer park knew Mr. Barnes, Sr. was dead. All except Jeff, that is. Someone had to tell him, and that job was given to Mr. Allen.

"Jeff, I'm so sorry, but the hospital couldn't help your dad."

"Oh, when is my dad coming back?" Jeff asked fearfully.

"Nobody could help your dad, so he went to heaven."

He saw Mr. Allen getting tears in his eyes.

"Then my dad won't ever come back. Never?" Jeff felt scared and confused.

"No, I'm sorry. Your dad won't come back."

Jeff cried and cried. Then the social worker came over with a policeman, and Mr. Allen talked to all of them. They said they'd take care of him.

"But where will I live? You've got to tell my dad so he can find me." Again, they explained to him his dad had died and wasn't coming back. Finally, he understood. And then Jeff got quiet and wouldn't talk anymore.

During his first few days at the orphanage, no one bothered to ask Jeff any questions. Because of his youth, he was ignored. Yet he knew things. He did have some memories. And some things were important, but he didn't know how to put them in any kind of order.

Jeff remembered many things. He had dreams about another man and woman and a little white dog. The images were blurry, but the woman came into his room at night before he went to sleep and gave him a kiss on the forehead. But he couldn't remember her face anymore, and he couldn't hear what she said.

* * *

During the next few years, Jeff couldn't make sense of the relationship between his dad, who'd recently died, and other people in his dreams. Who were these people? He didn't know. Why did they keep coming back? At first, he thought perhaps the man from the trailer park was his grandfather because he was older than other kids' parents. He always wondered, but never asked. Then one night when he was about seven and a half years old and supposed to be asleep, he'd wandered downstairs to the kitchen in search of food. This particular night was to be a turning point in his young life. An unforeseen occurrence completely changed his thinking and attitude. It was so dramatic that his future existence was changed forever.

Jeff was one of the few children at the orphanage who'd learned to use the stairs at night and still be able to avoid the creaks. This was a tough challenge. He knew that on the third and sixth step from the top of the stairs, your foot had to land to the right of the center area, but not quite at the railing to maneuver the stairs correctly. If you knew this, you could make it all the way downstairs without creaking the steps and therefore not get caught by the house-parents. The return trip up the stairs also needed caution on the same numbered steps using the reverse strategy, which made the accomplishment easier.

This particular night, having mastered the staircase, Jeff crept quietly along the dark corridor leading to the kitchen. He heard some voices talking from the area of the comfort room where the house-parents sat at night and talked or watched TV and had coffee.

"It's sad about Jeffrey, isn't it? He truly is a nice little boy."

He'd heard his name and stopped immediately. Had they seen him? He wasn't sure. He stood totally still, shaking a little and feeling defenseless. The voices continued. Was that Juanita Hernandez? He wasn't sure. No one came out into the hallway. That was good. Maybe he could hear what they were saying. He wanted to know something about his early life. No one would tell him anything when he asked.

They talked more. "Yes, he's probably one of the most likeable kids here. But he's such a serious lad. I wonder where he's from."

"No one knows for sure, but the man he was living with in that trailer park wasn't his birth father."

"Are they sure about that?" said one surprised voice.

"Oh, yes, they took blood tests due to suspicions and confirmed that the DNA established beyond a doubt this man couldn't possibly be his father. Furthermore, they said he couldn't even be related to him. No doubt about it."

This voice was firm and opinionated. There was no hint of doubt detected in her tone.

"What do they think this was about? It all sounds quite strange."

"Well, rumor has it that Jeff must have been one of those kids who was snatched away from his real parents. Who knows why? Maybe he was a lonesome old man. It was decided had he been the grandfather, they could trace his name and possibly come up with some relatives. But with no DNA match, they thought the name was probably made up, too."

"So no one knows for sure who Jeffrey Barnes is?"

"Nope, or even if he is Jeffrey Barnes."

"That's right. The name was probably changed."

Jeff felt strange. They couldn't be talking about him, he thought. He was Jeffrey Barnes.

"Sure, and if he was snatched, that means there probably isn't a trail to follow. I heard they'd posted his picture on TV and put up posters, but the police didn't believe he was from this part of the country. It's too bad because now that this man is gone, it would have been nice to find his real family. They've probably been panicking for a few years. But where do you start? Oh, yeah, they looked through all of the missing children's photos, but nothing came up. At least the old man took good care of him."

"Well, that's a sad story--very sad indeed."

"Do you want to watch TV for a while?"

The noise from the TV covered the rest of the conversation and brought Jeff back to the present. He'd been so glued against the wall of the corridor that he actually felt invisible and merged into the plaster. Feelings of horror at hearing the word 'snatched' were so severe his stomach suddenly ached sharply, and he had to grab it with both hands. He feared they must have heard him, but they just continued to talk and didn't even turn a head in his direction. And he was thankful he didn't have to face the house-parents, not only for his attempt at sneaking food, but, more importantly, for overhearing information that wasn't meant for his ears.

Jeff felt fortunate having remained motionless and able to fight his inner panic urging him to run away from this frightful scene. He took a quiet, long, deep breath and let it out slowly and carefully, hoping it would keep him from fainting. His mind raced with this new information. He'd definitely lost his appetite.

When he recovered from his shock, he inched his way ever so carefully back along the corridor he'd come from. He was almost undetectable as he climbed the stairs back to his room, being extremely watchful to avoid the two steps that squeaked even under his light weight.

Luckily, he made it back to his room without waking his roommate and immediately headed for the bathroom. That was the one place he could cry, and not be heard. He closed the door cautiously and grabbed a towel placing it over his mouth to muffle the noise of his tears. And there were many tears flowing out at that moment. For almost ten minutes he couldn't stop crying, so he let the tears come. Finally they subsided somewhat.

Gees, he cried, so many awful things happened to me. When will this ever stop? I'm trying to be good. I'm trying to do what I'm told. Then I learn new things about my life and it makes it harder. I keep learning things that upset me. Did somebody just grab me away from my mom and dad? Oh, my God. Maybe I really do have a mom and dad somewhere. How much more is there for me to find out? Nobody at the orphanage tells me anything. It's my life; I should have been told.

Now he remembered the memories that kept coming up in his dreams. That woman who came into his room at night and kissed him on the forehead was probably his real mother. How he yearned to remember her face. And the man who occasionally showed up in his dreams was possibly his real father. He did have someone who cared about him. At that moment Jeff knew somewhere in this world there were people who loved him, and that made the world seem friendlier. But he also knew he'd probably never find them, and that dashed him into devastating despair. He had real parents somewhere who wanted him, and he wanted them desperately. Yet, they'd probably never find each other.

That episode happened almost four years ago, and Jeff never told anyone. Whom would he tell? Would anyone even care anymore? Yet the drama did answer some questions for him but it also brought more dreams with memories always irritatingly in the background of his mind. However, with this new confirmation of events in his life, things were beginning to make sense to him.

He'd never made the connection at five years old that this man was not his father, at least not consciously. He never knew exactly what bothered him, but his confused feelings were proven right by this casual unexpected conversation. And even with the newer void settling over him, there was a symbolic satisfaction at knowing his remembrances were correct and not the result of an unbridled imagination. These were precious memories, and he was thankful for each of them separately and collectively. It was all he had of an earlier happy life, and he planned to savor the memories.

Sometimes just before an open house these memories came back in full force. Then Jeff realized this was what he'd been fighting today. I guess that's why I couldn't study, he thought. It's the past coming back and getting in the way. He remembered this happening before other open days, too. In a few days, I'll probably get back to normal, he thought hoping he was right.

As his mind kept working overtime, his young body had depleted itself by the energy used to figure out his complicated life. Before he knew it, Jeff was lying in bed realizing he'd just woke up, and it was now 7:30 a.m. Saturday--time to get up.

He knew he was allowed to sleep in a little longer on the weekend, and decided to take advantage of it.

Looking over at Steve, he realized he was still sound asleep and chose to cater to the luxury of the extra half hour or so himself. He could happily go back and forth between the twilight zone and reality for a while. And with that thought on his satisfied mind, Jeff nodded off again and was surprised when the alarms were going off at 8:30 in the morning.

The time had come to begin his Saturday routine of chores, study time and, of course, preparation for the open house on Sunday. There was only one more day before open house. Saturday would pass quickly, and before he knew it, the sun would be coming up over the horizon and Sunday, open-house day, would be staking its claim to be noticed.

# CHAPTER III

Jeffrey opened his eyes and felt his body shiver from the surprisingly cold weather taking place in the middle of September. Turning his head toward the window thermometer, he noted forty-two degrees. The low forties is cold for this time of year, he thought. Dipping into the fifties during early fall is much more common. If he'd known, the window would have stayed closed.

Wiggling his toes under the blanket brought him new warmth. He lay perfectly still. Any movement at all would remove him from the body warmth he'd created for himself. What a luxury Sunday was, he thought. Chores were finished on Saturday. Only a dribble of homework was left for Sunday, which left plenty of time for fun and surprises.

Then, in a sudden moment, Jeffrey's mood changed. Oh, no, he remembered. Today is open house day. Show and tell again. He knew there wasn't much chance of his getting selected. His stomach was already tightening up. He wished he could escape.

In an attempt to bolster his attitude, he turned on the radio. He enjoyed classical music at times, much to the disdain of the other boys. For that reason, he usually satisfied himself when he was alone. Steve was a heavy sleeper. It wouldn't disturb him. Then the announcer said:.

"Today, our temperature will only be in the upper fifties. That's cool for this time of year, but we've got a warm up coming. So stay positive about the sun, even when it isn't shining."

Looking over at Steve, he noticed his friend was sleeping right through the alarm clock. He laughed a little--so what else was new? Must've been a late night. Steve was still snoring, right through the second alarm. Should I wake him? he thought, but wanted to stay in bed himself. Maybe we can both get a few more minutes. I don't want to get up anyway.

A few minutes later, he realized that time was moving quickly when he would have liked it to creep slowly. Jeff called Steve's name a few times and knew immediately that he wasn't even making a dent into his dream world.

"Steve, Steve, it's time to get up." Jeff repeated his alarm-like tone of voice at twenty-second intervals. He got increasingly louder until Steve slowly started to move in his bed and resembled a small animal that just realized there were others around him trying to get his attention.

He saw Steve roll over slowly and sluggishly as he finally opened one of his eyes, then with effort managed to half open the other. Jeff saw Steve's surprise as he found himself looking directly into Jeff's serious eyes. His face, along with the rest of his body, was presently sitting in the middle of Steve's bed and staring thoughtfully as well as anxiously into his person. Despite his dreamlike state, Jeff saw him fake a slow smile at seeing his little friend so eager for him to get up.

"It can't yet be time to get up, Jeff. Are you serious?"

"Yes it is," answered Jeff enthusiastically. "Remember, today is open house, so we have to get up in time to eat earlier and get our rooms cleaned up."

"Oh, shit, I almost forgot," said Steve, interrupting and finally getting back to reality.

Stretching in several directions in an attempt to release tension, Steve looked considerably more awake to Jeff. He began talking rationally.

"Another open house. That's two since the beginning of summer--usually three or four a year is tops. Okay, okay, I know you want your room clean, little buddy, but just give me a few more minutes, okay?"

Jeff knew Steve's routine completely. He was the type of guy who was tough to wake up, but once awake, he seldom went back for catnaps as Jeff liked to do. He did like to lie there for a few minutes before he forced his body to make the vertical attempt since it was so comfortable in its present horizontal position. Knowing this, Jeff spoke.

"Okay, you're awake. I'm going to take my shower. See you in three minutes."

A three-minute shower allotment of time was the general rule, and Jeff always tried to follow the rules. But this was Sunday; everyone was lazy today. He could take a longer shower and still be okay.

\* \* \*

As always, Jeff was careful how he used his things in the shower. He cautiously unraveled his towel, washrag, and soap as well as his shampoo and toothbrush. He wished for a moment he had a lot of belongings like the other kids at school. All he owned could be packed into one grocery bag, possibly two if he were allowed to take his school uniforms, too. All the more reason for caution, he thought.

Although he took a longer shower today, Jeff hated it to end. He didn't feel at all guilty he'd pushed the rules to the limit. He needed a good feeling about himself before he faced this difficult day. His mind traveled back to one of his previous attempts in a foster home. They weren't pleasant memories. He thought this particular home for boys was possibly his favorite place to be. He knew what to expect here, and that was a comfort. His first experience at six years old caused him anxiety at the mere thought.

"I'm the real kid here, the first you know. I can't understand why my parents even brought you here. I don't want you in this house. Never. You're not going to stay, you know. I'm going to make sure they take you back."

This was eight-year-old Jeremy Sullivan. Jeff thought he talked crazy. And his eyes got a funny look in them as he paraded around saying awful things. This was how he talked to Jeff, when he talked to him at all.

"Why don't you like me?" asked Jeffrey trembling. Many times, he was scared. "You might like me if you gave me a chance." Why did they bring me here? Jeremy doesn't want me here, and he's mean. I'd rather be at the orphanage. The kids are a lot nicer there. He saw Jeremy pumping his fists again.

"There's nothing to like about you and besides, I like being an only child. I don't want anyone else around, understand? I sure don't want a stupid orphan living here. Your parents probably died on purpose. They didn't want you either. You're a loser."

Jeff saw a frightening and angry person standing in front of him. Jeremy was taller and at least thirty pounds heavier. Jeffrey's stomach hurt. He was scared. But then Jeremy could have scared anyone.

Jeff tried again to make peace. "But we could play together. Wouldn't you like to have someone to play with sometimes?" Even with his hands sweating and fear being close to paralyzing him, Jeff still made the attempt.

"No," answered Jeremy in a nasty insulting tone, "and if I did, it certainly wouldn't be you. Look at all these neat toys I've got. I don't need you. You're so stupid and ugly--just a stupid little orphan. Ha! Ha! You'll be my victim. That's it. I'm going to have fun with you. I'm going to make you so miserable you'll wish you'd never been born." Terrified, Jeff began crying and stood to try and get away. But Jeremy stood strong ready to hit him.

Crying, yet trying to stand up for himself, Jeff said, "I don't like you. You scare me. I'm going to tell dad about you."

"He's my father, and he won't believe you. Anyway, he loves me, you know. So whose side do you think he'll take?

Stupid kid. Don't you see, you can't win. Just go back to the orphanage why don't you?"

Just then, the father rushed in, and you could tell that he'd heard at least part of the discussion. He grabbed Jeremy's arm and told him to apologize. He did, but clearly he didn't mean it. Eric Sullivan was frustrated. He called Joanna to comfort Jeff while he tried to reason again with Jeremy.

"I'm sorry, Jeffrey, this isn't your fault," he said as he walked out tugging Jeremy's arm. Another attempt was made at a serious talk with his son, but nothing ever seemed to make a difference.

That's the way it was from the first day he'd arrived. The parents were nice, but Jeremy was a brother from hell. Too bad, he thought. He liked the parents, his bedroom, and their golden retriever named Parker. But he often wondered why they even brought him here? He didn't know.

One night, when he was supposed to be asleep, Jeff accidentally overheard a chilling conversation between the mother and father.

"I thought a nice, calm kid like Jeff would help Jeremy," Joanna said sadly. "It hasn't. He simply terrorizes him any chance he has. It's awful." Joanna was crying.

"I'm not sure what to do anymore, honey. Our plan certainly didn't work. And he's such a nice little kid. He doesn't deserve this. For God's sake, he'll start having problems soon if he keeps getting this kind of treatment. What a shame. He takes it all in and still tries to be nice to Jeremy." Eric's tone of voice wasn't happy.

Joanna asked. "What's wrong with Jeremy? I hate to say it, but I don't like our kid. He acts crazy. He gets everything he wants. What more can we do?"

"Well, I think we have to keep searching. Maybe we don't have the right kind of psychiatrist. I'm ready to try another doctor. This can't go on. I feel so sorry for Jeff. I wish Jeremy was more like him."

"Yeah, he has nothing, and yet he's so much more satisfied and happy. Crazy, isn't it?"

Gosh, he thought, they think I'm okay. I can't imagine why.

Eric went on. "But our problem is Jeremy. There's got to be a reason. He certainly can be fixed, can't he?"

"I sure hope so, Eric. But in the meantime--" Joanna's voice faded as if it had lost its strength.

"Yeah, I know. Jeff can't be subjected to this any longer. I'm going to hate to see him go. I've really gotten attached to him."

"Me, too. I wish we could keep him, but he's suffering every day. We can't let that happen. We'll have to take him back."

Jeff rolled over on his pillow that night and cried. He tried. He'd put a lot of effort in getting Jeremy to like him. But nothing worked. Now he had to go back to the orphanage. Would the orphanage be mad at him? He was told it wasn't his fault, but it sure felt like it was.

The Sullivans told the orphanage that Jeff had behaved as well as any boy could be expected to act. That's good, he thought. At least no one blames me. The headmaster, Mr. Edmond, thinks I'm acting good. I heard Mr. Sullivan tell him Jeremy is getting worse and I deserved better. I think he's right. I'm glad to be back here. No one here is as mean and nasty as Jeremy. I don't think he deserves such nice parents. What's wrong with him anyway? He has so much stuff and a nice home to live in. And he lives in the same house as his mom and dad. Some kids don't appreciate anything.

Jeff didn't feel as strong as everyone thought he was. He shed big tears in his towel that night, but no one could hear him. He wondered in that moment if anyone would think he was brave if they could see him now. But he did learn a few lessons. He should never get too close to people because in his position he never knew how long it would last. And, he couldn't get too used to his surroundings, new friends, and new so-called family environment because it hurt too much when he had to leave. This was a lesson he'd remember. He wouldn't be caught again.

\* \* \*

"Hey, Jeff, aren't you finished yet?" Jeff was shaken out of his memories with a shock. That was Steve, finally awake enough to want his turn in the shower.

"I'm coming right out," he yelled, feeling slightly vulnerable as he quickly yet carefully rolled up all of his belongings in his bath towel. He opened the door in time to see Steve leaning against the door, pointing to his watch. Even with a pleasant smirk crossing Steve's face, Jeff was worried that he'd upset him. If the truth were told, Steve was one of the few kids living here who mattered to him.

"Sorry, Steve, I just got carried away."

"Don't sweat it, little buddy; I'm only teasing you. God, lighten up, will you? You never do anything wrong. I'll be out in a few minutes, then I'm going tell you all about the great movie we saw last night. What a blast."

Jeff loved the way Steve discussed the activities of the older kids. He hadn't had a chance yet to ask Steve about his night out at the movies, and Steve was already volunteering to include him in. The other older boys would never do that. In fact, Jeff was sure they'd probably laugh at him if he even approached the subject. But they never laughed at Jeff when Steve was around; they knew better than that.

While waiting for Steve to finish in the bathroom, Jeff had enough time to get himself overly concerned about the open house. All of the usual self-degrading feelings crossed his mind, and the gloom returned. He knew he didn't make a good first impression with people. Although he didn't feel out of place, he didn't draw people to him by either a winsome smile, fantastic looks or appealing personality. Okay, but he had good points, too. It's just that his seemingly good traits were well hidden and had to be coaxed out slowly, which didn't happen during an open-house afternoon.

He looked around the room and thought he'd done a good job on Steve's side. He liked his room. He'd only changed rooms once since he'd been here. The décor in this room was rugged, and there was a big horseshoe over the entrance of the room with the opening at the top. He knew this meant good luck and wished from that day forward his luck would improve.

* * *

Steve appeared out of the shower room and saw Jeff startle to attention. He wiped his wet hair with a light blue towel and realized he still only felt half-awake. He resented the fact he had to get up so early on a Sunday. He wasn't angry exactly, just disgusted at the thought of another open house.

"Imagine, Jeff, some of the newer boys are excited about this open house."

Steve realized sadly that these boys hadn't been through enough disappointments yet.

"Yeah, I was, too, at the beginning, but later on it became routine."

Steve noticed a blasé look on Jeff's face.

"Me, too. Sadly, they'll learn soon enough it doesn't always mean a happy ending."

Steve hadn't yet been to a foster home. His life was complicated, yet occasionally he hoped he'd get into a small foster home. A quick parade of thoughts crossed his mind. Would he even want to go, if he got a chance? He'd have to leave Jeff, the closest thing to a family he'd ever had.

"Boy, Jeff, sometimes I wish you were older and could have come with us last night. We saw a real cool movie. It was one of those James Bond movies, and I love all the gadgets they use to get him out of trouble. Honestly, we all stayed and watched part of it for a second time. It was cool."

"Oh, Yeah? What was the best part?"

"Well, there was this girl … Gees, look at you. You just wait a couple of years, little buddy. Anyway, there was this girl, and she actually helped Bond get information and get out of a real mess. One of the bad guys was called Goldfinger, oh yeah, that was the name of the movie."

"Goldfinger was the name of the movie? Weird. Like a finger that's gold?" asked Jeff.

"Yeah. There were a lot of gold bullions scattered around. Everyone was trying to steal them. Anyway, you should have seen this beautiful Mercedes he was driving; it was gorgeous. Solid black and I couldn't believe how shiny it was. By the end of the movie, it was totally wrecked. What a shame, eh? Such a beautiful car."

"Sounds like it was quite exciting, except about the girl part."

"Ha, you just wait. I thought just like you a few years ago. Oh, Gees, I'd better get dressed or I won't have time to do anything."

"I'll make your bed and help you clean up the rest. I've done part of it already."

Steve looked at Jeff warmly. He's a good kid, he thought.

"You'd be great to have as a little brother, you know that?"

"Really, you'd like me to be your little brother?" The look on Jeff's face just melted Steve.

"I sure wouldn't mind at all. Hey, maybe we can pretend, okay?"

"Sure, I'd like that. I'd like that a lot."

Just then, the bell began ringing. That was the signal that they had fifteen minutes to finish everything and be downstairs for breakfast. And none of the boys wanted to miss Sunday breakfast. It was always special.

# CHAPTER IV

Young boys were always hungry, and it didn't take much time for Jeff and Steve to make it downstairs. As they entered the huge kitchen area, they were immediately lost in the aromas permeating the entire area. Most of the boys walked into this room on Sunday expecting something special. They were seldom disappointed.

Fresh fruit dishes were always available. Eggs with bacon or sausage and hash browns or fries and a variety of sweet rolls were offered with unusual breads, usually freshly baked. Early fall welcomed watermelon, but you had to grab your portion immediately as it seemed to disappear rather quickly.

Jeff and Steve sat together, as most boys grouped with their room partner. Conversation made a loud din throughout the room, with only moments of silence as the food appeared.

"It sure smells good in this kitchen. I wouldn't mind a little bit of everything," said Steve, rubbing his stomach for effect.

"Yeah, that's one good thing about open-house Sundays. We get extra treats and tender loving care from the kitchen," Jeff said.

Steve roared. "Tender loving care from the kitchen?" he repeated snickering. "What made you think of that?"

He noticed Jeff was still laughing. He liked to act funny and clown around but his shyness limited his antics to comfortable settings.

"Don't know. You know me. Weird thoughts just come to me," said Jeff impishly.

"That was funny, Jeff. It really was." Steve watched Jeff make a funny face and soon they were both laughing again. It took a few moments before they could control themselves.

The caregivers walking around were trying to find out what was so funny. When Steve told them, a few of the other boys overheard and started laughing.

"Hey, look, Jeff, Nick and Tim are way down the table. They still feel safer staying far away from me." Steve saw Jeff nod in agreement.

He continued. "I didn't even hurt them. And they started the fight anyway. They just couldn't admit it. Couple of wimps, if you ask me."

After they were served their eggs and sausage with hash browns and whole-wheat toast, Steve elbowed Jeff and said in a low tone for his benefit only, "Watch this, Jeff."

"Hey, Tim, would you pass me the ketchup? It's the only bottle on this side of the table."

"Sure, Steve," said Tim rather timidly. Steve could tell he was expecting more to come. Yet nothing more was said except, "Thanks, Tim." Steve could almost hear the deep sigh of relief from Tim.

Steve saw the caregivers take notice, but he just smiled, and showed them a congenial attitude.

He commented only to Jeff, "You know, Nick and Tim weren't blameless. They only pretended to be."

"Yeah, you were unlucky. The headmaster only heard what you said."

Steve knew Jeff understood. "That's what irritates me about them. When I cause trouble, at least I own up to it. Nick and Tim always blame somebody else. They can't even own up to their part."

"You know, Steve, I don't know if the three of you would ever be friends, but I honestly think they'd like to have your respect. But they haven't earned it."

"No, they sure haven't. Maybe someday, if they ever get any guts about them."

Jeff and Steve had chosen their big piece of watermelon at the beginning so that when breakfast was over, their dessert was ready. And they savored every bite. When all was over, there were many satisfied boys with contented stomachs at this breakfast table. Some were eagerly looking forward to the day, while others would be happier when it was over.

\* \* \*

Today the grouping of children was different. All boys from eleven years old on up would be grouped together, and Jeff was delighted. That meant he could spend most of his day with Steve. Everyone helped get the parlor rooms ready and by 12:30 p.m., everything was in order. The boys relaxed, did homework or played games, and at 1:00 p.m., the parents began to arrive. Jeff took a deep breath.

Mostly, when the parents arrived they wandered casually around the place looking the boys over, talking to them and getting acquainted. At one point when the director felt most of the parents had arrived, he'd gather all of the children and present them, stating their age and telling something about them.

Jeff hated this part most. He felt he was on display, like a show and tell game. Sometimes he wanted to scream ... 'I'm a real person and not a giveaway'. Yet common sense told him again that no one had bad intentions. This was the chosen way to get people to know you.

On the other hand, Jeff knew Steve didn't mind this part at all. He'd told him that while he was standing being looked over, he had a chance to look around, too, and evaluate the parents. Jeff knew this was the obvious difference between them, which ran deep. Soon the presentation was over. Thank God, he thought. Now he could relax. Food was offered which always put Jeff in a happy frame of mind.

Only a few parents even talked to him today. Still, Jeff knew he looked good in his brown T-shirt with elbow-length sleeves and his newer beige pants given to him from the local charity. His hair looked neat, and his personal hygiene was good. The parents who had talked to him seemed impressed. But they passed him up in a relatively short time and moved on to Randy Newman, a nine-year-old boy. They talked to him much longer. In fact, they all laughed and told jokes. Jeff often wondered how anyone could get so chummy with someone they'd just met. He couldn't manage to do that.

"Hey, Jeff, how's it going?" Steve said as he walked over. Jeff felt most comfortable sitting on the couch alone. He patiently waited for the day to go by.

"I'm okay, really. Thanks." He was grateful that his big brother had noticed him alone and came over. This showed that Steve really cared about him.

"Yeah, well, you know what?" added Steve caringly, "I think you look kind of sad. You're not, are you? We've talked enough about these days to get you past 'sad,' right?"

"Right," answered Jeff with a smile. By the look on Steve's face, he wasn't sure he'd convinced him. "But I'm not quite as social as you. And some of the other kids come and sit here, too, for a while. Not just me. I'm okay."

"Well, that's good because later we can play some games when this is all over, okay?"

"Yeah, okay, Steve. I'd like that."

Then Steve got called away, and Jeff went back to reading his history book. He didn't want to waste time when he could get in some study.

The day passed slowly for Jeff. Mostly he sat on the couch and watched the activities in front of him. He didn't feel as nervous as usual, but kept himself occupied as an observer and a detached participant.

At 4:00 p.m., Jeff drew a big sigh of relief. He could relax now. It was over. Yes, yes, it was over. He had to admit it hadn't been too bad, truly, but he wished his life was settled and normal. He didn't want to be here having other people look for a family for him. Happiness to him would be when he was old enough to take care of himself or if he found a permanent home. It seemed after today either solution was off somewhere in the distant future. His nervousness had used up a lot of his energy. He'd be happy enough to head back to his room and crash for a while.

\* \* \*

When Steve came back at the end of the day, they sat around in the parlor for a while.

"Well, we made it through another open-house, little buddy. Do you think it gets easier or not?" Steve noticed relief on Jeff's face.

"It's always easier when it's over."

Steve puckered his lips as he thought about it. Jeff had said it all in a few words.

"Well said," he answered in agreement. "You know, I always thought that people should see our bad behavior once in a while so they'd really know what they're getting."

Jeff looked surprised. "Yeah, but then, would they want us?"

"Hey, I don't think they expect us to be perfect. And you know me, I don't pretend. They'll know what they get if they choose me."

"You were talking to that one couple for quite a while."

Steve realized Jeff was right. He'd spent most of the day talking to one particular couple.

"Oh, yeah, the Hallick family. They have a foster home about two hundred miles from here. It's a family-owned type of foster home that's been in their family for generations. They're presently looking for a couple of older boys. I think they're traveling around the country checking out how other people run foster homes. Since they were in this area, they stopped to visit our open house. They seemed nice, but hell, they sure are strict. Probably wouldn't work for me. I don't think they're interested in me anyway. They asked a lot of questions about this orphanage."

"What did they think of it?" asked Jeff curiously.

"They thought our rooms were awesome," Steve said proudly. "I guess a lot of foster homes or other orphanages just don't have such great furnishings as ours. We do have a great room you and me."

"You know, Steve, I heard this old mansion was given to the city by a philanthropist who wanted to give some of the 'stray boys,' as he calls us, a nice place to live. Most of us guessed it was old Mr. Arrowhead. Did you ever take a close look at that picture over the fireplace?"

Steve realized he hadn't, but showed curiosity.

"Well, when you get a chance, look at it closely. I think it's him when he was a lot younger."

Steve enjoyed Jeff's enthusiasm. He'd obviously put some thought into his theory.

"Oh, yeah, you've got such an imagination, buddy. At least this place has some nice rooms. I think we've got the best room in this entire place."

"Yeah, I think you're right," answered Jeff, "and I just love my roommate."

"Me, too." Steve laughed, as he ruffled Jeff's hair. "I think I've got best roommate in this entire place."

"No, you don't, cause I do," teased Jeff.

"No, I do," retorted Steve, who proceeded to pretend he was punching Jeff in the stomach and in the shoulder as they both fell back on the couch laughing and giggling.

"Considering everything, I'm kind of happy with my life right now," Jeff said.

Steve acted shocked. "Boy, I always thought you were a little weird, but now I know you are."

* * *

Jeff noticed a few of the younger children walking around looking sad and dejected. Their shoulders were carrying a heavy weight of disappointment. You could see their gloomy faces and eyes that developed tears. It was a tough fact, as Jeff knew, to realize that you weren't chosen. It was still hard at times for Jeff and Steve, but they'd been through many of these sessions. Gosh, he thought, these days can be so tough. Some of the upset youngsters looked to them for comfort.

"Is it like this all the time? This is my second open house, and no one was interested in me." That was six-year-old Michael Mason. He'd lived at the home for about six months after his parents had been killed. He was so alone and had trouble accepting his fate. "I want to have a home. I need a mom and a dad."

Jeff watched as Steve placed young Michael on his knee and hugged him. After a few moments he said, "You know, Michael, you're a special little boy. Everyone here likes you. It might take time, but they need to find you some special parents. They're out there, and I'm sure it won't be long, okay?"

"Do you think so, Steve? Hardly anyone talked to me today. Why not?"

Jeff saw Michael's little face look trustingly into Steve's eyes for hope.

"Well, that happens to all of us sometimes. It just depends what people are looking for. But when someone wants a six-year-old boy who's really special, they'll pick you."

"Do you think so, really?" said Michael with his voice uplifting a little.

"I truly believe that. And I've never lied to you, have I?"

"No, you don't lie. I hope you're right. Do you think he's right, Jeff?"

Jeff continued with Steve's ideas. "Oh, Yeah, I think you're special, and soon I'm afraid you'll find a nice family and leave us, and then we'll miss you. But you'll be happy, so we'll be happy too, okay?"

"Okay. I guess so." Michael didn't look totally convinced.

Steve continued, "Listen to me, Michael. If you picture in your mind, you know, like when you're pretending, okay? Well, if you picture what kind of family you want, then believe in that picture, they'll come and find you."

"Really, they will?" Michael sounded much more hopeful. Jeff caught Steve's serious look.

"Yeah, they really will," answered Steve.

"Steve, would it help if I pray to God about the picture?"

Steve paused for a moment, and Jeff saw a frustrated look on his face. He could tell that Steve knew this was one moment he had to get beyond himself.

"You know, Michael, I think maybe God is waiting to hear your prayer. He sure will listen to a nice little boy like you."

"Okay, maybe I'll go and do that right now. Bye, Steve. Bye, Jeff."

And he jumped off of Steve's lap and began walking away. But then, he suddenly turned, ran back and gave both Steve and Jeff a hug.

"I'm going to pray for both of you, too." Jeff thought that those at this orphanage who thought Steve was only a troublemaker with no depth to his feelings should have seen him in these last few minutes. He truly had amazing insight for little children, and this had been one of his shining moments.

Neither spoke for a time after Michael left. There was something close to magic in the air and it was to be relished for a while. Finally Jeff said, "That was nice what you told him about God. I know it was hard for you."

Steve's voice sounded sad. "Yeah, I wish I could believe what I just said."

"Maybe someday you will."

Steve added thoughtfully, "I hope so. I sure hope so."

They both decided to head for their room when Steve got called over by Mr. Edmond, the headmaster. He turned and waved to Jeff and said, "I'll catch up with you a little later."

\* \* \*

Jeff watched Steve and Mr. Edmond walk into his office and close the door. Immediately he found that same feeling of gloomy apprehension flood his body and mind. He surprised himself with a sudden unexpected reaction. He was holding back tears. My God, he thought, he could still be so emotional. As quickly as possible, he headed to his room. He hoped Steve wasn't in any trouble. It was already late afternoon, so Jeff doubled-checked his homework and made sure his uniform was ready for Monday. Then he just waited and waited. It seemed like a long time.

As early evening crept forward, Jeff was still waiting for Steve to return. Feeling solitary and somewhat vulnerable, he worried when Steve had been called to the headmaster's office. Gees, he hadn't been in trouble for months, he thought. Steve's days of being called to Mr. Edmond's office with accepted regularity were actually behind him. Everyone had noticed his improved behavior. Jeff knew Steve had become one of the favorites at the orphanage by staff and students alike. And Jeff was tickled to be considered among his inner circle of friends.

Yet, Steve had been called once again to the headmaster's office. Jeff couldn't think of anything he'd done to warrant it. He felt that today had gone well, and he didn't observe any inappropriate behavior on Steve's part. In fact, he thought his friend had behaved exceptionally well. He'd talked and laughed with everyone and was considerably gracious with the attending parents. That was easy for Steve with his outgoing, gregarious personality. He seemed to exude warmth and caring, and he'd been particularly helpful with the caregivers on call. Yet he was called to the "big office," as the students referred to it, and Steve had been gone for an extremely long time. Jeff was concerned.

# CHAPTER V

As Steve sat down in the large formal chair offered to him, he had to admit his nerves kicked in quickly. Why was he here? Mr. Edmond looked somber at best. That usually didn't spell good news. He couldn't imagine what he'd done wrong. Just as Mr. Edmond opened his mouth to speak, the phone rang. He put up the palm of his hand to acknowledge it was an important call that he had to take.

Steve's sweaty palms signaled to him that waiting was hard. He fidgeted somewhat and looked around the room, but couldn't concentrate. His mind raced back over his life as he wondered again how he'd ended up in this orphanage and wondered what was ahead for him now. At this ill-timed moment, some of the haunting details of his life crossed his mind for consideration.

"Steve, you're wanted downstairs. You've got a visitor. I think it's your mother."

"It can't be. She never comes. Are you sure?" Steve suddenly felt nervous.

"That's what they said and they want you downstairs right away."

Steve was surprised. Gosh, his mother had only visited him twice in the past two years. Maybe she wanted to take him home. That'd be so great. No, he didn't think so. She'd always been drinking before the other visits. He didn't really think she was cured yet. He wasn't sure if he was glad to see her or not.

He thought back to his early life. His home life had been cut short he thought. His dad was the one who kept the family together and when he got killed on his motorcycle, family life as he knew it ended. It wasn't funny really, but his dad had been killed by a drunk driver. He often thought God must have a sense of humor. He missed his dad. Life was never the same. And of course, his mother drank a lot more after that.

Steve remembered when he said goodbye to her. She had to go for alcoholic treatment he was told. Then maybe when she was better they could live together again. He was taken to a foster home as a temporary solution. He wanted his mom to get better. He kept his fingers crossed everyday. And he prayed to God to help his mother heal. But nothing happened. Either God didn't hear his prayers or He didn't care. He remembered the first foster home clearly.

"Well, young man, you're going to like it here. We have several other boys, and we have a lot of fun," offered his foster mother. But Steve felt scared and had begun to retreat inward. It had started when he was alone with his mother.

"Come on, I'll show you to your room." With that, the woman picked up his bags and walked with him up the stairs to his new room. Steve followed along rather unsteadily, but realized this person didn't smell funny and talked better than his mom. His room was nice, he thought, but the place was weird. Sometimes he missed his dad so much his stomach hurt.

He was used to a small trailer park, and this house was confusing and frightening. It didn't take long before he realized he didn't like it here. His roommate at ten years old, had three years on him and could be mean.

"You've got to keep my side of the room clean, and then we can be friends. The new kid has to do all the work, you know. Those are the rules here. You can't tell the foster people, but that's how it works. Understand?"

"No, I don't understand," said Steve timidly. "I was told everyone made their own bed."

"Not in this room. Here, I'm boss, and you have to do what I tell you."

As the new kid in the house, Steve obeyed. He thought he was supposed to. Besides, he was the youngest and smallest kid.

\* \* \*

He came downstairs slowly and hesitantly hoping his mom was better. He couldn't help wishing he wouldn't smell the drinking on her. Usually she drank every day. Sometimes he remembered when she couldn't walk straight. Maybe she'd surprise him. He still hoped. But he didn't count on it anymore.

"Can you give your mom a hug, Stevie?" It was the usual story. She still smelled the same, he thought, but he could feel the caring in her hands. Her face looked at him with teary eyes and a longing that made him realize her life was beyond her control. Even as a young child, he knew this.

"You sure are growing. You must have grown a couple of inches since I last saw you. I think you're going to be tall like your dad."

Steve felt pleased. He wanted to be like his dad. "Where's your home, mom? Can I come and live with you?"

"No, not yet, Steve. But I hope soon. I'm not well yet, you know. Dad could take care of me better than anyone." His mom started crying a little, and he realized his mom was the same as before. She may not even make it, he thought, at least not before I'm a lot older. I'll probably always be in some kind of foster home because mom said I'm still hers and can't be adopted. Yet, I guess that's good, I think. It's like she still hopes someday we can be a family again. But I know it won't happen for a long time. I'm not sure mom knows this, but I do.

"I think I'm doing better, don't you think so, Stevie? I feel a little better. Do you think I look better?"

Steve felt he had to encourage her. "Yes, I thought you looked better when you first walked in the door, mom. Where do you live?"

"I live with a few women in a home. It's a nice place, not too different from this one. Anyway, we all try to help each other. What about you? How are you doing?"

"I'm okay, but I miss you and dad," Steve said. "Do you think about dad? I think about him almost every day. I miss him so much, all the time." Steve allowed a few tears to escape down his cheeks whenever he remembered his father.

"Yes, I do, too," said his mother, and he saw more tears in her eyes. "I think it's so unfair he had to die so young. He didn't deserve it. Life just isn't fair, you know. Always remember that."

Steve thought about what his mother said and believed most of it. His dad was a good man, and he took care of his mom and him. Now he was gone. Steve loved the memories, but he knew they were only memories now. He wasn't sure his mom did.

"We shouldn't have been left alone like this, Stevie. We didn't deserve it."

Steve felt he should encourage his mom, again. "Sometimes things just happen, I guess. Do you think dad's in heaven?"

"I don't believe in heaven. If there was a good heaven, this wouldn't have happened. I don't believe that stuff, and I don't think I ever did."

"Dad used to talk about heaven sometimes. I think he believed in it. Don't you, mom, even a little?"

"Your dad was a wonderful person, but he believed in fairy tales and magic. I don't think I ever did. Anyway, I'm going to have to go now. It might be some time before I can see you again," she added in a shaky voice. As she got up to leave, she remembered something. "Oh, here, Stevie, I brought you a picture of your dad. I found an extra one and thought you'd like it. I don't want you to ever forget him. Do you want it?"

Steve felt his face get brighter, and he was enthusiastic for the first time in the visit. "Oh, can I have it, mom? Can I keep it? I'd love to have it."

"Oh sure, I thought you'd like it. Wait a minute, I think I have another. You can have them both. Yes, here. The first one was when he graduated from high school. Wasn't he handsome? He was eighteen years old, and I think you look like him. This next one was taken about a year after we got married. He was about twenty-five." She handed over both pictures with a sad look in her eyes. Steve's hands shook a little as he took them.

"Gee, thanks. This is great. Mom, I'd like a picture of you, too. Don't you have one of you?"

"I might have one at home. I'll bring it next time, okay?"

With that comment Steve tried to hold a pleasant look, but knew next time could be several years from now, if ever. Yet he had a picture of his dad and could now remember what he looked like. At least that was something.

Steve felt more withdrawn after this last visit. He knew his mom would never get better. She's always going to drink, he thought. And he'd always live in these foster homes. He began to think life wasn't fair. He had no hope left, and always felt alone. There wasn't much fun in his life, but even more important, he didn't feel his future would be any better.

* * *

After his mom's visit, Steve developed anger. Why did his father have to die? He felt abandoned, and many times, he was scared. Another new roommate was older, bigger, and a bully. He'd have to decide to forever be somebody's puppet or take a stand.

Steve started defending himself. He'd not be warred upon anymore. He got roughed up and acquired a reputation as a troublemaker. He got more new roommates. God, he thought, more guys who need to be the boss. More noticeable bruises and more scuffles followed. Steve got blamed most of the time. After a few months and several more incidents, Steve was moved to another foster home. Not long after, he was moved again. He remembered his dad's quiet strength, but hadn't been able to master that style. Sometimes when he looked at his dad's picture, he still shed tears. No one knew.

At eleven, he ended up at the Cambridge Home for Boys, and he brought a tough reputation with him. I've moved seven times in five years, he thought. I don't trust these people. His temper was always on the edge of exploding, although he fought hard to keep it under control. He was tired of moving around and thought this home was better than some. Kids here didn't want to fight as much. Some were even friendly. He hoped he'd get to stay a while.

Steve met with a few psychologists. They said he was uncooperative. He didn't think so. He didn't want to talk about his inside pain. It hurt too much. They said they wanted to help him. How could they understand? As a result, not much progress was made. He was always trying to find a way to help himself. He believed there must be an answer.

Then one day, they had a substitute teacher in his sixth Grade Science class. If any subject caught his interest, it was Science, especially the order of the universe.

"I'm Mr. Langtree, and I'll be with you this week. Your teacher, Mr. Winegarden, will be back next Monday, and he's asked me to delay demonstrations on magnets. He has special plans for that. So I'm going to talk to you about various attractions and vibrations and waves that happen in this world of ours."

For the next few days Mr. Langtree talked about various attractions. He said a magnet was an object that exhibited a strong magnetic field and attracted materials to it, like iron. Steve kept notes. Okay, that's interesting, he thought. He'd seen how magnets work. The teacher talked about the two poles that magnets have, the North and South poles. Steve continued with his notes realizing how complicated was this universe.

Then on the last day of the week, Mr. Langtree talked about other applications of attractions he'd never heard.

"You know, we speak about the Law of Gravitation, which draws and holds together the atoms of which matter is composed. We recognize the power of the law that attracts bodies to the earth and holds them in their place and others that hold circling worlds in their places, too. But we ignore the Law of Attraction in the Thought World."

"Gees," said one student, "you mean our thoughts have attractions, too?"

Many students laughed.

"Yes, that's exactly what I mean. Our thoughts are also a force--a manifestation of energy--and they have a magnet-like power of attraction, too."

"You mean every time we think, we send out waves and vibrations, too?" Several students laughed again. Steve didn't.

"Oh, yes. Thoughts send vibrations or waves of energy into the atmosphere, and there they look for other thoughts like themselves, of the same vibration."

Steve asked, "That would mean these thoughts we send out are attracted to the same type of thoughts. I mean, if I send out positive thoughts, then my thoughts are out there looking for other positive thoughts."

"Hey, you guys are getting this. That's exactly what I mean."

A few students laughed and thought it was silly. Steve was thoughtful.

Steve asked another question. "And if I send out a real positive thought with a lot of emotion attached to it, then that will have a higher vibration, from what we've learned today, than a thought with just a little emotion, right?"

"Right, and now Steve, you're getting into this deeper than I planned for this introduction, but you're right. And when these thoughts are out there looking for similar partners, it doesn't matter if they're positive thoughts or negative thoughts. They look for their own."

"I get it," mentioned someone. "That's what's meant by 'like attracts like.' And they have their own vibration rate, wave velocity, probably, and I don't know what else."

"Yes. Yes, you students definitely have the idea. I only wanted to let you know that the Law of Attraction was something happening every day in your lives. The universe operates that way. And you personally are utilizing it, physically all the time. Well, the hour is almost over and I'll be done with my job. Thanks for your attention. You've been a good and sharp class to teach."

As he was leaving the classroom, Steve couldn't ignore his need to talk to the teacher a little more. He felt enthusiasm about something for the first time he could remember. Something inside of him was vibrating at this moment. It was hope. He made sure he was the last student to leave and approached Mr. Langtree as he was packing up.

"I enjoyed your talk about the power of our thoughts."

"I'm glad you did, Steve. That's a wide open subject, and there's so much to learn."

"I'd like to learn more. How can I do that?"

"The library should have some information. But you know what? I happen to have a few booklets that discuss this thought force and its implications. Here, you can have them."

Steve knew his face lit up. Mr. Langtree looked pleased.

"Thanks, this is great. This is a good start for me. I'm sure these will help."

"Well, those are only some small booklets. But it will reinforce what we've talked about and probably give you more to think about. I think they have other references for you to check out."

"That will certainly get me started. Thanks a lot, Mr. Langtree."

The teacher then said something that Steve liked and remembered.

"Your mind is always with you, Steve. Make it your best friend and not your worst enemy."

As Steve left the room, he thought, what an idea. What a great idea. He felt enthused and it was still with him when he got home from school. He felt better. He knew he looked better. He had a plan now. That's all he needed, a path to something.

Steve started experimenting. He studied the booklets. He tried to think more positively. Some days it worked, and some days it didn't. But it never hurt. So he tried again and again. And he found out during his experiments that, even when they failed, a positive effect remained. And he believed it was because he was trying, really trying to improve, which was a positive thing. During these times, he wasn't being negative. He felt he was developing his own system, which made a big difference in his attitude. His relationship with others improved, and by thirteen years old, he was finally starting to relax and feel a little better inside.

\* \* \*

Steve's latest therapist noticed an improvement. Of course, Mr. Ingram thought he deserved the credit. And he probably did provide some help. Still, Steve felt, it was his different way of thinking. He realized when he thought and concentrated on his father's tragic accident, his alcoholic mother, and his crappy life, it dredged up a type of anger at fate or some universal being many called God. Though he admitted it to no one, being alone terrified him. Yet, if he turned off the negative thoughts in his mind as soon as he began reminiscing, and concentrated instead on more positive aspects of his life, he felt better. He'd calm down. With more practice, he taught himself to control his thoughts, to a degree.

He was beginning to experience some agreeable experiences. He found some of the other kids at the home actually learned to like him. It wasn't they just tolerated him anymore, but they actually liked him and had a distant respect for him.

"Hey, Steve, you can be so funny at times. Where do you get all those funny stories?"

"I don't make them up, Nathan. I just watch the world around me. Adult behavior can be even funnier than ours, don't you think?"

That sent Nathan, a shy eight-year-old boy into fits of laughter as he answered, "I'll have to start watching them."

To which Steve answered, "Don't forget, Nathan, they'll be watching you when you're watching them." And Nathan, along with some other boys, laughed hysterically.

These new exchanges of pleasantries and playfulness between Steve and other children were emerging slowly, and soon were a common event.

* * *

Acknowledging Steve's behavioral improvements pleased Mr. Edmond, but the final hurdle was finding Steve a compatible roommate. He'd been moved many times at this home with problems following him from room to room. Who'd want to be a roommate with him? Everyone knew Steve's reputation, but maybe someone more agreeable would be helpful. Jeff Barnes was the only answer. He approached him to see if he'd consider having Steve as his partner. Jeff had a good rapport with most of the household, but it was only respectful to ask if he'd be willing to have a roommate who owned a difficult reputation.

"Jeff, what do you think of Steve Johnson?" asked Mr. Edmond seriously.

"Oh, he's okay. But he does get into a lot of trouble, doesn't he? Although lately, he's been much better."

Mr. Edmond watched Jeff's face as he answered. He was polite as usual.

"Yes, he's had a difficult life and seems to have developed a lot of anger. But he has some good points, too."

"Yeah," admitted Jeff, "he can be real funny, and he tries to make people feel better. I think he hurts inside."

"Very observant of you. You've had a tough life, too, yet you seem to handle things differently. How do you do that?" Mr. Edmond saw Jeff get rather pensive for a moment.

"I'm trying to take life as it comes. I hurt sometimes, and I get scared, but this is a good home." Smiling awkwardly he added, "I'm not trying to score points here--it's what I believe. I've heard about other homes, and they're not as nice as ours. Steve's lived in some bad places. He's told me about them."

"You're mature for eleven years old, and you seem to have a good head on your shoulders. You're doing well in school and you get along quite well with the other kids. Now I'm not trying to score points with you either," said Mr. Edmond, adding a wink, "but I know that to be the truth."

They both laughed.

"Yeah, I try. I like to get along, but I don't like everyone. Some of the older boys are tougher for me to connect with."

Mr. Edmond saw Jeff shift uneasily in his chair. "It's hard to get along with everyone. Even adults can't manage that. I have a question for you. Would you say okay if I put Steve with you as a roommate? It'd just be a trial setup, and if things didn't work out we can move him somewhere else. But I thought you might be good for him."

Mr. Edmond knew Jeff had been caught off guard. He saw him pucker his lips in deep thought. Then he said, "He's moved around quite a bit since he's been here, hasn't he? We seem to get along okay, but I know it's different if you have somebody as a roommate. But, okay, I guess I could try."

"Okay, then, and just between you and me, I was hoping some of your good sense might rub off on him."

Jeff gave him a satisfied smile. "I can't guarantee that. I'm sure not perfect by any means. But if you think it might work, I'll give it a try."

"Thanks, Jeffrey. I appreciate your cooperation."

\* \* \*

Try as he may, Steve couldn't maintain his hard heart when Jeff was around. As a roommate, he had a caring and congenial friend. He remembered when he first moved into his room.

"Look, Steve, they gave me the left side of the room when I came here, but I could move to the right side if you like."

Steve just stared at his new roommate. "You've got to be kidding. Don't you know you got the short end of the stick? Nobody wants me for a roommate. They stuck it to you this time."

Steve wasn't angry exactly, just frustrated. He knew he got along with most of the kids now, but only on a casual basis. Again he had another new roommate to get used to. This was his biggest problem that got him into trouble. He liked Jeff; he seemed like a good kid. But as a roommate, he hoped it would work.

"Jeff, the right side of the room is just fine. Actually this is a nice room."

"Yeah, it's my favorite. I've only had one other room, but it was filled when I came back from a foster home, so they put me in here. But I like it. Did you notice the horseshoe over the doorway? The opening is at the top and that means we can trap good luck and keep it."

"Do you really believe that?"

"Well, I like to believe it," said Jeff hopefully. "And it could be true. It's like believing in Santa Claus. I'm sorry I found out that he wasn't real. I was happier when I believed."

Steve noticed Jeff's positive little face, which made him realize he was now bunking with an optimist.

"Look, don't let me drag you down, okay? Sometimes I don't always look on the good side of life, you know?"

"Neither do I," commented Jeff, which surprised Steve. "But when I remember, I try because it makes more sense to me. Anyway, do you have all your stuff here? I can help you carry it back. We could probably make it in one trip together."

"Well, I don't have that much stuff. I'll get the rest of it soon. But thanks anyway."

"Okay."

God, thought Steve, this kid is so congenial.

"Hey, Jeff, you don't swear at all, do you? I was thinking I've never heard you swear, not even once. I do sometimes."

"Well, Gees, I've been in Catholic school for four years. That's probably why. I never got in the habit. A few guys at school can really let some juicy words go by at recess. Anyway, I've only heard you swear a few times."

Steve said, "I'm not horrible, but I've been known to displease a few people."

"Oh, well I do swear a little. Usually only shit or hell, damn, words like that."

Steve laughed. "Many would consider that nothing. But you know, Jeff, I don't like how it makes me feel, so I'm stopping myself a lot. Just between you and me, okay?"

Jeff laughed, but Steve saw him wink. "Sure, just between you and me."

\* \* \*

Several months later Steve realized Jeff had become a confidant and friend. He had his first familial feeling he could ever remember, except, of course, his dad. Jeff melted Steve's heart, he had to admit that. And he protected him from the older boys who could be bullies at times. It gave him a purpose in life, as kind of a protector for his little friend. Steve was agreeable most of the time now and, except for occasional outbursts of anger that he couldn't always control, he was beginning to make a better reputation for himself.

"You know, Jeff, I didn't realize we had so much in common. I don't have any relatives either. Well, there's my mom, but she has her own problems, and I've told you I don't see her much."

"Are you okay with that, Steve?"

Steve was silent for a moment before he began. "Yeah, I am. At least, I accept it now. I know she loves me, but she has problems. If she'd been able to overcome them, I think I'd be living with her again. If she ever conquers herself, which I hope she will in time, I think I'll be an adult by then."

Steve looked at Jeff and saw he shared his pain.

"Yeah, that's life," Steve said sadly. "Just look at the kids around here. I know I've got anger inside, but at least I try to deal with it. I mean, I'm almost fourteen now, and I should be able to handle my life. Other kids, even as old as I am, just complain and whine about their lives. That used to irritate me about them. I'm glad you're not like that." Steve saw a proud look cross Jeff's face.

"My teacher, Sister Margaret thinks there are good things that come along with the bad. I agree, don't you?"

"Yeah. When I can put my anger aside, I know that no one gets a free pass in this life. Everyone will get their share."

Steve saw Jeff nod. They agreed on a lot of things, he thought.

"Do you believe in God, Steve?"

Steve thought for a moment before he spoke. "No, I don't think so. Nothing ever pointed me in that direction. But I'll bet you do."

"Well, it's hard to avoid it going to Catholic school. But I've learned to think for myself. I don't think of God as something up in the sky who gives out all sorts of hard lessons. I used to, but not anymore. I think he's more like a power that allows me to think and make my own decisions."

Steve could tell that Jeff was enthusiastic in his belief. "Then you don't think there's a God who's ranting and raving mad at people if they make a mistake? That's what turned me off."

"No, I don't. I used to, and that scared me when I goofed. But now I don't think God sends anything bad to people at all."

Steve said, "The word God never did much for me. It actually irritated me. I must have bad memories."

"Personally," Jeff said wisely, "I like to think of it as a power or universal intelligence; that's the popular term now. I'm more comfortable with that."

"Hey, I like that a lot better," Steve said with renewed interest.

Jeff continued, "I think it's like a neutral power, you know? We can use it if we can learn how to connect with it."

"If it's neutral, how come you and I don't have any families? And other kids, some worse than us, seem to do better. I didn't ask to be born into this life."

"Steve, I don't know all the answers. I'm not even sure what all the questions are. Gees, I'm only eleven. But it's starting to make a little more sense to me. That's all."

"Yeah, well it's certainly another way to look at life."

\* \* \*

Later that night, Steve looked over at Jeff, whose eyes kept shutting and were close to sleep. He liked feeling like a big brother. His mind wondered how he truly felt about him. Suddenly he heard a sharp voice saying, 'That's how much I cared about you.' He immediately thought the voice sounded familiar. It was so real he was sure someone had walked into the room. He looked around quickly, but no one was there. The door was still closed, and the window was shut. What was going on? Had he been dreaming? If it was a dream, then his dream was talking to him about his present life. How could that be?

Could this be the God or that Power that Jeff talked about? Maybe, he thought, this Power could take me into different realities, like daydreaming in several directions at the same time. Maybe I can be here physically, but get information from somewhere else. I reckon if I told Jeff about this, he wouldn't even be surprised. I know he wouldn't laugh.

There had been times Steve thought he felt his father's presence around him. Weird as that sounded, he knew his father was there with him. He'd never told anyone. He wasn't about to ruin these memories by speaking about them to anyone. He sometimes believed that if he did mention these occurrences aloud, they'd disappear, like writing being erased from a blackboard. He wasn't willing to take that chance.

# CHAPTER VI

Steve was edgy being called to the headmaster's office. Luckily, Mr. Edmond seemed to be in a good mood after his phone call. That was a plus. He trusted he'd acted quite properly during the open house, and his confidence edged up. Mr. Edmond had seemed congenial and friendly when he closed the door and walked back behind his desk. At that time Steve watched his every move, waiting to hear the reason for this unexpected meeting. Now, with the phone call behind him and without any more interruptions the time had come and Mr. Edmond began

"Another open house day ended. But I think it went well, don't you?"

Steve knew Mr. Edmond was making casual conversation. He hoped he'd get to the point soon. He felt he should answer his question.

"Yes, I think so. And the food was good, too."

Steve's mind raced back through the happenings of the day to brace himself for whatever Mr. Edmond's summons would entail. He didn't have to wait long as the headmaster got right to the point.

"I'm sure you remember the Hallick family. You spoke to them for quite a while today. They found you to be intelligent, cooperative, and very informative. They're offering you a spot in their foster home, if you care to accept it."

Steve saw Mr. Edmond relax in his chair and just look at him. This was a most unexpected offer. Steve thought he was expressionless, either by shock or by choice. He did fidget somewhat, trying to process the new information. It was like a huge weight had been placed on his chest, and part of it was light, pleasant, and exciting, but another part was heavy and quite scary.

"Wow, Mr. Edmond," Steve responded finally. "This is so unexpected; I don't know what to say." Steve answered with the first words entering his mind, feeling he should say something. One part of his person was terrified, as he never thought he'd have to face this day. He wasn't considered adoptable, and felt at his age no one would want him in their foster home.

"Do you have any reaction at all, Steve, just curious? I realize this is most unexpected."

"Most of me is shocked, you know," he answered honestly. "Part of me is excited because I'd always hoped to live in a small foster home. Yet, I'm kind of scared, too. Didn't think I would be."

"That's totally understandable, Steve. Unknown adventures usually do scare us. But this could be a good move for you."

"Yeah, I'm sure that's true. There'd be new experiences and a view of the outside world that I really need. Do they have only one spot? I was thinking maybe Jeff could come, too."

Jeff had crossed his mind immediately. What about Jeff? He wasn't sure how he'd handle this. They'd become a team, and possibly Jeff would fake being happy, but mostly he'd be devastated. Jeff was a big part of his decision, and once again, Steve realized how important a bond they'd formed.

"I believe they only have one spot at this time, Steve."

He immediately got the feeling that Mr. Edmond didn't like the idea. He was told to consider what was best for him.

"Although you'd be separated from Jeff, you'd have the opportunity to keep in touch with him. Making lasting friendships is as important an experience as any others."

Steve was thinking as fast as he could. He didn't know what to say. Time was standing still for him at this moment.

"I'm not expecting you to make up your mind at this moment. At your age, we don't force a child to make this big of a change. However, I'd like you to know as of late you've made great strides here. We're all proud of your improvements. Yet a mature person must begin to realize changes are part of life, and some adjustments are necessary for everyone. You, as well as most of the children here, know that better than some."

Steve kept taking deep breaths. Was this for real? He never would have imagined this could happen to him.

"You know, Mr. Edmond, there was a time I'd have jumped at the chance because I've always wanted to know what it was like to live with a family. The Hallicks said they have one child of their own and one foster child at this time. They live in a large colonial home on about one acre, and have a few dogs, a cat and other animals, horses I think. I don't remember everything they said. I know in my mind that this would be a great chance for me. Yet lately, I've been truly happy here and I do think of Jeff as a younger brother. He's family to me."

"That doesn't have to change. Members of families move all the time when children go off to school or someone moves away for a job. Most families don't live forever together in the same house or even in the same town."

"Yeah, I know that's true." Steve talked slowly and thoughtfully. "This could be like me going away to school for a while. And of course life for kids like me is always a guessing game. You never know if I might be back."

"I think you have to think this over. You could even discuss it with Jeff. Families do discuss things with each other, and it could help make up your mind. I want you to take time to think about this. Look at all sides. You could turn this down, and then Jeff would get adopted. How would you feel about that?"

"I would want what's best for Jeff. I know he'd keep in touch with me. Jeff and I will always be there for each other."

When Steve looked up at Mr. Edmond's smiling face, he realized what he'd just said. He knew in that instant that Jeff would want the best for him, too. Why did life have to be so complicated? Why couldn't this foster home be in a nearby city and not so far away? Why couldn't they have one more opening for Jeff? Why did life have to teach so many lessons all the time?

"I think we've done all the talking we can for now. I'll give you a week to make up your mind. That seems fair doesn't it?"

Steve agreed.

"Okay then. I want to tell you honestly I'd be happy if you chose to go, only because I truly believe this would be a great opportunity for you. But, if you decide not to go and you want to remain here, I'd be happy to have you make that decision, too. This has to be your decision, Steve. Just let me know when you're ready to talk again."

* * *

Leaving Mr. Edmond's office, Steve felt he was walking inside someone else's body. He didn't even feel like Steve Johnson. His entire life seemed unreal to him, and he didn't know how to cope. As he climbed the stairs to the upper floor, he landed on the creaky step. He had to smile. Jeff had taught him how to take the steps without making any noise. But his mind was spinning and his thoughts were all mixed up. Turning around, he decided to go outside and think.

Looking at the sunset from the long white veranda of the orphanage, Steve felt smaller than he usually did whenever his mind wandered and considered the heavens and the amazement of the universe. Every time he gazed upward, he got the impression he was only one small spot in this entire universe and wondered if there was an energy or spirit or something out there that cared about him personally. Jeff had told him he believed there was, but he still wasn't sure. It wasn't he didn't believe in God because he did in his own way. But he didn't believe in a punishing God or a vengeful one, which some of the Catholic schools taught. He couldn't agree you had to be a near perfect person to get into heaven, whatever heaven was.

Most people he knew weren't even close to being that good, which would mean that most people would be lost. And why would a loving God create a world called earth where most of the people would try to improve their lives and still end up going to some kind of hell? He'd been brainwashed with this negative and depressing philosophy as a young child. He couldn't live a life with such discouraging rules and self-doubt. He liked Jeff's way of thinking better.

A sudden cold chill helped Steve realize that time was passing quickly, and he'd best return to his room. He still hadn't made any decision, not even much headway, but his thoughts and emotions had settled down somewhat. He was ready to face Jeff. He didn't have to tell Jeff anything; he knew that. But he wanted to discuss this decision with him. Although Jeff was younger, he had a maturity that Steve hadn't even found in some of the older boys. How lucky they'd been to be partnered together. The only difficult part would be the initial telling to Jeff. How would he tell him? What words could he possibly use to make the initial statement? And, Steve wondered, how would Jeff react?

\* \* \*

As he opened the door to his room, Jeff was sitting on his bed waiting for him. Steve was sure he would be. Jeff smiled as wide as he could and started immediately to speak.

"Hi, Steve. I already know. The Hallicks want you to go and live with them, don't they?"

Steve hadn't even entered the room. He was still holding onto the doorknob. But there was no real surprise. Jeff had a way of knowing things that he couldn't possibly know and, against all odds, he was usually right. As he stood there, staring at Jeff's face he saw a child who looked smaller than usual waiting patiently and expectantly for any comment he'd throw at him. His little face looked as if it was holding its breath and wouldn't last much longer without some supporting statement. Steve decided not to prolong the inevitable.

"Yeah, they made me an offer," said Steve entering the room. "Can you believe it? I thought it'd never happen. Here I am fourteen years old and someone wants me in their foster home. Can you even imagine it?"

"Well, of course, they'd want you," Jeff said proudly, "who wouldn't want you? Everyone would want you if they knew you and they were smart."

In that moment Steve's old whimsical personality returned for a brief moment, and he felt like laughing on the inside and outside at the same time.

Steve had wandered over and landed on Jeff's bed in a sprawled-out position relaxing his lengthy body as best he could. There was a tension inside that wouldn't slacken, so he took a few deep breaths trying to calm down. He knew Jeff never missed anything.

"That must be scary for you. I know it'd be for me. You and I just sort of expected to remain here, both of us together, and you get hit with this." It seemed that Jeff couldn't stand the suspense. "What did you tell them?"

"The Hallicks had already left. I've got a week to make up my mind. Mr. Edmond told me that I don't have to go. I guess since I'm older now, I get a choice."

"Wow, you have to make the choice. When they put me in foster homes I was too young to choose," Jeff paused. "Any feelings about what you want to do?"

Although nothing was said out loud, Steve knew Jeff was holding his emotions inside. Neither of them had been honest yet. Slowly a real conversation began.

"Honestly, Jeff, I have to tell you, I thought about you immediately when they told me about the offer."

Steve wanted to see Jeff's reaction. It was true surprise.

"You did really? You thought about me?"

"I did, Jeff. I do think of you as family and my best friend, and I'm not sure I want to break up the only family I've ever known. I know I've told you I remember my dad a little, but he's gone, and he isn't coming back. Until I met you, I had no family. I guess I never thought that we'd be separated, at least not for a long, long time."

Steve had to hold his emotions tight. His voice did crack a few times, and he was sure his face betrayed his feelings, but that was okay. He wanted Jeff to know how much he cared about him and the important position he had in his life. As he sat talking to Jeff, he truly couldn't imagine him not being around.

"I know what you mean, Steve. I've often thought about the spot you're in now. For me, I know I'd be mixed up about it. I think of you as family, too." Then Jeff got slightly preachy. "But while you think about everything, you have to do what's best for you. That's what I'd want you to do. I'm your little brother, you said so. And I'd never want to hold you back. Do you think this would be a good move for you?"

"I did talk a lot to the Hallicks. They seem like nice people. They have three children. It would be a much smaller home. I think I'd like that."

"Let me ask you this. If I wasn't here, would you want to go? Think about it."

Steve looked over at Jeff and thought, Is he really only eleven years old? That's one of the best questions, and I didn't even think about it. If Jeff wasn't here, it wouldn't be difficult to make up my mind. In fact, it would be no problem at all.

"Gees, Jeff, you sure know how to phrase things, don't you? I never thought about it that way because you are here, and you're most important in my decision."

"But you didn't answer me," Jeff said strongly. "If I wasn't here, what would you decide to do? Do you know? Be honest, Steve. You and I have always been honest with each other."

Steve spoke honestly, "Jeff, if you weren't here, I wouldn't even blink about it. I'd probably be packing right now."

Steve felt tears in his eyes when he made that admission aloud. Jeff made all the difference in his world. Otherwise, one orphanage or foster home was pretty much like another.

"That's what I thought," Jeff said in a sad tone. "Remember, you told me that you always felt like one of the pack here. If you don't take this chance and it's because of me, I'd feel terrible. Don't get me wrong, I'm going to hate to see you go, but I think you have to do it. First, you must have loyalty to yourself. We've talked about that, remember? And if I don't ever get a chance to get adopted, you can tell me what you've learned. That's how we can remain a team."

"Jeff, are you sure you're only eleven years old?"

Steve watched as Jeff fell back on the bed laughing. He liked to make Jeff feel good, but it was true. Jeff seemed so mature to him. And discussing his decision with him was like talking to a family member. Steve was sure about that. Having a little brother was something he'd always wanted. What should he do? He hated making this decision. But he had to.

"You have to take me out of the equation while you make up your mind. Please promise me that. Don't lay that burden on me, okay? Don't you do that to me." Jeff was definite on this point.

"Okay, Jeff. I have a week to make up my mind. I'm glad I don't have to tell them right now. It'll be hard not to give you consideration in my decision, but I understand what you're saying. I know I'd feel the same way. There are a lot of other things I have to think about, but I'd still like your opinion okay?"

"Sure. That's what families are for. And you and I will still be a family, no matter where you are."

With that said, and without saying another word about the Hallick decision, they both became rather quiet. Time was inching by and they both kept some private thoughts to themselves. Steve, needing to change the subject, brought up a few funny things that had happened during the day. Some of the boys had acted silly, but no one got into trouble. Overall, it had been a good day, and Steve watched Jeff laugh and giggle for about an hour about all of the antics that went on in that famous parlor room during open house.

* * *

Steve made his decision. He only had one choice. He must take the chance. Tugs at his heart of happy memories with Jeff made him wonder if things would ever be the same between them. He'd heard other people talking and promising to keep in touch, yet the friendships didn't last for the duration of the months and years that passed.

Still, Steve couldn't imagine a time he wouldn't want to talk with Jeff through letters, emails, possibly some phone calls and hopefully occasional visits. Jeff was his younger brother, and not just by a mental decision he'd made. It was by a feeling in the deepest part of him.

What was family anyway? Some kids he knew at school truly hated their brother or sister, and not for just a few weeks. Parents who were considered families often divorced and went their separate ways. So what did the term family mean? To Steve it didn't mean you were accidentally born into some family, and therefore you had to care about each other. Many times that didn't happen. Family, he thought, should mean that you really cared about someone and that person didn't have to be a blood relative. And in that way, Steve and Jeff were brothers in the best sense of the word.

* * *

When Jeff entered his room after school on Friday and saw Steve sitting in unusual silence, he knew.

"Hi, Steve. You look sad. What's wrong?"

"I'm not sad really, but I've decided to go, and I hope I'm making the right decision. How can you know anything for sure?"

"I guess you can't. Life has to leave some surprises, right?"

Steve laughed. "Yes, I guess so."

Jeff smiled and waited because he knew from the heaviness of Steve's shoulders he had many things on his mind. He didn't really need a conversation; he just needed a listener.

"You're the only one I'd tell I'm kind of scared. I know what to expect here and I don't know what I'm getting into. Maybe I'll hate it, and I won't learn anything. Maybe it'll be one big mistake."

"That's one possibility," said Jeff thoughtfully. "On the other hand, the Hallicks have a great reputation, and their success rate is excellent. Sounds like you've got the jitters, but who wouldn't? This is one of those times we talked about, isn't it?" After a brief pause, Jeff continued, "Remember, you told me you have to keep your mind riveted on the things that are good for you and what you want to come into your life."

Jeff saw a forlorn look on Steve's face. It was obvious that he was reminiscing. Between the two of them, they'd formed a great philosophy for their lives.

"You know, Jeff, it was good when I met that teacher. And just at the right time, too. I used to feel lucky about it, you know. I mean, gees, I've changed schools so many times. Who'd have guessed I'd be in that class on that day when that substitute teacher came?"

"Yeah, who'd have guessed?" Jeff watched Steve get brighter.

"Of course, that's when I believed in coincidences. Now I don't ... we don't. It was meant to be. And it sure changed my life. I mean, I know I've got a long way to go, but I've got a system now. And I'm gaining all the time."

"Yeah, that's true. But you were ready and willing to change. That's what makes all the difference. You put effort into those thought exercises."

"But when I start to get off track, which I do now and then, who's going to point it out to me? Who's going to help me get back on track? This isn't a good partnership to break up."

Jeff watched Steve's reaction as he began. "You know, Steve, you've shared plenty with me about your thought system. I use it too, now and it's helping me. I don't think we can ever know anything one hundred percent. Sometimes you've got to be willing to take a chance."

"You really feel that I should go?"

Jeff realized Steve was trying to read his face before he spoke.

"Yes," he said thoughtfully. "I do. It's a good chance for you. It doesn't mean that everything will be perfect. But, it's a chance."

Jeff could see that Steve was beginning to smile and lighten up a bit. The obvious was in front of him. He knew Steve hated some of the decisions of life.

"I know," added Steve, "but why can't I feel it inside? That'd help so much."

"That'd be nice. But sometimes, you've got to go with your gut feeling, you know? And we both know what you're gut feeling is, don't we? You've got to trust yourself."

Steve looked serious as he spoke. "I have to say this honestly, Jeff. If some of the adults around here heard some of the things that come out of your mouth, they wouldn't believe it. Most of the time I feel you're older than me."

"Well, I'm not. Who says an eleven year old who's been alone most of the time can't figure out life a little? I'm scared a lot of times when I have to do things. I wish I was more outgoing like you, but I'm not. I guess that's why I became more of a thinker and a watcher."

"You're much more than that, Jeff, and I don't think you realize it. I think someday a lot of important people will know the name of Jeffrey Lancer Barnes."

"Sure, they will," said Jeff, giggling in his eleven-year-old voice.

"Where did the name Lancer come from? Was it from your family?"

Jeff felt himself retreat inside a little. He'd never told anyone about his middle name, except of course, Sister Margaret. But he wanted Steve to know because he was sure he wouldn't laugh. Big brothers could be great that way.

"Actually, I gave it to myself," said Jeff as he suddenly felt shy and stuttered slightly as he continued.

He cleared his throat and began. "When I was in the 2nd Grade we had to go around the classroom and tell our names and something about ourselves and our families. That was always a tough thing for me. I didn't have any family to talk about, and there was nothing about my life I wanted to share. Gees, I didn't even have a middle name."

"That's okay, Jeff. A middle name isn't everything."

He knew Steve was trying to help. "Usually I'd have liked to dig a quick hole next to my desk and fall in. But, of course, I couldn't do that. All the kids knew I was an orphan. A few snickered because I didn't even have a middle name. Have you ever heard of that? No middle name. Whew! So I talked to Sister Margaret and asked if I could give myself a middle name and would she acknowledge it in class. She loved the idea and said it was okay with her."

"So you got to pick your own middle name? That's cool," Steve said approvingly.

"I thought about what name to choose for a long time. It had to mean something so I could be proud of it. I was so timid and wanted so much to be brave. Then I read the story about Sir Lancelot from the Knights of the Round Table. He was the greatest of King Arthur's knights, and he was brave. And brave was something I wanted to be. So I took the name of Lancer, a shorter form of Lancelot. Now, every time I hear Sister Margaret say it or if I have to tell someone my full name it makes me feel brave and that's what I'm trying to become. I've made great strides already."

"Wow, that's a great name. My middle name is Owen-- that was my grandfather's name, I'm told. So I'm Steve Owen Johnson. Your name is more impressive."

"Not really. Wasn't there a famous person … a ballplayer or someone named Owen? I think so. I can't remember, but I'll try and find out."

"There's only one Jeffrey Lancer Barnes in this world, and I feel lucky to know him." Jeff loved the proud look on Steve's face.

"One is probably enough, but yet that's why we're all so unique. When are you telling Mr. Edmond of your decision? Or did you already tell him?"

"No, oh no, I wanted to tell you first. I'm going to tell him tonight, after dinner. But I'm not sure when I'll have to go. Usually it's pretty soon afterward."

"Oh, really? We probably won't have much more time then."

"Probably not. Think I'll sack out before dinner. Decisions take a lot of energy."

Jeff saw Steve stretch his legs as far as he could on his bed. Jeff smiled, and slowly he, too, succumbed to wonderful sleep that took him to another magical world.

# CHAPTER VII

Steve would leave for the Hallick Foster Home on Monday morning. Part of him was sad since this orphanage had been his best home so far. He remembered his rule of never getting too used to a place or too close to people. Jeff, of course, was the exception. He kept analyzing his decision. Was he making the right choice? He smirked as he remembered Jeff had said kids like them had to take advantage of anything good that came along because maybe there was a reason. It might be part of Steve's "grace along the way," and to snub your nose at a good chance in life wasn't the smartest thing to do.

On Sunday mornings, Jeff always went to the religious service. This time, Steve joined him.

"That preacher was okay, Jeff. He wasn't at all what I expected. Are they usually like that?"

"No, not always. But that's Jonathon Watters. He's a deacon from a nearby Catholic Church. He does have a good philosophy, and I was surprised when I found out he was Catholic. Usually I heard they were hell and damnation thinkers. Yet Sister Margaret isn't. I wonder if they know each other."

"Maybe they do," said Steve laughingly. Yet he realized what Jeff was saying. Maybe they're from a new breed.

"I wouldn't have liked some of the old religions that scared you. What kind of a thing is that to do?" Jeff said.

Steve added his own thoughts. "Doesn't make much sense to me and it never did. That's usually why I never went to these services. One foster home used to make us sit through these services every Sunday, and they scared me when I was younger. I couldn't wait to get out of there. But I liked this one today. I really did."

Steve listened to Jeff's explanation.

"Well, Jonathon is one of the better preachers. Some of the others are okay, but some still try to scare you. Like they know how God is going to judge every single person. They're only one person, too, so how would they know?"

"That's right, Jeff. I've always wondered how they could possibly know what God thought."

"Yeah, and that's another thing. If you heard two or three preachers talk about the Bible, they didn't even agree with each other. One said it meant this and the other said it didn't, so I figured they don't even know for sure. Maybe my ideas are as good as theirs."

"Hey, that's right. Good thinking, little buddy."

Steve was again amazed at Jeff. He did so much thinking, but it made sense.

"What are you doing today, Steve? It's your last day."

"I have at least a two hour meeting with Mr. Edmond. I think it's just to get some things straightened out. He told me it was nothing to be concerned about. He wants to give me some pointers about a lot of things. Who knows?"

"Oh, okay, I've got some studying to do anyway."

Steve smiled. Studying was always part of Jeff's day.

"And then we're going to have your party later this afternoon. But I want to have some time for us to talk again before you leave. I figured maybe later in our room. I still have a few things I'd like to tell you. Okay?"

"Oh, yeah, for sure, Jeff. I figured we'd talk for a while tonight."

\* \* \*

Jeff retreated upstairs to study when Mr. Edmond came looking for Steve. Climbing the stairs to his room, Jeff always avoided the creaks in the stairs as a triumphant act, but as he reached his room the melancholy had already started to sink in. Soon Steve wouldn't be here, and he'd be alone again. Somehow, this feeling wasn't as scary as it used to be. Maybe it was because he was getting older. Jeff remembered he had a birthday coming soon, then he'd be twelve years old. He couldn't imagine being twelve.

It was late afternoon, almost dinnertime, when Steve returned to the room. He had a lot of heaviness on his face, but assured Jeff that nothing was wrong. He was realizing the decision he'd made. Steve felt that growing up enough to make your own decisions wasn't all that great sometimes.

\* \* \*

Stomping up the stairs together after dinner, Jeff was happy the home had given Steve a nice party. Steve reminded him that he knew where to land on the third and sixth step and would probably never forget it, no matter how many years he lived. Jeff went into endless giggles.

He saw sadness slowly cover Steve's face. This last night was tough, so Jeff reminded him of good moments at the orphanage. They both tried to enjoy themselves, but a somber atmosphere was quietly settling in the room and interfering with their gallant attempt to be nonchalant.

Jeff began. "This is really it, isn't it? This is our last night as roommates."

"Yes, it is," answered Steve, "and since I've lived here with you it's been one of the best times of my entire life."

They both sat calmly and quietly as the ending sank in. Then in his usual successful manner of turning around a glum situation, Jeff added, "But it isn't the end at all. It's a new beginning for you ... a great new beginning. We have to remember that. You'll always be my friend and my big brother wherever you are. No distance can take that away."

Hard as he tried, Jeff had to fight the tremor in his voice. He was sure Steve had noticed. He knew what he said was the truth, and he wanted the best for Steve, but his heart and body already ached at the idea of missing him. Steve wouldn't be there when he came home from school tomorrow. He wouldn't have anybody to wrestle with anymore and, most important, he'd lost his ally among the older boys.

"That's the one thing I must keep in the front of my thoughts. You're always my best friend and little brother. Someday we'd have to separate anyway. Life is just that way. But it always hurts when it's time to part, doesn't it?"

"Yeah, but I've learned a lot from you, Steve. I'm going to remember all the good times and that'll keep me close to you. But I'll miss you a lot; I can't deny that."

"I know you'll always be okay, Jeff. You're one sharp little guy. You'll probably graduate at the head of your class as much as you study all of time. And with a good education you can do anything you want."

"I hope so. My teacher told a story once about a puny little tree planted in the middle of an acre of land, and everyone thought it would die. There were other sturdier trees planted near the barn and another one near the house. Those trees were sheltered and were supposed to grow better. But you know what? That puny little tree had to learn to bend and go with the wind and snow and rain, and it had to survive all of the bad elements. It was the puny little tree that became the best and the strongest tree on that farm. It had learned to grow strong on its own and didn't always have others around protecting it. That's like you and me, Steve."

Steve nodded.

Then Jeff continued. "We've learned to get by. We didn't have parents around solving our problems. And look at us. We've done quite well, I think."

Jeff's voice did crack a few times, and he felt a small tear escape from his left eye that he didn't even bother to wipe away. It traveled all the way down his cheek and found a way to curve toward his lip. After this statement, Jeff sat and stared at Steve sitting cross-legged on his own bed savoring their conversation.

"There's one thing I'd like to tell you, Steve. It's important, and I've never, ever told anyone in my whole life. It's not that I didn't trust you, but there was no need until now."

Jeff noticed Steve's interested look.

"I've always keep your secrets. What is it?"

Jeff knew that Steve was surprised at his extremely serious and deliberate frame of mind. It was a side that he seldom showed.

"Well, this isn't easy to say, even to you. I know you're aware of my story; I'd lived in a trailer park with my father until he died. With no known relatives, I was brought here, and I've remained here for six years. Anyway, one night I was sneaking downstairs to get something to eat. I paused by the sitting room because I heard a few voices talking, like whispering a secret. Anyway, as I passed by I heard my name mentioned. At first, I panicked because I thought they'd spotted me, but then I realized they hadn't seen me at all. They were talking about me and my situation, as they called it. They thought everything about me was sad. But then they said something that shocked me."

"Gees, Jeff, if you overhear house-parents talking about you, well, we both know that's the only way we ever hear the truth. Rotten as it is, no one tells us the truth. God, Jeff, what did you hear?"

"Well, first of all, I found out that the man I lived with in the trailer park wasn't my father."

"What? He wasn't your father?" Steve was visibly shaken. He stuttered, "Well, who was he? Maybe he was your grandfather. You said he was older?"

"No, that was my first thought, too, but the house-parents said the police tested his DNA and found that he couldn't possibly be related to me. Now, I don't know how they can be sure about that, but that's what they said."

"Wow, that must be confusing and hurt like hell. What else did they say?"

"Yes, well ... and this is the hardest part. They said the police believed I was one of those kids who were snatched from somewhere."

Steve sat in shock with his mouth open. Jeff knew immediately he felt his pain, and somehow that made the burden a little lighter. As he got lost in his own recollection for a moment, he noticed Steve waited patiently until he was ready to continue.

"Yes, 'snatched' was the word they used. The police said they didn't think I was taken from around here, but probably from far away. Still, they posted all kind of information on television and placed posters all over the place. No one knew who I was--at least no one ever called."

"Wow, and you've never told anyone what you heard?"

"No, I wasn't supposed to be there anyway. I was supposed to be in bed. I almost passed out right there in the hallway, but I managed to hold on. I sure wasn't hungry anymore, and as soon as I got my wits about me I went back upstairs thankful I'd mastered the stairs and didn't get caught."

"How do you handle this, Jeff? How do you feel about something like this?"

"Well, I did cry a lot at first. I was around seven when I found out. I figured I had parents out there somewhere who wanted me, you know. Somehow, that helped me feel a little bit better. Even the house-parents said it was too bad that they couldn't find my real parents because now with this man dead I could have been returned to them. But no one ever found my parents or any other relatives."

"Life really sucks, doesn't it? You probably have parents who panicked when you were taken and would love to have you back."

"Yeah, that's why I work with my dreams now. I've had some dreams about a woman coming into a room where I was sleeping, and she'd kiss me on the forehead. I'm only guessing but that could be my mom. There was also a little white dog that licked me a lot and made me laugh. Then I've had images of a man that I guess might be my real dad. Some people think that dreams are just crazy, but I don't think so. A few of them made a lot of sense."

"That's too bad, Jeff. I'm so sad for you. But it does make me admire you even more. You're so much stronger than even I thought you were. You've kept this to yourself. Why?"

"I didn't think it would make any difference. People would feel sorry for me, and I'd hate that. I've never even told Sister Margaret. But sometimes I think that if anything ever happened to me, I'd like one person in this world to know I'm aware what happened to me. And I just wanted you to be the one."

"You're really something, Jeff. And I don't even think you know it yet. What's inside of you makes you so strong?"

"I don't think I'm strong. I wish it hadn't happened and that I was living with my parents, and had my original life. But this did happen, and nothing can change that. So you either whine about bad things or not. I'm learning, little by little, life just is, you know, like we've talked about. We have to go with the best we're offered, and that's why you're going to the Hallick Foster Home tomorrow."

"I know. I know. Don't you think it'll be interesting in about thirty years from now when you and I are looking back over our lives and we'll think about this moment. I know I'll always remember what I'm feeling right now. I don't think I can ever forget it." Steve looked very sad at that moment.

"Yeah, I'm sad, too, but life should be a wonderful adventure. We can make it that way."

"Good idea." And that ended Steve's part of the conversation.

\* \* \*

Jeff watched as Steve rolled over slowly in his bed, stretching his legs as far as they could go. He was getting sleepy. This ended a stressful day. Within a short time Jeff realized he'd completely forgot to tell Steve an important thing. He called his name.

"Steve, I forgot to tell you something."

There was no answer from the other side of the room, so Jeff tried again.

"Steve, are you still awake?"

At that moment Jeff heard what seemed like snoring coming from Steve's bed. Jeff knew Steve was a heavy sleeper, and waking him was always tough. In his excitement to get everything said, Jeff realized he'd missed something important. He decided he'd write it all down and put it on top of Steve's heavily packed brown duffel bag where he couldn't possibly miss it. Looking back on what he wrote he knew Steve would be pleased. It read:

Hi Steve,

I guess this is my first letter to you. I forgot to tell you something I found out about your middle name Owen. I knew it was just as important as mine, maybe even more so. Look at the important people with the name Owen, either first or last name.

Freeman Harrison Owens--1890-1979--Changed the movie making industry when he perfected the process of putting sound on film. He was an inventor with over 200 patents. Very respected by Eastman-Kodak Company.

Michael Owen--great soccer player. At eighteen years of age, he was the youngest National Team Member of England's 1998 World Cup Squad.

Wilfred Owen--He was one of England's great English poets of World War I. He was brave in battle and wrote about his experiences.

Jesse Owens--Awarded the Medal of Freedom--In 1976, Jesse Owens was awarded the highest honor a civilian of the United States can receive. President Gerald R. Ford awarded

him the Medal of Freedom. He overcame racism and bigotry and became one of the best athletes in the world. He set several world records in the 1935 and 1936 Olympics.
AND LAST BUT MOST IMPORTANT
Steve Owen Johnson--Details will be added later.

Best of luck to you--I really love you, Big Brother.

Jeff

Jeff now felt satisfied inside that he'd shared everything with Steve. He could relax enough to welcome sleep. Life could be good at times, but he knew Steve wouldn't be there anymore. He tried to keep himself awake since he could still look over at Steve sleeping. This would be the last night for that. So many things would change for both of them, he thought. Their lives had begun a new adventure, and Jeff hoped it would be good. With his eyes closing constantly, Jeff was fighting the impending sleep. He realized he was losing the battle, and soon he'd be awakening for school and Steve would be gone. One more look across the room confirmed there really had been a Steve Owen Johnson in his life, and that part wasn't a dream. Blissful sleep was taking over, and the time had come to accept the future.

# CHAPTER VIII

Jeff adjusted as best he could to Steve's departure, although his heart ached at times. He learned what it meant to miss someone you love. He had a big brother out there somewhere and was anxious to see him again. Steve, good to his word, had written within a week with the promise of more to come. And he'd even put a postage stamp in the envelope so Jeff could write back easily. That settled Jeff's heart considerably. Just knowing his connection was still there added a dimension to his personality that couldn't be explained, except by an understanding of the heart.

Sitting in his favorite seat at the back of the bus, Jeff pondered what fate had in mind for him now. Steve being gone was the most singularly difficult episode of his life, so far. To have found a bosom buddy, big brother, and best friend all in one and have him move many miles away was difficult. But more was to come, as had been confirmed by a recent conversation with his other friend, Frank Anderson.

"Hi, Jeff. I'll bet you were surprised to find out I'm moving," said Frank as he sat in the empty seat next to him. "My dad's being transferred, and we don't have much time to pack or anything. I sure hope I'll like the school there. I won't know anybody. You're lucky to stay here."

Jeff was surprised to hear anyone call him lucky, but Frank did look gloomy. "I'm sure you'll do fine, Frank. Your family will be with you, and you make friends easily."

"Yeah, but it's hard to find your way around at first. And by the time I get there, all the kids will already know each other. I hate being the new kid on the block. I wish we'd stay here, you know."

"I hate to see you go, Frank. Life is just that way sometimes. It doesn't give us a choice." Frank looked at him thoughtfully and said, "Yeah, you're right. That's true, isn't it?"

Frank was a casual friend, but Jeff liked him, and he didn't have many others he could talk to. Looking out the dirty window of the bus with his elbow on the windowsill as usual, Jeff thought the world could be mean to young boys like him who had little choice as to where they could live and what they could do. When he was older, he'd visit everyone he wanted to see. First, of course, it would be Steve, then maybe Frank, if he kept in touch. He could travel, make new friends and visit places now only an interesting idea in the pages of a book. Yes, when he got older he'd have many more choices for his life.

What will happen to me in the future? Who can I confide in now? There's always Sister Margaret, and she's great, but I like to have a guy to talk to, and Frank's father has always been nice to me. But he'll be gone soon enough. Tears wanted to come, but at twelve years old, he knew he could keep his emotions under control, even though it was hard.

"You know, Frank, my friend Steve left a while back, and I really miss him. Now you're leaving, too. I'm going to miss you, too. I wish we could all stay together."

"I'll write to you and maybe we can talk on the phone or email sometimes. My dad says we can keep in touch. That'll be great, right?"

"Yeah, that'll be great," answered Jeff, not convinced that Frank was one who'd keep in touch. As sadness descended on him, Jeff remembered what Steve had taught him. It was a scientific fact that like attracts like. He knew that what you concentrate on grows in your life and what you ignore can disappear. Steve cautioned him to concentrate on good things. Jeff thought he might as well begin right now and think about his older brother and when he'd see him again. Staring at a distant spot outside the window, Jeff wondered how Steve was doing in his new life.

\* \* \*

Steve realized he enjoyed living in Mt. Pleasant, Michigan on an acre of land in a five bedroom colonial. It allowed him room to roam about occasionally, and the atmosphere was nice. He enjoyed the animals, and there was enough property to give him a place to relax. Gees, he thought, it's great to walk around this property.

"Hey, Steve, where did you go?" That was Skitter, age seven, always asking questions.

"Just for a walk, then I stopped to see Mafia." That was the new horse recently acquired.

"I was looking for you. You want to play some ball?" Skitter, real name Jonas, was always trailing around after him. He was an okay kid, but quite whiney and always looking for someone else to entertain him. At fifteen, Steve didn't feel it was his job.

"No, not right now." He felt bad as Skitter walked away looking dejected, but he had no connection with him.

Jason was another foster child. He was seventeen and always busy doing something. Steve didn't have much to do with him. He only saw him at dinner. Everyone had to be home for dinner -- House Rule No. 1. Mostly, Steve wandered around after school. He walked the property and did a lot of thinking. He'd gotten some books on the scientific explanation of thought waves. And he was learning. Yet applying his new information wasn't always easy. He smiled, thinking he was becoming more like Jeff. God, he missed that kid.

Boredom settled in deeply within the first year. His schoolwork was suffering, and Jeff wasn't there to help him. Others tried, but he didn't connect with them. He tried a few after-school activities. That didn't work. He tried finding a part-time job, but transportation made it difficult. Maybe next year would be better. He wandered around a lot. His foster parents talked to him. His anxiety showed, and they were concerned.

He helped around with the horses. He liked that. But he was bored. He didn't fit in anywhere. He thought maybe a little more time would help. That never happened. His happy-go-lucky attitude was disappearing, and his negative attitude and sporadic anger outbursts were returning.

"Damn it, Skitter. I don't want to play with you. Go find something to do on your own." He immediately felt bad. And John Hallick had overheard.

"Sorry, Skitter, I'm not in a good mood today." But feelings weren't mending so easily anymore.

I don't fit in here, he thought. I don't know why. Everyone's nice, but I'm lost. I don't get along with these kids. They're okay, but we don't think alike. Jeff and I thought the same way most of the time. Here I have no one, just like before. The parents talk to me, but I don't connect with them. This has been a big mistake. I wish I could go back. Why can't I feel like I belong? I feel strange. They want me to talk to counselors again. No, no, not more counselors. They never helped. What's wrong with me? I can't get out of the fog anymore. I feel so alone. I'm angry again. Oh no. I've got this whole thing to fight again.

Time moved quickly. Steve liked being sixteen. It got him closer to eighteen, when he'd be able to manage his own life. Two more years, he thought. It seemed like a long time. And so much anger and hate to conquer. Stupid things I've done. I've got to get back in control. Letters from Jeff were always helpful and he opened the latest one and reread it.

Steve,

Hey, big brother? How's it going? From your last letter I know that you're worried about your anger returning. Okay, you know what you have to concentrate on. Remember, even though we're physically apart, we're still one team. You do have a choice of your thoughts. You can switch to something more positive, remember? It may be harder right now, but hang in there, okay? You taught me how to make it through; you can do it, too. Remember to take those deep breaths and relax. It does help.

The school sounds a lot tougher than Roosevelt. It does make it harder when there are a lot of bad influences around. But the world's like that, too. You have to stand your ground. Concentrate on the positive. I know you said this move was a mistake, but it doesn't have to be. Don't think of it as a mistake, but rather as another lesson--a challenge to be overcome. You're sixteen, now and soon you can move out on your own. You said the foster parents were nice, but you've lost your feeling of belonging. I know that's tough, especially for you; you're such a feeling person. But I know you can do it. You'll make it, no matter what.

I've got a great surprise for you. Remember little Michael Mason? Well, guess what? He got adopted. He was so excited and happy. I got a note from him, and he sent one for you, too. I've enclosed it.

I'm always here believing in you. And no matter what happens, I'm in your corner.

Love you,
Your little brother, Jeff.

Relaxing on his bed, Steve let his mind wander. He thought one reason for his unity with Jeff was he felt like a big brother, and that made him feel needed and valuable to someone. Also, Jeff looked up to him and expected great things, so Steve felt he couldn't let him down. He didn't want to let him down even now, but sometimes his rages were so uncontrollable. His light-hearted humor had disappeared. He wished he'd never left the orphanage. But Jeff had mentioned in one letter that maybe his anger would have flared up again no matter where he was living. It was just something that needed to be conquered again. He thought that Jeff was probably right.

Remembering the enclosed letter from Michael Mason, he opened it.

Hi Steve,

I hope you remember me, Michael Mason. Guess what? I got adopted. And you know what, Steve? It was exactly like you told me. I got the family I pictured in my mind, just like you said I would. I got a big brother. His name is Andrew, and he's eleven years old. I also got a little white dog, Daisy, and that's just what I pictured. I did a lot of praying to God. But I kept that picture in my mind and pretended. That's what you told me to do. And it worked. Thanks, Steve. I'll never forget you. And I'm going to say a prayer for you every night for the rest of my life.

I love you,

Michael Mason (Bouchard) --- that's my new last name. Isn't it great?

Steve actually felt a little numb and reread the letter a few times. He definitely had tears in his eyes. He knew a little child believing and praying could create miracles. He wished he could believe like that. That was just a little incident, and it happened a long time ago. Who knew that one little act would mean so much to someone. Steve felt good inside. This little Michael believed he'd done a lot to help him get adopted. And he'd only fed him one little idea. Who could possibly have guessed the results? He put the letter in his shirt pocket. He'd keep it.

He decided to write Jeff immediately and share this moment. He also wanted to admit to his latest problems.

Hi Jeff,

Your letters mean a lot to me. Sorry to be dumping on you, little buddy, but I always thought you had more sense than me.

Thanks for sending me Michael's letter. It's performed magic on me. Kind of like a shot in the arm, which I need right now. It's good to know that one of the orphans made it, and is happy.

Presently, I must admit that I've been getting in deeper and deeper and can't seem to find my way out anymore. I know you've said this is probably another lesson for me, and maybe so, but I'm not sure how it will end.

Don't be too upset, but I've gotten into trouble with the police twice. I've made some stupid decisions, but I'm not myself right now. Those guys I told you about, well, we stole some tires and got caught. The first time I got probation. That was about two months ago, and I swore I wouldn't be stupid again. I didn't tell you because I didn't want to upset you. But now, I must tell you. This time we were smoking marijuana. We lucked out and got probation again, but with counseling for three months. So here I go again. And I know so much better. I'm so dumb and ashamed of myself. I'm going to do better and turn my life around. Maybe it took this to do it.

Don't worry about me Jeff, I'm going to make it. I'm sure you'll worry anyway, but maybe my life had to take this downturn. I don't know what to think anymore. I still believe in our system, but lately, for some reason, I can't seem to get my thoughts together. Actually, that's not true. You see, my thoughts are together, but they're on the negative side. And that proves our theory, too.

Send me good, positive vibrations, okay? And keep those letters coming.

Your big brother, Steve.

* * *

More letters from Jeff in the next year didn't impact Steve the same way. Jeff even started sending some books by Thoreau and Emerson he was presently studying in school. These opened a new world for him with great insights making a strong impression. But it took time. Steve thought of his brother, and it wasn't quite the same since Jeff didn't live in his present location. His feelings were ruling his life. They couldn't discuss things face to face. He needed that. There had been a certain attachment when Jeff was around, a great feeling of belonging that defied explanation. Sadly, it had slowly faded away, and was replaced with awkward feelings of exclusion and seclusion at various times.

Yet Steve tried to walk straight. He'd made great strides, and his attempts were recognized.

"Steve, you're home too much. You need to do more." That was Janice Hallick. He liked her, but getting out in the world was dangerous for him.

"Well, I do better here. Can I help you with anything?"

"No, no, you've done your chores. Why don't you go to the game tonight? You said some of the guys asked you. You can't be a hermit. All you do is read and help around here. Extremes on either end aren't healthy."

"Yeah, I know."

"You're trying so hard to find yourself. You've been doing good for a long time now. You could probably let up a little."

"Maybe you're right. I'll call about the game. Take a chance, right?"

"You know right from wrong. There's always going to be wrong things to do. You've got to face up to it."

Steve did start to go out more. And he maintained his course for a while. He found new friends and continued studying Thoreau and Emerson, who made sense to him in small doses, and he also improved in school.

Yet less than six months after Steve turned seventeen, he was caught with the same boys breaking into cars. This time cocaine was found on one of the boys. Steve said he didn't know about the drugs, but the boys were all together, and the police didn't believe him. Steve didn't even blame them.

No probation. Steve shuddered when he heard those words. He'd really done it this time. How stupid he was. Now he'd have a felony on his record. God, what was wrong with him? Then a choice came from a conference between the attorneys and the judge. The judge agreed that Steve wasn't completely lost yet. It was jail for three years and a felony on his record, or he could join the army with the condition that he'd stay in until the age of twenty-one, with one month of in-depth counseling before he left.

Prison scared him more than anything that ever happened to him in his life. It scared him more than the bullies he'd known, more than all the awful things that happened in some of his early foster homes, even more than his uncertain and confusing future. The army sounded better. And he had his foster parents to thank for that. They still believed in him; bless their hearts. And they, with their attorney, convinced the judge.

* * *

Steve had one month of intensive counseling before he left for the service. And two days before he left, he was allowed a phone call to Jeff. He was nervous about the disappointment he knew he'd hear, but had no choice.

"Hi, Jeff. Bet you're surprised to hear from me."

"Not really, Steve. I had a feeling you'd call me soon. What's up?"

In spite of himself, Steve had to laugh. "Of course, what am I thinking? You probably had an intuition, right?" He heard Jeff laugh.

"Yeah, I still get them, Steve. Are you okay?"

"Yes and no, Jeff. I've got some news to tell you."

"What?"

Steve began slowly. "The bad news is I'm joining the army. The good news is it'll keep me out of jail."

Steve waited for Jeff's reaction. And it came soon.

"Wow, Steve. Are you okay? What happened? I thought you were doing better."

"In some ways I was doing better, but it took all of the control I could find. The Hallicks are good people, and it was mostly their help that kept me out of jail. But I never fit in there and didn't know how to adjust. I think you'd have done better than me. I couldn't seem to make it. I was so lost. Maybe I'm getting older and need to move on, I don't know. But now I'm leaving in a few days for boot camp in Ft. Jackson. It's in South Carolina." Steve waited hopefully. He didn't want Jeff to give up on him.

"Wow! Well, that's okay, Steve. This is just a detour for you. And you know what? I'll bet you can even finish high school there. Maybe you'll like the army, you know? It can be a challenge mentally as well as physically, and that'll suit you."

Steve laughed. He'd hoped Jeff would be upbeat. "You're forever the optimist, aren't you? I didn't even hear you once tell me that I acted stupid or reckless. You didn't even blame me, and I was the one to blame."

Steve heard Jeff talking softer. "You know, Steve, maybe this wasn't a mistake for you. Maybe this is the way you had to go. You've got another chance to make things good in your life. You're going to make it. This is simply a little detour."

"Somehow, Jeff, I think you might be right. Some guys hate the thought of going into the service. Maybe it wouldn't be my first choice, but I don't feel I really mind. I'm not sure why. And after boot camp, which I hear is awful, it's just like having a job. Maybe I'll fit in better."

"I hear your old attitude coming back, Steve. Isn't that funny? You'd think now would be your worst moment, but you sound better than when I talked to you six months ago."

Steve realized Jeff was right. "Six months ago I was in a lot of trouble and trying to get my life back on track. My attitude was awful, and I didn't feel sure about anything. But right now, for some reason, I'm more comfortable and calmer than I've been in a long time."

"Yeah, I can tell. You do sound calm like when we used to talk in our bedroom, you know?"

"I think you're right. I'm okay with this. I'll be writing to you, but boot camp is for eight weeks. I should be able to write to you, but I'm not sure. I'll be in touch as soon as I can. I trust everything is going okay for you. You usually do have your head on straight."

"Oh, I'm doing okay. But I really miss you. So you be careful, okay? And I'll keep those positive vibrations coming and going for you."

Steve took a deep breath. They really understood each other, he thought.

"Thanks, that's best thing you can do. Just a minute."

Steve was back in a moment saying, "I have to go now, but it's been great talking to you. You're always such an encouragement to me. And I'm taking Emerson and Thoreau with me. I'm learning from them, only in little doses, but I'm learning. I like them."

"Yeah, and I have more things to send you. I love you, Steve. Keep a positive thought, okay?"

"Okay, little brother. Bye."

"Bye, Steve."

# CHAPTER IX

Steve felt exhausted on the bus ride to Ft. Jackson. He'd have liked to fall asleep and wake up when it was over, but he didn't. His mind wouldn't relax that much. He was now on his way, he thought. A new chapter in his life was beginning. Where would it take him? He didn't know. He wasn't sad really, but he wasn't happy thinking of all the weird stories he'd heard about boot camp. Yet it beat going to jail.

He decided this time he'd straighten out his life for sure. This was his last chance. He wasn't a child anymore. He was now responsible for his decisions. And after boot camp, this army life might open up something good for him. He didn't have anything else going on anyway. It wasn't like he'd had to give up college or a great career to be here. He'd keep an open mind. But first was boot camp.

He'd heard those first eight weeks were awful. Several guys he knew had been in the service, and they'd said that boot camp was a nightmare. But once you got past that, it wasn't too bad. Still, they hadn't been in the service during war time. Right now, the U.S. was fighting in Iraq and Afghanistan, and Steve was worried he might end up in one of those war zones. Well, that was in the future; right now was boot camp. He remembered what John Hallick had told him in their last discussion before he left.

"Do everything they tell you, and do it right away with a good attitude. Try to make sure that your drill sergeant never learns your name. Once he knows who you are, you're screwed."

Steve laughed.

"I'm not joking. They'll always pick on anyone they know as an example, and I guarantee you don't want to be an example. Life is miserable enough in basic. Don't add on a drill sergeant."

"Okay, I get it. I'm to behave and lay low. Sounds like a good idea."

"It's the only way to get through it easily. Well, there really isn't any easy way to get through it, but this'll make your life simpler."

He smiled as he remembered that both John and Janice Hallick had come to see him off. He was glad they didn't take his bad behavior personally. It wasn't about them. They finally understood when he'd explained it. That left a satisfied smile on their faces.

As the bus slowed down, he knew he'd arrived. He was at the drop off point. Now the bus from Ft. Jackson arrived, and quite a few recruits boarded. After another hour or so, they passed through the gate of Ft. Jackson and continued on to a building that said, Military Training Reception Center. The bus stopped. At this point, a rather large man wearing an impressive hat boarded the bus and yelled, "I'm Staff Sergeant Ray Ramirez. You'll address me as Drill Sergeant. You'll address anyone who wears a hat like this as Drill Sergeant. You are Recruit. From this point on, I don't want to hear the words, 'I', 'me', or 'my' 'they,' 'us,' or anything else from your lips. The correct phrase is 'this recruit,' or 'those recruits' or 'that recruit.' Do I make myself clear?"

The bus responded somewhat in a low tone form of "Yes, Drill Sergeant."

"I can't hear you!" he shouted.

Everyone accepted the challenge. "Yes, Drill Sergeant." This was considerably louder.

He screamed much louder. "I can't hear you, you weak-lunged maggots!"

They all shouted back, "Yes, Drill Sergeant!"

Steve now realized for sure he was in the army. And boot camp probably wouldn't be a lot of fun. However, he immediately realized he had to get himself into a positive frame of mind. Maybe it wouldn't be too bad. He didn't believe that. If it did prove to be as bad as he'd heard, it wouldn't last forever. Yes, that he could hang onto.

Surprisingly, the first few days were quite laid back. There was a lot waiting and many long lines, he thought, but that was easy. Waiting your turn for a diagnostic Army Physical Fitness test, I.D. cards, record processing and uniforms was boring, but that was all. There was also orientation briefings, drills, and ceremony instructions, and the beginning of physical training. He was assigned to a platoon consisting of approximately seventy recruits. God, the process never seemed to end.

During his moments of waiting, Steve scribbled off some notes to Jeff. He knew he'd be anxious to hear from him, and God, from what he'd heard, he might not have the strength to write during the first few weeks. He acknowledged this training would be tough, but others had made it through, and he'd definitely be in better physical condition later. He'd received one brief note from Jeff. It read,

Hi Steve,

I'll keep this short because you'll be too tired to read it. I just need to know when I can call you "Private Johnson."

Hang in there--your attitude sounds good. But I'm not really surprised.

Your little brother--Jeff

Weeks 1-2 was the Red phase and mainly working on physical fitness, learning about communications, basic first aid, and DNC (Drill and Ceremonies) and bayonet training. And before you could move to the next phase, soldiers had to successfully complete the knowledge and skills test. Steve passed. He felt good.

He'd been harassed, yelled at, hurried, and stripped of his hair and individuality within a few hours. He'd learned that his drill instructor (DI) was king. And he'd felt sorry for himself and wished he'd behaved better and not landed in the army at seventeen. Nevertheless, he found out soon enough he wasn't alone in his misery. Everyone in his platoon was experiencing the same thing. They found comfort in each other. Steve was slow to commiserate at first, but found out it did help.

For a time they all hated their DI. He was the one who made them do drills along with agonizing physical exercises, but was never happy with the results. As the weeks passed, their minds got tougher. They were starting to stick together and they thought, he says we can't do it, but we'll show him. And they worked as a team. This was new for Steve. He was now part of a team, and he felt he belonged. It made a difference. He shared with Jeff in a quick, short letter.

There's a lot of grumbling here Jeff, I've got to tell you. Some of the common and lighter ones are: "I hate that God damn DI and I hope he rots," or another version, "I'm so pissed off to be here." Then, "I just want this to be over before I kill him." I felt like that, too, at first, but now I'm beginning to understand what it's all about. It's getting us to work together as a team, you know? Imagine me talking about teamwork. But it's true. When one of us is having trouble with something, we all try harder. We don't want to let the team down. It's a new feeling for me, but I like it. Honestly, Jeff, I feel like I belong to something, finally.

Every night I try to grab one quick phrase from Emerson. I don't have much time but I must continue learning. It must be great to be studying him in class. Last night it was "Each man has his own vocation. The talent is the call. There is one direction in which all space is open to him." Honestly, Jeff, I love this guy. Have to go.

Your Big Brother—Steve

\* \* \*

During the third week, which was the White phase, they were learning about rifles and chemical warfare and more bayonet training. Steve didn't feel good. He'd had a stomach ache for a few days and couldn't quite keep up. And he felt crabby. He found out the army didn't care. Unless you were ready to expire, they didn't believe you. Steve learned the hard way to hide his feelings.

"Okay, recruit, you don't feel well. That's too bad. We all feel sorry for you, don't we?" The DI was acting nasty.

No one said anything. So he continued.

"I said we all feel sorry for Steve, don't we?"

"Yes, Drill Sergeant."

"Yes what?"

"Yes, Drill Sergeant, we all feel sorry for Steve." And they screamed it loud.

"That's right. Now, does that help this little boy feel better?" He said this about two inches from Steve's face as he mocked him. "Maybe he needs his mommy to come and hold his hand."

That did it. The DI hit a bitter note. Much as he tried to keep his composure, he was close to losing it. He hadn't said anything out loud, but the DI saw his face go sour.

"Oh, yeah? Take ten laps, Recruit Johnson. That'll make you feel real good."

Even though he felt ill, Steve headed out for the track happy he hadn't answered the DI out loud. He started running. He was livid. He ran faster. He forgot about feeling ill; he was still fuming. He forced his body to continue running. And then he found out something very important. He had the DI's face in front of him and some of his nasty comments on his mind when he'd first started to run. But then, after a few laps his anger subsided. He still didn't like his DI, but he felt better. He started to run faster. Then he knew. He was running the anger right out of his body. Wow, he didn't know this could happen. It was as if the anger was leaving his body as he pushed himself physically. This was good to know. It was another tool to stay in control. When he returned after his laps, the DI met him immediately.

"Well, Recruit Johnson, how are we feeling now?" This was said in his usual sarcastic tone.

"Better, Drill Sergeant." He didn't want to laugh, but he could have. He felt better and was sure the DI noticed.

"Well, okay then, join your platoon," was all he said. Usually he said much more.

Steve felt satisfied. He could tell there was something on the road to respect in his DI's eyes, and he'd discovered another tool for future use.

The first chance he had, he sent Jeff a letter. He wanted him to know why he didn't have much time to write. He shared his typical day.

5:30 a.m. - Wake up
6:00 a.m. - Physical Training
7:00 a.m. - Breakfast
8:30 a.m. - Training
1200/Noon    - Lunch
1:00 p.m. - Training
5:00 p.m. - Dinner
6:00 p.m. - Drill Sergeant Time
8:00 p.m. - Personal Time
9:00 p.m. - Lights Out

At first some of us didn't even make it to 9:00 p.m. I was one of them. We fell asleep immediately, and you could hear the echoes of sighs all around the barracks. We were totally exhausted. But it started to get better as we all got in better shape. We do get a little more time to ourselves on the weekends, but not much. Hope things are going well with you. I miss you.

Love you,
Your Big Brother--Steve

* * *

Weekends were a little better. Drills, exercises and training were still in full force, but somewhat relaxed. There was more spare time. Steve felt this was probably so that no one totally cracked mentally. A few lighter days helped tremendously.

"Hey, Steve, want to play cards tonight?"

That was John Freeland from Spokane, Washington, John from Spokane as he came to call him. He came from an extremely well-to-do family and had chosen to get his service out of the way before he completed college. Steve knew John had taken a liking to him because he felt they had a lot in common. Steve couldn't begin to imagine what John thought they had in common. John never had to be concerned about earning a living, never had to worry about where he'd live or what he'd eat or whether he'd get kicked out of another foster home. Yet, John formed an attachment to Steve.

"I'm not in the mood tonight. But thanks anyway," answered Steve dryly.

"Oh, come on, Steve. You're the one we need," said John laughing.

"You need me because I'm a lousy poker player," joked Steve, who really didn't enjoy the game. Steve looked at him thoughtfully while appraising him.

"Well, we don't have any hot shots here anyway. You're as good as most of the guys here."

Steve just laughed as he watched John scheming. Steve explained. "You're not even close, John. I'm one of the worst. but becoming a good hot-shot poker player isn't my life's dream anyway."

"Okay, I'm going to give you one last chance, my friend," John said deviously. "Otherwise, I might have to move on to someone else. Devron's playing. You know how funny he is with those stories he tells about Harlem. He's hysterical. And Rodrigez is in. Come on, we need you."

Steve chuckled. There was kind of a riddle about John, although carefully hidden. "No, no, I'm too broke. Maybe some other time."

"Oh, come one, I'll give you a twenty. No pay back needed. No big deal. We need another guy or two."

"Thanks anyway, but no thanks. Try George, he's free tonight."

Steve said this tongue in cheek since almost everyone was free for the evening. They weren't allowed off the base during basic. Also, no one liked George Holland much. He was nervous and clingy. Nervous George, as he was referred to, tried too hard to make friends and frightened people away.

"I think I'll see who else I can find. Later, Steve."

"Yep, later."

* * *

As most filed out to another place for the card game, George meandered over to talk to Steve. Steve watched him as he sheepishly wandered around the barrack and peeked over at Steve as he passed. He could tell George was hoping it was okay to stop and talk. Steve had to wonder how he ever got into the army.

"Want some company for a few minutes, maybe?" George asked hesitantly. Steve noted his usual approach. Something to the effect of, 'I'd love to talk to you if you might possibly want to talk to me.' Steve often wondered what it must feel like to live inside that anxious body.

"Sure, sit down. What's going on with you?"

"Nothing much. I'm a little edgy and, trying to relax a little." Steve decided to jump on this opportunity. George's choice of words had opened a door for him to walk directly into without being accused of nosing into an uncomfortable situation.

"Can you, George? Can you relax a little sometimes? I get the impression that unwinding would be hard for you?"

Steve saw George look quickly and nervously directly into his eyes, seeking a motive behind his words. Other guys in the barracks often laughed at him for his uneasy and sometimes unstable behavior. Yet Steve's eyes tried to convey another message to him. It was close to concern at best, and at worst he was only making conversation. Steve saw George inhale ever so slightly as satisfaction crossed his face.

"Well, relaxing is tough for me, even on the best of days. But sometimes when I can get it all together inside, I'm calmer." Steve thought he must have decided to trust a little.

"That's good you can relax sometimes. A person does need to relax and let go at times, don't you think? Kind of gives them a chance to reinvent themselves."

Steve had chosen his words carefully and had spoken them slowly and deliberately. Then he paused and waited for the reply.

"Sure, I do that, too, but it's easier for some people. I like the way you can be calm and not worry. I wish I'd be like that. Maybe the others would like me more and sometimes include me in things. I know they don't like me. I mean, I don't think they hate me, but they don't really like me. And I hear them when they make fun of me sometimes."

With that, George stopped talking so abruptly that Steve looked over quickly to make sure he was all right. And he was. It seemed he wondered if he'd said too much. He'd gotten quite pensive, and the tone of his last few words conveyed a small lump developing in his throat.

"Well, everyone has their own unique way of being in this world," began Steve slowly. "You think I'm always calm and never worry? No, not even close. I work hard at being able to fool other people, even myself sometimes. Sure, I worry. I was worried about passing the Red Phase, but we both made it into the White Phase, right?"

"Yeah, we did." George looked satisfied.

"Right now I'm worried what will happen to me in the future. I don't want to upset these drill sergeants." Steve stopped to wink at George, and he laughed. "And later, I sure don't want to go to a war zone, but if I do, I hope I'm not in some hot military zone, you know?"

"Yeah, me, too. I don't want to go to war ever, if I can help it. But the way our world is today, I might have to face that. Thinking about going to war is strange for me. In some ways, it'd be easier than facing some people I know. Sounds pretty crazy, doesn't it?"

Steve noticed George looking at him questioningly for understanding.

"You seem to care a lot about what other people think. You have to remember that it's impossible to please most of the people anyway. Why not just please yourself and let the others take you the way you are? Or not."

"Steve, don't you ever worry about what other people think of you?"

"Well, there are some people I'd hope would have a good opinion of me, but my first responsibility is to myself. People have to like me for who I am. We're all so different. There's no way any of us are much alike, know what I mean?"

"Sort of. Are you saying that I should just be me and not worry about what other people think?" George had an inquisitive yet surprised look on his face.

"Exactly, exactly. That's exactly what I mean. What good does worrying about other people do for you?" Steve waited for George to continue.

"You know Steve, for so many years I tried to please everybody. My family was difficult; I guess dysfunctional is what they called us. My father drank too much and so did my mother at times. They always argued, and I'd try to please them both, but I couldn't please either of them. I used to retreat to my room and cry when they fought because I was so scared. I was about five or six years old at the time, but I still remember how scared I was. Then my father would drag me out and slap me because he said I was a wimp, and he wanted me to a good little soldier."

Steve just listened as he knew George wasn't finished.

George paused for a moment, then continued. "I was taken away from them and lived with my grandmother. She was nice to me, but I was still very nervous. And when my dad and mom would come occasionally to visit, they always reminded me that I was a laughable failure." Then George stopped talking and Steve could tell he was in his own world of thoughts.

"Wow, George. That must have been tough for you. Any brothers or sisters?"

"No, there was only me," George said pursing his lips.

It did appear that George was starting slowly to trail off, which was good as several loud recruits wandered back into the barracks and the chance of any further conversation was lost. Shortly after the card-playing crowd returned and almost everyone felt the need for sleep.

George said quickly as he left, "I hope we can talk again sometime."

"Me, too," answered Steve appreciating the satisfied look on George's face.

\* \* \*

The next two nights after dinner some recruits seemed anxious to return to their card game while others wandered around outside. It gave George more chances to corner Steve for a talk. It was getting to be a nightly affair.

One particular night George seemed to have something on his mind and was hesitant about saying it. He'd talked openly about himself overcoming his timidity. Steve saw George open his mouth twice to speak, but didn't.

Finally he got the courage, "Steve, I always do the talking. I'd like to know how you feel about yourself and your life, if you don't mind talking to me about it."

"Well, George, there are times I don't like myself at all. I get angry with myself for some of the stupid things I've done. We're not that different, you know."

"You're just saying that, right?" answered George, as if confused. His face showed surprise at being compared to Steve. "The guys around here like you, and they invite you to do things. They want to hang around with you. They don't do that with me. Except for you, I usually don't have anyone to talk to past the words, 'Hi, how are you?' Then they immediately move on."

Steve noticed George stop talking abruptly and then stared at Steve's face, waiting for him to continue.

"Let me tell you something about myself," Steve began. "As you've trusted me with details of your life, I'd like to trust you with mine."

The look on George's face was complete astonishment. He seemed to have trouble accepting the idea Steve would take him into his confidence. He was so thrilled his demeanor changed drastically and he leaned forward staring directly into Steve's face without a blink. Although this could have made Steve feel uncomfortable, he realized this was a purposeful position taken by George to let him know he was totally interested in every little syllable he was about to speak.

Inwardly, Steve smiled because being able to trust George was easy for him. Nobody talked to George, so he wouldn't be repeating his stories. And Steve felt he might be able to help him. He had learned things about thoughts and believing. He had figured out how to think about life and expose himself in appealing ways. In a future time he planned to share the basics with George, sort of 'invest in him.' But right now he needed to earn his trust, and be his friend. And although George desperately needed a friend who cared about him, so did Steve.

He proceeded to tell George his life story. He mentioned his alcoholic mother, his father's tragic motorcycle accident, being expelled from school, and his turbulent life in several foster homes culminating in his forced entry into the army. Finally, he connected their stories.

"It's great that your grandma cares about you, George. It's important to have someone on your side that cares no matter what you do. But I didn't have anyone. I've only seen my mom a few times since I was seven years old, and that's true to this day."

"Wow, Steve, you've had a hard life. I never would have guessed it. You seem to have everything together."

"When I was eleven years old, they put me in an orphanage. For some reason I did better there. The place itself was nice and I kept thinking if I got kicked out I might have to go back to one of the other places. So I started to learn to control my temper and ease my anger. You see George, I found out I could change."

"Really, you did this yourself … all by yourself?"

"Actually I did. I'd been sent to many counselors and psychiatrists, but it was hard to trust them. I held back and didn't always tell the truth. Anyway about this time I became roommates with another kid from the orphanage, Jeffrey Barnes. He's the one I get a letter from at least once a week. Together we started to figure out some of the problems we were having and put some effort into a thought and belief system. But that's an entire story on its own." Steve purposely threw out this little morsel to see George's reaction. He took the bait.

"Wow! What do you mean a thought system? I'd like to learn about that."

"And I'd like to tell you sometime, but for now, I'll just finish my life story, such as it is."

"Oh, okay, that's what I really want to hear anyway."

Steve paused briefly and realized it was doing him a lot of good talking about his life, his mistakes mainly, but also his small victories. Looking up, he saw George with an impatient expression on his face, so he continued.

"Well, when I was fourteen I chose to go to another foster home. It didn't work out very well for me. I didn't fit in, no matter how hard I tried. Eventually I got in with some bad kids. I got into trouble with the police several times and the last time I was going to jail. But the judge gave me a choice of jail or the army. I didn't want to go to jail so after some focused counseling, they enlisted me in the army at seventeen. You see, George, my story's not too good."

"Wow I don't know what to say." It was obvious that George had been mesmerized during Steve's entire story. "You seem so laid back and I thought nothing would bother you. But there's an anger that's always there, right? It's always there when your parents treat you bad. I know I have it. I never talk about it because no one would understand, but I know you would. I have tons of anger but I always keep it inside. Maybe that's why I can't be strong. I hate to say it, but at times I've cried about feeling so worthless."

"Don't be ashamed of crying. I've done it, too," admitted Steve easily.

"No, you don't cry, do you?" asked George in amazement.

"Yes, I have, and I do. There's nothing wrong with crying because it helps you feel better, like it releases something inside. My problem mainly was being angry about feeling like a nothing person. I took it out on the entire world. No one could talk to me, and I never shared. I simmered down after I met my brother, Jeff. Then I moved on and lost the close connection. Again, I resorted to hating myself, hating the world and everyone in it. And if you'd asked me what I wanted instead, I couldn't even tell you."

George got quiet, as did Steve who felt totally worn out after putting so many of his feelings out there. They both sat for a few minutes, and then George broke the silence.

"Steve, I'd like to ask you something."

"Sure, what's on your mind?"

"If you say no, I'll understand, and it's okay."

Steve heard this sad person sitting on the opposite barrack cot from him and realized how much he needed something to put a fire inside of him, and make him realize just how important he was.

"Just ask me."

"I wonder if you would consider being my friend during the rest of our stay here. I know you have other friends, but I don't, and I think I could learn from you. I'd like to know about this thought process you talked about, and how you changed things in your life. What do you say? If you did it, maybe I can do it, too."

Steve looked at George with a slight pain in his heart. "I thought we already were friends, George, but if you need a special statement, then yes, I'd like to be your friend."

"Thanks," said George with a satisfied look on his face. "And could we have some more conversations like this and you could help me improve myself. Okay?"

"Love to, but you have to remember, I don't know it all-- hell, I'm only seventeen. And I've made tons of mistakes. But I've figured out some things that have worked for me, and I'll share with you, absolutely."

"Thanks, thanks a lot. I feel so good right now." And that statement made Steve feel quite useful about himself. He wondered why it was when you forgot about yourself and tried to help somebody else that you felt so darn good.

Again, the time came when some of the other recruits began to repopulate the barracks, preparing for bed, as another intense day in basic training was inevitable. George had told Steve he felt a surge of hope rising as he started to believe there was a way for him to improve.

\*\*\*

Steve felt good inside for having done some sharing with George. It was funny, yet strange how expanding yourself for someone else could give you a wonderful inner glow. But something else was going on he hadn't figured out yet. When you extended yourself for someone else, something changed inside of you. Since Jeff had the stronger religious connection, he could better understand. Yet Steve was reminded of "cooperating with grace along the way." And Steve did feel an alliance with grace at this exact moment. He'd make a mental note and mention this to Jeff.

He remembered a conversation they'd had about 'grace.' Jeff could never figure out what it was and Steve was no help.

"Is grace a kind of luck?" he asked Steve.

"Gosh, I'm not the one to ask, not being very religious. I mean I believe in God sort of, or at least I believe in some of the aspects of Him, like love and truth. I do believe that he'll give us help if we try. I don't think he helps lazy people much, you know the ones that want everything done for them."

Jeff laughed. "You do have a way with words. Yet I know what you mean. And you just gave me an idea. Maybe grace is that extra something you get when you're really trying. Maybe that's it."

"We may have hit on something. That make sense to me. Like an extra helping hand when you're heart's in the right place."

Jeff seemed satisfied with that answer.

"As we get older, Jeff, we may really figure out what that means. Some things take a while to figure out."

Jeff nodded. He seemed to like that thought.

They hadn't spoken again about grace since Steve left the orphanage shortly after. But it was still a lingering thought on his mind.

# CHAPTER X

Steve felt proud. He'd made it through the Red, White and Blue phase, along with George and John. He could now tell Jeff he was a Private. There was an impressive Graduation ceremony. Steve met George's grandma and another family friend. Although Steve didn't have anyone attending for him, he got a congratulatory letter from Jeff, which he expected. But he also received a best wishes telegram from the Hallick family. That meant a lot.

Another satisfaction was the phrases he'd never again have to hear. Examples: "You maggots! Get off your butts now. Move it. Move it." Another was "Get up, you lazy SOB's. Out of those racks right now." Another favorite was "You have 45 seconds. Move it, you lunks, move it!" Steve wasn't sure if he'd have some new ones ahead of him, but hopefully these rather offensive lyrics would now be retired.

John Freeland, George Holland, along with Steve Johnson were all going to Camp Shelby, Mississippi. Steve was happy. His new friends would be with him. Devron Pitfield and Ray Hernandez were going to Ft. Leonard Wood in Missouri. He'd miss them. No one knew where the final destination would be. That came later.

John had confided to Steve that he was quite upset. More combat training meant they'd most likely be sent to a war zone. He wanted his father to get him transferred so he could stay in the United States. Steve calmed him down, but couldn't help thinking that it must be nice to have someone get you out of this.

And, of course, Steve knew George was happy to be staying with him. He was glad, too. He was used to George. And Steve was living one day at a time. Jeff had sent him more books on Thoreau and Emerson cautioning not to be overwhelmed. Take it slow and read just a few paragraphs at a time. Soon enough he realized that a few snippets at a time was more than enough. God, he thought, look at me reading Thoreau and Emerson. Of course, he still studied about thought waves sent out in the atmosphere. Somehow that was his comfortable zone.

* * *

Steve and George read over the brochure they'd received upon arrival at Camp Shelby.

It was one of the largest State National Guard and Reserve training sites in the nation and had a long history of serving the country. Units across the country used its assets to support a variety of missions. It had been used as a special training ground since before WWI and had the capability of training at any given time 12,000 army, Air Force, Marine Corps, Navy, Special Operation Forces, National Guard, and reserve and joint operations personnel in stressful, simulated combat conditions.

"Gees," said George. "I wonder what we're in for here. You're supposed to feel that you're in Iraq or Afghanistan."

"Yeah, this'll be different than Basic, that's for sure," said Steve curiously.

"Yeah," was all George could say as he looked at the pictures of the brochure.

"Hey, George," said Steve as he watched his worried look, "one day at a time. Right? Others have done it, and we'll make it, too."

George smiled.

After orientation, the first few days were shocking. First, they were pushed and shoved by a gang of Iraqi impersonators who yelled and called them names, as their patience grew dim. The crowd kept getting larger, and though they tried to calm them down, the people got angrier. Shortly, a bomb detonated near them. Wounded and innocent people were everywhere and the tension rose. The soldiers had to respond. Their first taste of this type of training was frightening. Later they talked.

John began. "That was done on purpose to show us what we didn't know. Gees, that was scary. It didn't feel pretend to me."

"No, it wasn't supposed to, I don't think," Steve said broodingly. "I thought I'd crap when that bomb went off. It sure seemed real to me. I guess this was to make sure we'd pay close attention to the training coming up."

"Those people were scary. You couldn't see any weapons but you didn't know for sure if they had them hidden." George looked confused to Steve.

"Yeah," said Steve, knowing the feeling. "Looking down the line of those screaming people was unreal. I can't imagine what you're really supposed to do."

"Guess we'll find out soon enough," said John. "Tomorrow we're supposed to see some stuff on video. I guess there's a lot of things that can happen. We've got tons to learn, don't we?"

"That's what they do here at Camp Shelby. All we can do is learn what we can. Right now I'm going to sleep. Tomorrow will come soon enough." With that, Steve turned over and was asleep quickly.

\* \* \*

The next few days and weeks was more of the same. Steve was the first to go to the Forward Operating Base (FOB). He and his partners were exposed to IED's 24 hours a day. He realized that it did help to gain situational understanding and awareness of the threat.

"It's weird," Steve told them. "You actually forget about yourself, forget about being scared and just concentrate on where that IED's coming from. It's amazing."

Other times they were in convoys, being fired upon on all sides and still had to watch out for IEDs and maintain awareness. The whole concept of getting in a convoy was to stay together while looking around for anything odd. Everyone had a job to do, including keeping your eyes moving and taking in everything while staying in communication with other vehicles and their headquarters. Steve didn't feel it would ever get second-hand.

"This sure makes everything real. I guess I know where we're heading," said one of the guys.

"Yeah, does anyone know any way to get out of this?" joked another.

"The world could end," interjected a third, "then we wouldn't have to worry about anything." Jokes helped relieve the tension, but the final journey was always on their minds.

\* \* \*

Three months seemed to go quickly at Camp Shelby. The trio felt pleased and somewhat comfortable with their new skills. Always was the thought, however, that there was more to learn. Yet now they had some basic tools, and when graduation approached, a level a confidence was achieved.

Nervous George led two convoys and, although he blanched when he was first chosen for the task, he immediately took control of himself and led as well as any. He felt proud and although surprised he'd performed so well, a sudden belief in himself began to develop.

His buddy Steve had led several convoys, and he'd gotten three soldiers killed in the first one. All had learned from that difficult experience. Encouragement was always given to each other, and George's last convoy was almost perfect. Even John was impressed and asked George how he felt.

"I feel great. I know I accomplished something good. At first, I almost passed out when they called my name," George added laughing, "but then I remembered some of Steve's ideas of excellence and wouldn't let my mind wander back to anything else. I feel good."

"You should feel great. You did a fantastic job," answered Steve proudly.

"What ideas are you talking about? What do you mean by 'ideas of excellence'?" asked John almost sarcastically.

Looking over at Steve quickly and wondering whether he should divulge some of the theories involved, he noticed a slight shrug and a smirk that said it was up to him. So he continued.

"Well, at the moment they chose me to lead, I simply couldn't believe it. It was as if I went numb and thought I can't do this. But then, Steve told me that anything anyone else in the world can do, I can do also. I must believe in myself. Also, in this particular case, I wasn't alone. I had an entire convoy with me. So I forced the muscles in my body to move in the correct direction and with the movement came somewhat of a decision as to the confidence that would come from somewhere as I went along. It's like you get help from within if you let it come. And it did come."

"I felt good being led by you," added Steve and George saw a huge grin on his face.

"It was funny. At first, I reacted in my old scared way. Then I took control, and the interesting thing was after I started giving the orders and moving with assurance in my muscles and my step, I believed in me, too. I just thought I had to get my men to believe in me. But then I realized if I believed in me, others would, too."

"Way to go, buddy."

George saw the proud look on Steve's face as he slapped him on the back and held his hand on his shoulder for a moment.

"I'm not sure I understand what you two are talking about, but whatever it is, it made you a good leader today."

"Thanks, John. I appreciate that," George said, obviously pleased.

"I can't believe the long days we put in here," said John. "I never get enough sleep, but at least we're getting decent food and showers. Did you know that some places over there don't even have running water? That's what we have to look forward to. Well, hopefully not me, but you two probably will."

George and Steve had begun to understand and ignore this part of their friend's personality, but other recruits thought he was a total jerk.

"What's wrong, Steve? You look down. Sorry, that's probably a dumb question. You're waiting to see if it'll be Afghanistan or Iraq, right? That's the answer."

Steve smiled, and even George noticed that many times John did all his thinking out loud, which left little to wonder what was on his mind.

"I don't know. Something is just bugging at me, you know? Sure I'm a little edgy about waiting for our orders, but there's something else. I don't know. Happens sometimes, know what I mean?"

"Yeah, I guess so. I mean, I get bugged a lot, especially waiting for my dad to do his thing."

Steve added. "I usually just accept life as it happens. Maybe it's just something I ate." They all laughed, and it lightened the air, which had gotten heavy in the last few days.

All of the soldiers were edgy and tense lately with one thing on the forefront of their minds. They all tried to hide it. Then finally, it was roll call, and at least they'd know.

* * *

Waiting for that roll call was tough. Steve's forced his mind to return to Jeff and the calm moments they shared in their room. They had discovered, even as young children, that they could face whatever came their way. And the familial feeling that they discovered they had for each other helped them brave any situation. Steve took a deep breath and tried to relax. At this exact moment, he tried to remember the feelings he had when he felt totally at peace with himself. What was one of those great sayings that Jeff always seem to come up with? He helped his mind relax as he waited, hoping something would cross his mind. And some ideas appeared, just when he needed them. He didn't remember who said them, but it didn't matter. They still helped.

.   Life is not a final, but daily pop quizzes.

.   My life has a superb cast, but I can't seem to remember the important plot.

.   He has not learned the lesson of life who doesn't every day surmount a fear.

.   Life is simple, it's just not easy.

Then attention was called and his wonderful moments of trying to encourage himself ended. He would now hear his fate and hope his strength would endure.

*\*\*\**

CAMP PHOENIX--KABUL, AFGHANISTAN. Steve looked disgustedly at the black words that kept fading in and out from the white paper. His hands shook. He felt faint. Oh God, he didn't want to faint. He'd come so far. This couldn't be true. It must be a mistake. He was going to Afghanistan. He'd have to serve until he turned twenty-one. Having just turned eighteen, he'd be there three years. God, he'd prayed hard. He didn't want this. He'd begged, no war zone. Anywhere in United States. He'd show people he'd changed and could be accountable.

Again he felt some dizziness. Okay, Steve, he thought. Take a deep breath and let it out slowly. His thoughts were murky. His own stupidity had gotten him in the armed forces at seventeen years old anyway. How dumb. If only he'd known. If he'd been alone in the room, Steve thought he'd probably cry. He took another deep breath and looked again at the paper. It hadn't changed. He was going to Kabul, Afghanistan. Okay, that was now a fact. What was it that Jeff always told him? Oh, yeah, life just is. That didn't seem to be a great comfort right now.

Others around him were moaning and groaning at their assignments, too. It turned out that only two soldiers were staying stateside, and all others were being split between Afghanistan, Iraq, and a few other places he didn't even know. Then, Steve thought, what do I know about Afghanistan? It's a country clear across the world, unfamiliar to me. I don't know anything about it. I wonder what language they speak. Well, that probably won't matter since we'll be living on a base, I think. I need to run and think. I don't want to talk to these other guys right now. I don't want to talk to anyone. I need to be alone.

Steve jumped off his top bunk and headed quickly for the track where he could run off his confusion, anxiety, some anger, and most definitely fear. He was afraid. Yet he didn't want to edge under the radar to pessimism or futility and hopelessness. Therefore, he started running, and he kept running and running. I'm so mad at myself for the spot my life is in. I'm mad at the world and the way it's treated me. I'm mad at everyone and everything, but mostly I'm mad at myself. Look at the dumb things I've done. Look what I've done to my life. How stupid those angry years seem now. I'm so scared. Oh, God, I'm so scared. What do I do now? What do I do now?

Steve couldn't believe he was still running. He'd always wanted to do five miles without stopping, and he'd done it and wasn't even aware. But now, feeling totally exhausted since he'd run at full speed, he couldn't catch his breath. He sat right where he was, in the middle of the track. He felt so depleted of physical energy that his emotions were in full control, and he began to shed tears of despair.

It was already getting dark and since no one was around, Steve really let go. He cried about his anger the year his father had been killed. He needed him. He wanted his dad. Then he cried about the years he'd hoped over hope that his mother would straighten out her life and take him out of those miserable foster homes. He cried about the bullies who'd made his life miserable. He even cried about getting a D on a math test in the fifth grade. He cried about everything he could think of and then finally, he stopped. He simply stopped crying and realized that he couldn't cry anymore. It was all gone. And he felt satisfied inside. For years, he'd wanted to cry about the anger and hurt he knew infested him inside. Now he knew how wonderful it was to be free and feel the pleasure of releasing a lot of the pain of the first eighteen years of his life.

He knew the experiences wouldn't ever be forgotten, and they weren't totally erased, yet now he felt in control again. That allowed him room inside for better things. He sat there, still in the middle of the track, and looked around. When he was little, he'd have been afraid to be out at night by himself like this. But he'd outgrown that fear. He'd overcome the fear when he found out he was joining the service or going to jail. He suddenly remembered being in that courtroom and what the judge said to him.

"Young man, I'm not sure what to do with you. This is your third offense, and we gave you a break the first two times. Probation the first time and the second was probation with counseling. We can't give you probation again, understand?"

"Yes, Your Honor." That was all Steve said. He was too scared to say anything else.

"What am I going to do with you? You see, Steve, I don't think you're a lost child, not yet. I simply don't feel that way about you. I get a lot in here whom I wouldn't hesitate to send to prison, but I don't feel that with you. I agree with your counsel on that fact. What am I going to do with you right now? What do you want to do?"

"I don't want to go to jail, Your Honor. I really don't."

"No, I'm sure you don't. It's not like I believe you deserve a choice, but I don't feel you're completely lost to society either. Here's what I'm going to propose. I'm going to give you a choice. Your sentence would automatically be three years in prison and five years' probation with a felony on your record. That's not a good thing. Your second choice would be after a month or so of concentrated and intense counseling, you'll join the army, and you'll have to stay in the service until you're twenty-one years old. What do you want to do? I'll give you five minutes to confer with your counsel and your foster parents."

After a short conference, everyone realized that there wasn't a choice. The army was by far the best option.

"Your Honor, I'd rather join the army than go to jail."

"It seems that you do have some intelligence after all. You could probably finish your high school and hopefully see life in a different light. Good luck to you. It's so ordered."

"Thank you, Your Honor."

"Just make the most of the last opportunity any court will ever give you. That'll be thanks enough." With that, the gavel came down, and Steve heard the finality of the next three years of his life with a small bang.

The service was a better choice. He knew that. Why am I so afraid of Afghanistan? Because a lot of soldiers die there. Yet many make it home from war zones. And a lot of people die at home from car crashes and plane crashes and a lot of other things. No, that's not it. I'm not really that scared of dying. Oh, I know. I get it now. I know what it is. I haven't lived yet. Sure, I'm only eighteen, and I've spent a lot of those years angry at the world and only recently started to see life differently. Oh yes, in a quick sudden pain to his heart he thought, I really miss my brother.

Still sitting in the middle of track, Steve looked around and realized he hadn't noticed a lot of things. This had been his home for three months, and yet so much went unnoticed. The barracks from a distance looked rather attractive in their uniformity. He'd been comfortable here, especially after the first few weeks when he got into the routine. He'd done surprisingly well, completing all assignments and being chosen to help others in certain areas of physical fitness. That had gone well with his new image of himself.

Then, in a quick mystical moment, Steve felt like he wasn't Steve at all. It was like his thoughts and ideas were in slow motion, and he definitely had a surreal feeling. He thought again of his young life and tried to picture his father, but sadly, he couldn't. He tried again, but still couldn't quite get an image of his father's face. Yet, although he heard no words, he knew his father was near. He had felt this before, usually when there was a crisis in his life. It was as if his dad was watching him from afar, but was coming closer in time of need. Steve held his breath and didn't move a muscle. He didn't even blink. This moment must last a while, he thought. The warmth and loving sensation enveloped his entire body, and he found no necessity to breathe. For this one moment, he was happy, satisfied, and aware he could accomplish great things in his life.

Suddenly the moment was gone, but the feeling stayed. Steve put to memory this amazing experience and knew his father would always be there whenever he needed him. That calmed his heart. Time was moving fast and he needed to return to the barracks. He was back to being Steve again, but better. Gone was his feeling of urgency. He felt calmer inside. Gone was his need to know all the answers to his future immediately. He could live daily without heavy worry. Something out there was watching over him.

And it wasn't only his dad, although he felt that was part of it. There was something else, a huge and magnificent something else still hovering over his person yet, affecting him inside as well. It felt like a personal protection still surrounded him, and he felt as if he was walking in a bubble, and this bubble followed him and shielded him from the outside world. This was the something he invited inside and now he wasn't afraid to call it God, or the One. As he neared the barracks, the sensation ebbed a little, but not completely. He realized that his mind was in two realms at the same time.

\* \* \*

Entering the barracks, he came face to face with Nervous George and John from Spokane who'd been looking for him. They didn't look happy and had the same frustrated expression as most of the others. A heavy weight had come down on them all.

"Where have you been? We've been searching for you," asked George, who depended on Steve for support. Steve saw the usual uneasy look on George's face. Yet, to be honest, everyone was uneasy.

"Actually I needed to be alone for a while and think, you know? This was stress-plus for me. How did you do, George?"

"Kabul, Afghanistan. Can you believe it? I was hoping to go back home or at least somewhere in the States. I do think it's better than Iraq, but not much. I'm uneasy about it."

"And you, John from Spokane? Where are you heading?"

John laughed and sneered at the same time. His usual cocky look was showing, although Steve did detect some unnerving qualities showing forth through his self-made armor.

"Kabul, Afghanistan. At least that's what the papers say, but my dad knows many influential people, like senators and others in Washington, and I'm sure he'll work twice as hard as soon as I tell him where I'm assigned. I've already put in a call to him. I'm sure he won't like this at all."

"And what about you?" asked George, nervously waiting for an answer. "Where are you going?"

"Well, guys," replied Steve almost with a slight touch of humor, although he knew for sure, there was no funny side to this situation. Yet, he paused for a long moment trying to keep it a secret a little longer. Who would have thought that they'd all be going to the same place?

"Would you believe Kabul, Afghanistan?" he answered as he stared directly into their faces and watched their sudden reaction. John almost sneered in disbelief, and George had no reaction other than gratefulness since his best friend and mentor would be with him still.

"Really? You and I are going to the same place. That'll certainly help," George said thankfully. "It'll help a lot."

"Wow, who'd have thought?" said John, "but like I said, I'm going to get my dad to change things, so I probably won't be joining you."

"Well, for me," said Steve, "things just are the way they are. I don't know anyone who'd help me, even if they could. So I guess that's where I'm destined to be. I don't know anything about the place, but I'm sure I'll learn. Yep, George, it'll be you and me for sure. Who else from here is going there?"

"I don't know. I do know others are going to Afghanistan, just not to Kabul. Is that good or not?" asked George, hoping desperately to get some encouragement from Steve.

"I have no idea. Truly, I haven't. I'm edgy about this assignment, but I guess what will be will be. Anyway, right now, I'm hungry, and I'm heading for the chow hall. Anyone want to join me?"

As expected, George followed him.

* * *

John stayed back, hoping to get that call from his father. He was angry he'd get such an assignment. With his family's position, he felt he should have gotten preferential treatment. After all, his father donated to important causes in the United States. That should count for something. He was sure after he talked to his dad there would be better news. Therefore, John sat on his bunk and waited for that phone call.

John was feeling low at this point. Why hasn't he called? I was sure he'd call as soon as he heard. Doesn't he even care? He's probably too busy again. But he can't be too busy to make just one phone call. Some things never change. Thinking back in time, he remembered.

"John, where are your parents? I haven't seen them yet." That was his third grade teacher, Ms. Perry, who was staying later than usual after open house.

"Oh, they couldn't come today, but my sitter's here. Would you like to talk to her?"

"Oh, I guess that would be okay. Did they make the last open house? I don't remember meeting them."

John looked down sadly, as he answered, "No, they couldn't make that one either."

"That's okay, John. I'll talk to your sitter." She looked embarrassed. John felt better when she smiled at him. He didn't feel so disappointed. His teacher talked to the sitter at every open house of his third and fourth year. She was also the one who'd appeared at his soccer games, but usually he had other representatives at PTA conferences. When the school complained at the lack of parental participation, heavy monetary donations were made to pacify everyone.

He felt lonely at times and still had to hear how lucky he was that his parents held such prominent positions. John wished they held prominent positions at home as well. Life wasn't always what it seemed on the surface. John had always wished, even as a young lad, that his parents had less money, less influence in the city, and spent more time with him. But that never happened.

In some ways, John admired Steve. He knew Steve would have been amazed at that statement. Yet Steve was the one who seemed to have it together inside, where it counted. He knew Steve hadn't had the best life, yet he had a reality and a belief about himself hard to put into words. Look how he'd taken

George under his wing and was working with him. And Steve had only recently turned eighteen. John was already twenty-two, and he hadn't even thought about his personal philosophy. Although his life seemed smooth and luxurious to others looking from the outside, John preferred to admire one person who hadn't had any privileges.

In some ways, John even had a tender feeling for George and would have liked to be his friend. However, he could never get outside of himself. He'd never even found a way to help himself because he didn't know what he needed. He acted a part all the time until he didn't even know for sure who he was. Sometimes he was the sarcastic know-it-all; at other times, he lorded over people about his wealth and his family's influence. And many other parts of his personality were just as futile and yet, that wasn't even John. He'd have loved to be himself, but how could he begin? And who was he really? That was his biggest fear. He didn't know who he was.

\* \* \*

Entering the dinner area, he spotted a seat near Steve and George and appreciated the warm welcome they always gave him, even though he acted like a jerk at times. He realized they didn't want to go to Kabul either and were probably nervous about it. Anyone would be. Yet all he'd talked about was getting out of it because his family had influence. For the first time, John was embarrassed and decided at last to let his guard down just a little and say something.

"Look, guys, I'm sorry about my comments. I should have thought about how you were feeling about your assignments." He sat down, carefully keeping his eyes lowered. He felt frustrated, disappointed, and in turmoil, but he knew his remarks had surprised both Steve and George. This wasn't the type of comment expected from him. He remained silent for a moment, which gave Steve an opportunity to speak.

"That's okay, buddy. I have to be honest. If I knew anybody at all who could pull strings for me, I'd do it, you know. That's just normal."

"Yeah, we don't blame you. After all, nobody in his right mind wants to go to Kabul," added George in a hesitant manner.

"But I feel I was throwing it in your face. That's not what I meant. I know that I'm a selfish bastard a lot of times, but I didn't mean what I said that way."

John knew that some underlying currents of emotion weren't being kept very guarded anymore and one day would probably explode. He was quite sure Steve was noticing some of his unrest. Steve didn't miss much. Even John was seeing that his picture perfect life was probably no better than anyone else. Everyone had challenges, and no amount of money or family position could help all the time. Sometimes, it probably could hamper you as you waited for favors instead of preparing yourself to handle your own problems.

John hesitantly continued. "I put a second call to my mother, but I haven't heard from anyone yet. I thought they'd have called back right away."

John's tenseness began in his shoulders and traveled down throughout his body, yet he believed both Steve and George felt the same inside. Their tension was knowing they were going to Kabul and nothing could be done about it. John felt he had the added pain of wondering if his family could possibly help, and whether they would help, if they could. He was walking a long, hard road alone, hoping he'd make it to the right side.

* * *

By the weekend, everyone was starting to pack for their destination. All of their uniforms and equipment were bundled, and they had to be ready to leave on a moment's notice. For many, the anxiety huddled in the background of their minds as the immediate tasks took up all their focus and attention. They were all going somewhere, mostly overseas, and that fact couldn't be tampered with. Steve noticed a slight maturity in George that impressed him. He accepted his fate quite well, not happy about it, but realizing this was his life for the next few years and determined to make the best of it.

It was four days before John actually talked to his dad; he was told that his mother was too upset to talk to him. Yet she bragged about her brave son in Kabul. Steve saw anger and pain on John's face. He said his father had asked for favors from a few powerful and persuasive people, but hadn't received a response yet. John's dejected look worried Steve. He hoped he could hold it together while he waited for positive news.

# CHAPTER XI

Jeff had Steve constantly on his mind. Although letters and emails made the separation more bearable, the inside pain of missing someone you loved and worried about was constant. But that was life and they both eventually adjusted.

And Jeff's life was moving along. He couldn't believe his luck--or grace. At fourteen years old, he'd been accepted at Hillman High, a school mainly for gifted children. He didn't fall into any gifted category, that was for sure, but their extended view also included a few hard-working dedicated children. He definitely fell into that group. This had been Sister Margaret's idea; she'd sponsored him. After careful investigation into his background, Jeff was accepted.

He'd finally grown taller and felt proud that his height matched most of the other students. It was easy for him to be congenial with the gifted children. He admired them. Most stayed in their own little group, and the competition among them was fierce. But Jeff was no competition. This helped them to accept him.

During the second year he was set up to take some math classes. Never his strong subject, Jeff realized immediately he'd probably need some tutoring. That's okay, he thought. It's offered. Yet another significant event happened, and it occurred on the first day.

Walking into his class, he spotted a rather young looking kid sitting off by himself. It seemed everyone else was with their usual group. Jeff couldn't believe how young this student looked. Why, he couldn't be more than eleven, if that, he thought. Is he in the right class? Then he heard a few of the other gifted students talking about him. Ross Inglewood was his name. He was extremely bright, and crude remarks were made about him. Jealousy was obvious, and the competitive attitude was already in full motion. These guys might be smart, but they were acting like jerks, Jeff thought. Didn't they know he could hear them?

"Gees, I didn't know he'd be in this class. I heard he beat everyone hands down last year."

"Well, he's going to have more competition here. We can guarantee that." That was Martin Bailer, who managed to take top honors in math most of the time.

"Oh, yeah, you're here." One of Martin's friends laughed. "But he's pretty good, I hear."

"Well, he can sit back there by himself. Nobody wants to talk to a child who thinks he's so smart."

"How old is he anyway? He looks young, and that bright red hair and horn-rimmed glasses makes him look creepy." Jeff realized that these boys weren't going to let up.

"Maybe eleven or twelve. Who knows?"

"Looks too young to be in Grade 10, don't you think?"

"I heard he's skipped quite a few classes."

"Well, he's going to get a lot of competition here."

Part of what Jeff heard was the common rivalry always noticeable among these kids. Yet there was an added nastiness he'd never heard before. Looking over at this Ross person, he could tell he'd heard most of the remarks, and it hurt him. What was wrong with these guys? Jeff got up from his chosen seat and selected another spot, right next to Ross. He introduced himself.

"Hi, I'm Jeffrey Barnes, but don't call me Jeffrey, okay? I like Jeff." He winked at Ross as he said it.

"I'm Ross Inglewood. I'm glad to meet you. But as you've heard, I'm not very popular with those guys."

"That's okay. They're not my favorites right now either."

He noticed a sweet smile coming from Ross. He continued.

"How old are you anyway?"

"I'm going to be twelve in a few months. Don't tell them. They think I'm already twelve. How old are you?"

Jeff laughed. "I'm fifteen. But I've got to tell you, Ross, at eleven I was struggling through my Grade 6 math. You must do pretty good to have made it this far."

Several heads turned in their direction from the other group. Some looks were disapproving. Ross looked down.

"You might become an outcast like me now."

"Who cares? The way they've been talking, they're not the group I want to be with. Don't get me wrong, Ross, sometimes when they're not all together they can be nicer, but I don't care for their group mentality no matter how smart they're supposed to be."

Ross was a little shy, Jeff noticed, as he said, "It would be nice if you sat back here with me. I'd like that."

"Okay, then, but I should tell you something right up front." Jeff threw out the bait and waited.

Ross responded. "What?" He looked concerned.

"I'm not one of the gifted children. I'm one of those other few who squeaked in on a prayer. I do work hard because I want to do well, but I'm not gifted. Not even close. That's the only reason they talk to me. I'm no threat to them."

Ross laughed. "That's good. I think sometimes it might be better to be like you than me. I don't have many friends. Some like me okay, but I'm much younger. They don't talk to me very much."

"Well," said Jeff, feeling good about Ross, "if it's okay with you, I'll sit back here, and we can talk. Okay with you?"

"Yeah, I'd like that, Jeff."

At this moment, the teacher walked in and class began. The first day was always easier, but Jeff could tell what was coming. He decided he'd head right down to the admission's office today after class to request a tutor.

A few weeks later, while standing in the hallway talking to a few guys, Ross came walking by, alone as usual. He looked up at Jeff, smiled, but kept walking. Jeff called to him.

"Hey, Ross, come over here."

Ross looked surprised, but approached the group.

"I want you guys to meet my friend here, Ross Inglewood." Then he proceeded to introduce him to everyone. Because Jeff accepted Ross, his friends did, too, and the look on Ross' face was reward enough.

Several weeks into the class showed Jeff how brilliant Ross was. He was better than anyone else in this class. Now he understood the jealousy. He didn't agree with it, but figured it must be hard for some of the other gifted ones to get toppled by a twelve-year-old genius. And Ross was a genius, as far as Jeff was concerned. There were a few occasions when Jeff felt the teacher wasn't even sure of his answers.

Yet this teacher was cool. He didn't mind Ross' obvious brilliance, and Jeff found a lot to admire in Ross himself. He was unassuming, a kid at times, but mostly a person growing like everyone else, except his mental growth was much faster. They'd formed a close friendship. He felt like he was to Ross as Steve had been to him, a friend, confidante, and somewhat of a big brother. Life was amazing at times.

* * *

Jeff's first philosophy class totally amazed him. By the second year, he was looking into the possibilities of mind power and some of the things Steve and he had dreamt of. Some learned and respected men and women believed in a tremendous power that could be accessed and used by those who worked with this power and not against it. To work with this power, you had to understand and believe in it. Sister had mentioned grace, and Jeff wondered about a connection. With this theory in mind, Jeff began serious work about his personal philosophy of life.

At one of their occasional dinners, he discussed with Sister some of his preferences. He liked what Emerson said:

'There is a time in every man's education when he arrives at the conviction that envy is ignorance; that imitation is suicide; that he must take himself for better or for worse as his portion; that though the wide universe is full of good, no kernel of nourishing corn can come to him but through his toil bestowed on that plot of ground which is given to him to till.'

"So you like Thoreau and Emerson, do you?" asked Sister Margaret.

"Yes, I do, and I'm actually starting to understand them," Jeff said laughingly. "Of course, there are still a lot of things I don't understand, but I'm working on them. You know, Sister, I'm still trying to figure out what grace along the way means. That may take years."

Jeff knew Sister made sure her expression gave no clue.

"Of course it will. If you've figured that out, you're already on your way. Many things develop as we grow over the years. I personally still don't know exactly what that phrase always means in my life."

"Really?" replied Jeff, as he felt clearly jolted. He studied Sister's face as he sat back more deeply in his chair and got slightly pensive for a moment.

"You know, that might have helped me a lot if you'd told me that years ago." Jeff seemed amazed at Sister's admission.

"Well, first of all, I don't have all the answers all the time. No one does. Young students many times think that their teachers know everything. I don't, and I'm sure by now you've figured that out. As you grow and mature, you change a lot, then the same ideas mean different things. I didn't want to rob any of you of keeping your minds perfectly open and clear. I didn't want to corrupt you at a tender age and admit I didn't always know what it meant. That would have discouraged you into not even wondering. That phrase will mean something different to each of us."

Jeff saw Sister try to stifle a grin. He remembered she used to love jokes and riddles in class. Then he realized this was probably one of her longest running capers.

"Where did you hear that expression?" Jeff asked.

"Umm, I'm not sure. It seems I've always known it. Maybe I dreamt it long ago. But it seems I've always used that term to understand the happenings in my life."

About this time, the waitress came by with more coffee. Both succumbed as their conversation intensified.

"You know, Sister, for you being a nun and all, you and I are more alike than different. When I first met you, I thought, oh my gosh, a nun, you know, and I was a little kid and you seemed uh--"

"Strange is a good word," supplied Sister. There was that impish grin again. Jeff laughed, and abandoned his attempt to be delicate.

"Yeah, strange is good," he repeated with a quiet laugh. "But I never thought we'd ever have much of a connection. Life is funny, isn't it? You're probably the biggest grace I've had along my way. Lately I've been understanding the concept a little more." Jeff completed this thought with a wink.

"Looking back," Sister said, "I believe you were a perfect match for Hillman High. I've never had any regret recommending you, but then I didn't think I would."

Jeff nodded. "You know, I've never believed in luck. You have to prepare, so when an opportunity comes by, you're ready. Remember what Thoreau said--it's got to be one of my favorites.

If one advances confidently in the direction of
his dreams
And endeavors to live the life which he imagined,
He will meet with success unexpected in common
hours."

Jeff sat quietly for a moment and then added, "I'm glad you recommended and supported me. I think it's a perfect fit for me."

"By the way, how's our friend, Ross, doing? He's quite brilliant you say."

"Ross is a most fascinating person. He told me he skipped Grades 2 and 4. Remember me? I was barely getting into my own in Grade 4. But he was so far ahead of the others that they put him in Grade 5. Then Grade 6 was too easy so they put him directly into Grade 8. He graduated at the top of his class in Grade 8. I'm hoping they'll keep him in Grade 10 for a while."

"I imagine he's quite fascinating?"

"It's like I told Steve. We sure could have used him in grade school. He's only twelve years old right now, and I'm quite sure he could have handled Grade 11 or 12 last year without any real problem. But, his parents felt they didn't want him to get with students too much older because his emotional and social personality was important, too. They wanted a balance. He's getting extra assignments so he doesn't get too bored."

"What are they doing for him?"

"Right now he's reading War and Peace and some Shakespeare plays and must write some deep and involved critiques about them. Also, he's doing some college work in math that will qualify as credits later on. Can you imagine me and Ross as friends? Until you taught me some better study habits I wasn't doing very well in Grades 3 and 4, except of course, in history." Jeff's excitement caused him to shift in his chair. "What's funny is we talk almost even keel about history. I've even told Ross some things he didn't know. Imagine that? To get the best of Ross is quite a feat, believe me."

"And how does Ross relate to the other students?"

"It's tough for him. He'd like more friends, but most keep their distance. Honestly, he can be intimidating whenever he opens his mouth because he knows all this stuff. Most of the gifted egos can't handle it. Honestly, Ross's I.Q. is almost off the charts. They know he's got them beat without even trying."

The waitress brought the check. Time had moved quickly, and the evening was ending.

Sister mentioned, "There are disadvantages to being so intelligent, although it seems life should be a breeze for them, especially in school."

Jeff saw Sister purse her lips. He agreed with her.

"I know. Ross has a couple of things against him. For one thing, he's small, remember, like I used to be. But besides that he has bright red hair and wears horn-rimmed glasses." Jeff laughed at Sister's reaction. "He's just like the movies would have a total nerd look like, but he's so brilliant. For instance in math, my word, Sister, he can multiply numbers in his head before most of us have them entered into our calculators. This makes a lot of kids angry, so our math teacher told him to hold back a little. Now some of the other students snicker, thinking maybe he isn't overly smart after all. Yet he knows the answers like before, he just doesn't say them out loud. Ross says it makes his life a little bit more comfortable that way."

"Ross seems to have good insight for a young kid. That'll do him well."

"Yeah," said Jeffrey honestly, "and he has a good heart."

\* \* \*

At the orphanage, Jeff almost got another roommate. They were moving ten-year-old Jackson Dudley into his room. The move was almost complete when Jackson got unexpectedly adopted. Jeff was happy for him, but still wondered why his day never came. In a way, he thought, maybe that was good. He'd learned to depend on himself.

Good news came the day Jeff turned fifteen. He no longer had to attend open-houses. Finally, he had a choice. He could also choose not to be adopted. By now he felt comfortable at this boys' home. He'd lived here almost ten years. It was home. If he was around he helped out on the big day. Although it was optional, he watched the younger children and saw their reactions. He remembered how he'd felt. Some needed help after a disappointing day.

One afternoon after school, he was summoned to Mr. Edmond's office.

"Jeff, I've noticed how well you handle the younger children after a tough day at the open-houses. You show a lot of caring and compassion, and you do make a difference to them."

"Thanks, I enjoy helping," Jeff said honestly.

"If you don't mind me saying so, you're still somewhat of a shy nature. but you do well extending yourself with the younger children."

Jeff was quiet for a moment, then confided. "I remember how I felt, you know. Those days can be so hard. You get your hopes up, and then no one wants you. That's the real hard part."

"That's true. But you help these kids feel better and we appreciate that. You're good with them."

Jeff saw the proud look on Mr. Edmond's face. He wanted to make sure it was well placed.

"Steve taught me. Did you ever watch him and hear how he'd talk to those little ones? He was impressive. He'd tell me later he wished he could believe some of the things he told them. He wanted to give them hope, you know? Steve had a big heart. He just didn't show it all the time."

"Yes, I know he did. He had hurt and pain, and sometimes it came out like anger. Yet inside, I think he was always good."

That satisfied Jeff.

"Jeff, I have a couple of things to discuss. First, I'd like to make you a Junior Advisor here. It's one of the positions we've created lately. It takes someone like you. You've experienced this life, and you know how these kids feel. You understand them. You're the type who can relate to them. You needn't worry about your school work or anything else. It would be a part-time position. But with it would come a salary. I know you're trying to save money for college, and this could help. Would it interest you?"

"Yes, it would." Jeff felt excited. "That'd be great. Wow, you think I could do it?"

"Jeff, you're doing it now. But from now on, you'll get paid for it."

Jeff knew Mr. Edmond saw his happiness and enthusiasm.

"This is the type of thing you could put on your resume for college recommendations. They always look for community help and humanitarian work. This would look good."

Jeff was beginning to see possibilities. This opportunity fell right into his lap, like another grace.

"One more thing, I want you to know. I would have given you a great recommendation anyway. You've been a model child and student ever since you came here. You were never a problem and never caused trouble. I think you helped Steve a lot."

"We helped each other. I think we were what we both needed at the time. And I gained a big brother for life. Thank you so much, Mr. Edmond. I can't wait to tell Steve."

"You're welcome, Jeff. We're lucky to have you."

* * *

Just before mid-terms, Jeff had twice noticed some of the older boys giving Ross a rough time. It was nothing physical, but it was unpleasant. Ross always scored better than they did on tests. It was their jealousy again. Ross handled it well. Jeff didn't. What was wrong with those guys? This time Mr. Cadent, the math teacher, overheard. A few general statements made in class ruffled a few egos. Later, both Ross and Jeff were asked to stay after class.

"Look, Ross, these guys are acting badly and I can't let it go on. You never complain. Why not?"

Ross simply answered, "I'm used to it by now. That always happens to me."

"I know you've heard it, Jeff, probably a lot more than I have."

"Yeah, and I don't get it. Those guys are smart, too. They're just so jealous of Ross." Jeff shifted in his seat as Ross reacted. "Pardon me, but you haven't ever said nor done anything to antagonize them. You go out of your way to calm them down and simply walk away. He does, Mr. Cadent."

"I'm going to be talking to a few people."

Ross interrupted, "Please don't. It just makes everything worse. After a while, they'll get more used to me or simply start ignoring me. That's okay. It's how it is."

"Ross, getting an education and maturing is more than scholastic work alone. These students, and I know who the worst ones are, have to learn social skills. If they go around acting like that in the real world, they won't make it. I'll keep everything simple, but we must begin to let them know their behavior is not okay."

Ross looked upset.

"Don't worry, Ross. It won't come to them as a complaint from you. I'm much too clever for that. I know a few ways to make them want to act better. If any of these kids got bad remarks on their sessions, their parents would be quite upset. You see, colleges look at schoolwork, but they also look at behavior. They all know I heard them today. Notice how quiet they suddenly were in class? That's how I'll approach it. I just wanted to let you know."

Turning to Jeff, he said, "Ross will never complain and I don't expect you to complain either. But if something happens that's over the top, I expect to be informed. Like I said, we teach a complete education here, and good common sense is part of that. Okay?"

They both nodded and left.

Several weeks later, Mr. Cadent stopped them and asked about progress. It seems Ross didn't have any further problems. Some students would never become his best friends, but life was simpler for him the rest of the year.

\* \* \*

Sister wondered what Jeff had on his mind. He'd only twice before asked for a special meeting with her. Having no family and his friend Steve away in the service, Sister always tried to be available. She felt a close connection with him.

"So many things we have to learn in this life. Not all of it is passing exams in class either, is it?" mentioned Sister, watching Jeff as she put away her never-ending paperwork.

Jeff had told her of Ross's problems. "They've sort of asked me to be a big brother to Ross. That, along with some quite pointed parental/student discussions with those troublesome students have made his life much easier."

Sister watched as Jeff's face took on a purposeful expression.

"That's a good idea."

"Ross and I've had some good philosophical discussions, too, just like Steve and I used to."

"I think you and Steve have created an inroad into some of the mysteries of the mind. How is Steve? Have you heard from him lately?" Sister watched a special expression cover Jeff's face as he thought of Steve.

"I got a letter from him last week. He's on his way to Kabul, Afghanistan any day now. He has to remain in the service until he's twenty-one, so it looks like he'll be there awhile. I want to see him as soon as he gets back in America. I haven't seen him for three years already. We'll both be so different by then. We were both kids when he left. We'll be adults when he gets back."

"Has it been that long? That part of the world is so different. I'm sure he'll have a lot to talk about when he gets back. How did he feel about going?"

"Honestly, he's somewhat scared. Many soldiers are killed over there. We talked a lot about fate, universal laws, and how we believe. And we talk about girls, too." Jeff winked and slapped his hand on the arm of his chair. She noticed his feet now touched the floor. So he thought he'd caught her off guard, did he? She had her comment ready.

"That's a deliciously normal statement, and I'm glad you find time to have fun."

Jeff settled back in his chair and was rather reserved for a few moments. He had a certain tilt of his head and mannerism with his hands that only occurred when he wanted to discuss a difficult idea. Sister noticed his signal immediately and just waited for him to speak.

"You know, we had an open house last week at school. At first, I wasn't going to go. Then I decided that I couldn't spend the rest of my life pretending I didn't have the life I have. I met Ross's parents. It was kind of funny to hear them say that sometimes they don't even understand Ross, and have to go check the Internet or books to know what he's talking about."

"Really? He must be interesting to live with." Sister heard herself laugh. This was a habit for Jeff to take an aside to a subject that was painful for him to face directly. Sister realized Jeff was searching for a particular comfortable approach to begin his subject. She waited.

"The only sticky moment was when they asked if my parents were there."

"Ohhhh, what did you say?"

"At first, I got the usual sick, queer feeling in the pit of my stomach, but I promptly realized I had a choice in my reaction so I just answered the question and said, I live at the Cambridge Home for Boys, and I don't have any parents."

Jeff looked fine, thought Sister. He handled this well.

"They were embarrassed and apologized, but I said none of that was necessary. I told them I accepted my life quite well."

"You're getting comfortable in your present status, aren't you? I mean, you seem to be able to handle yourself in uncomfortable circumstances."

"Somehow, yes. Something inside of me has been making it easier. I can't quite put my finger on it, but at this point in my life I'm just an accepting person, without trying or putting much effort into it. My life is as good as anyone else's and better than some."

"I'm detecting an early maturity from you and a good foundation to build on."

Sister saw Jeff lean forward as he said, "I need to confide something. You know I've wanted to mention something to you over the years, but somehow it was never the right time. But I need to share this with you now."

Jeff paused again before he could continue. "When my father died in that trailer park, I was moved to the orphanage because no one could find any relatives. Apparently the police were suspicious, and they tested my father and me and found out that we couldn't possibly be related."

"Oh no, I never knew that," Sister said, watching a serious young man. "You mean, Mr. Barnes wasn't your father. Who was he?" She tried to keep her voice even and casual.

Jeff told Sister the story of how he'd discovered he was a "snatched" child. When he'd finished this discourse, he took a deep breath and sat back in his chair, a habit he'd picked up when he needed to think and relax. Sister just watched him. She knew his confession came at a high price. He was waiting for her reaction and when she thought he was ready, she began.

Slowly she leaned forward, and asked, "How long did you keep this information to yourself, Jeff?"

"I guess it was almost four years. I finally told Steve the night before he left. I thought if anything ever happened to me, I wanted someone in this world to know I knew I'd been snatched."

Sister pursed her lips. "I've always thought you were a strong and powerful child, a shy child, but a deep thinker, even for a little one. That was a tough secret to carry around with you, and you being such a little boy at the time. How do you feel about it today? How have you processed this information as you matured?"

That was a searching question and she saw Jeff swallow a few times before he answered. Slowly he began to share his thoughts on the subject.

"Well, of course, at first I cried a lot, privately. I was horrified anyone would find out. Then they'd ask me all kinds of questions and probably put me in counseling and feel sorry for me. So I was careful to try and behave the same way I always had so no one would suspect I knew the truth about me. But it hurt a lot to think there are parents out there who love me and want me and I'd never find them. I've told you about some of the dreams I used to have and now, of course, they make more sense. I've written them all down so I wouldn't ever forget them, and maybe someday piecing them together may help."

"Do you have hopes of finding your parents?"

"I don't really know. Many times, even now, I just feel numb about the subject. I don't think anything is totally impossible because out there somewhere are answers for everything, but I'm not putting the rest of my life on hold to search. Honestly, I wouldn't have any clue how to go about it. Yet I'd like to know them and where I came from. I think of it more now that I'm getting older, thinking about college and gearing myself to become a useful and responsible adult, I hope." she saw Jeff wink. "Of course, I'd like to know where I came from, and some nights I have trouble with it. I think I've turned out pretty good, and I'd love my parents to know they could be proud."

"I'm sure they desperately tried to find you. I really can't imagine their turmoil and pain in losing a child in that way, and never knowing if something awful had happened--even if you were dead or alive."

"Yeah, life is strange isn't it? The story at the orphanage was that the old man took good care of me and seemed to love me. They thought probably he was just a lonesome old man who took me for companionship or whatever. Who knows?"

In his reminiscent state of mind, Jeff couldn't help but have tears well up in his eyes, so he quickly and carefully moved his hand to his face to hide his emotions. Sister knew young boys on the verge of manhood were always conscious their behavior couldn't include crying like a child.

"When you look over your life now, how do you think about it?"

"Honestly, it's still tough at times. It was bad enough being an orphan, but being snatched is a totally different situation. I'm not even Jeffrey Barnes. Good grief, who am I? It's not that I think I'm nobody in the usual sense of the word, but I'm a person who doesn't know who I am, where I was born, my parents, my relatives, if any, nothing. I'm just sort of out there somewhere in space and time with no real history. It's overwhelming at times."

Sister offered a challenge. "You've had so many thoughts about this, and most likely, some thoughts haven't even reached the surface yet. But think of this, Jeff. What's in a name anyway? I was called Katherine, as a child and now I'm Sister Margaret. Yet that doesn't define who I am. I decide who I am and who I want to be. I decide where I'm going, and what I'll do with my life. There are so many examples out there of wealthy families whose favored children squandered their inheritance or ruined the family name. So who they were and where they came from wasn't the answer for them. And it isn't for any of us."

Sister paused for effect before she continued. "Do I think it would be easier and better if you had all that information? Sure I do. I liked knowing my mom and dad and my brothers, but they weren't me, and they didn't determine what I'd become. I did. You know God gives us certain families for a reason and perhaps you didn't need that reason past the age of four or five. If that sounds trite, I'm sorry, but I'm deeply committed to the philosophy that we're all separate beings, and we only connect with some people for universal reasons, which we probably won't understand in this world. Everything is

God, and God is everything. So maybe you can dwell on that and see where it leads you."

Jeff's thoughts began in a newly refreshed frame of mind. What was identity? That was something he'd have to think about.

# CHAPTER XII

What's in a name? What's in a family connection? Sister was right, thought Jeff. That doesn't determine our path. Look at Ross Inglewood. His parents are average people. Yet their child, Ross, is a super I.Q. person with inexplicable abilities. Obviously he was nurtured by his parents, but his adeptness was his own and not an offshoot of his family.

Then there was Steve Johnson. His mother was an alcoholic, and he barely remembered his father. Yet after a few mistakes, Steve was moving positively with college dreams and a good philosophy of life. So his family didn't determine his life. What really made people belong together? As people grew and matured, many of them completely changed whom they related to, and some actually hid where they came from. Where was the continuity? Where was the common thread?

To begin making sense out of his own life, Jeff realized he'd have to start at the beginning alone and yet, not alone. No other humans had answers for him, and they couldn't be expected to understand what seemed mysterious anyway. So when quiet time came one Friday afternoon, Jeff set about to discover who he really was. He barricaded himself in his room at the orphanage. This was easy since he didn't have a roommate again. In his favorite position on his bed, he began to submit to a type of meditation. In this light, he tried to discover himself.

Okay, I'm not Jeffrey Barnes, and I've got no known family. I'm not related to anyone on earth whom I know. I'm in a body, but I'm not always aware of it. I don't want to think of myself as being a student at Hillman High because that defines me. I want to think about the feeling I get when I go to the beach and sit in the sand, and look up at the blue sky and feel the warmth of the sun. I know the sensation of hugeness and littleness at the same time, relating to being out of myself. That feeling makes me realize I belong as a part of everything, interrelated and yet separate.

I think of the trees I love in the forest and become a part of nature, and I know I belong. Sometimes I stop and feel the bark of the trees. I must admit I've talked to them, feeling part of the same existence. These trees have been here for thousands of years, and they still exist. How? Who makes sure they'll grow and continue their existence? I'm a part of all this. I'm not a person living in Scranton, PA; I'm a person living and connecting with everything that's universal. I'm looking around and becoming aware of all that's here, the movement of the people and the drama of life without getting into any detail. I'm detached from the entire world, traveling around mentally and spiritually, and observing. How do I feel? How do I feel?

I feel a part of everything, and realize everything has a purpose with nothing being accidental. Everything is occurring for a reason, and the business of nature has its calm, serene moments and its upsurges along the correct timeline. I sit here and observe. I'm on the peripheral part of the universe, detached from all I can imagine, and yet attached. The universe goes on and on into areas and dimensions I not only cannot see, but cannot imagine in my human mind. I sit here, watch, listen, and accept. I know that--.

Jeff was startled out of his thoughts by a loud knock on his door. Darn, he thought, I think I was getting somewhere. Good ideas were coming to me. Gees. His disappointment caused irritation as he answered the door.

"Hey, Jeff, Mr. Edmond wants to see you right away."

"Okay, thanks. I'll be right there."

Taking a deep breath, he thought immediately, there are no coincidences and wondered what was happening now.

\* \* \*

Entering Mr. Edmond's office he found him pacing back and forth. This was quite unusual for him. Immediately upon seeing Jeff, he looked relieved.

"Hi, Jeff. Come in, come in. Take a seat."

"What up?"

"We've got a problem, and it has to do with Takoda Lightfoot. He's had a pretty rough day at school, and he's upset. I need to tell you briefly. Some kids in his class made fun of him, his name, and his Native American background. They were mean and nasty the teacher said."

"Gees, what's their problem?"

"Teacher wasn't sure, but he had to get help to break it up. They were about to get physical, and there were about six boys involved. Actually it was one of the other boys who ran for the teacher, so some were on his side. Right now, he's in the other room crying his eyes out. We haven't been able to settle him down even a little. And he's asking for you."

"Oh, okay. I'll talk to him. I hope I can help. He's mostly scared, right?" Jeff looked to Mr. Edmond for confirmation. He could tell Mr. Edmond was about to take him into his confidence.

"That's only part of it. He feels awful being an Indian right now. He wishes he could be something else. He wants to change his name. As I've said, he's having a difficult time right now. I want you to be prepared."

"Okay, I'll do what I can."

\* \* \*

Jeff opened the door to the other room and saw a distressed and wounded little child. Takoda was seven years old and in the best of circumstances, he was shy and sensitive. God, this must have crushed him completely.

When he saw Jeff, he immediately ran to him and put his little arms around his waist. They stood there in a mutual embrace for a few moments, as Takoda wouldn't let go. Finally, they stood apart for a moment, and Jeff could see a sweet little face, painfully hurt and showing the effects of recent tears.

"I heard you had a tough day at school, Takoda. What happened?"

Wiping his tears with one hand, Takoda had trouble talking through his emotions. Jeff told him to take a deep breath, and they both sat down. Jeff didn't take his hand from his shoulder and stroked his back to calm him.

"They think my name is stupid. Both my names. They said Indians were stupid and bad people. Jason told me there were stories in his family that his great, great grandfather had been killed by Indians." Takoda stopped and took many interrupted gasping breaths as he continued. "They said they hate me because I'm an Indian, and I should go find a reservation and live there. They didn't think any orphanage should take care of me. I hate them. I hate them when they hurt me."

With this said, Takoda started shedding big tears again, and Jeff held him until he calmed down. Tears could be helpful, as Jeff knew, so he waited for them to ease the pain.

"Why is being an Indian so bad, Jeff? Why?"

"There isn't anything bad about being an Indian, Takoda. You should be proud of who you are."

"But they laughed at me and said mean things. They all laughed at me."

"Takoda, did they all laugh at you? Did every single person laugh at you? Or was it maybe only a few who laughed."

Takoda thought for a moment and answered. "Not everyone laughed, but a whole bunch laughed. And I was hurt. I hurt a lot. I'm mad. I don't want to be an Indian anymore."

"They were mean, I think, because they don't understand our history. What they said wasn't true. Not really."

"You don't think Indians are bad, do you, Jeff?"

"No, I don't. They're as good as Italians, French, Mexicans, African Americans or anyone else. You've got to be proud of who you are."

"But they said the Indians killed a lot of people in America. Is that true?"

"Yes, that's true but that's only one part of the story. Let me tell you a little about our history, okay?" At this moment, Jeff felt happy history was his best subject.

"You've studied a little bit about Christopher Columbus, right?

"Yeah, he discovered America. And he came over on the ships Pinta, Santa Maria, and another ship. Right?"

"Yeah, that's right. The other ship was the Nina. Gees, you're smart, Takoda. Well, when Columbus came here and discovered America, there were a lot of Indians who lived here already. You see, they were here first. Later, when more settlers came, the Indians were afraid of losing their land, so there was a war. Actually, there were many wars in this country. Some had Indians in them and other wars didn't have any Indians at all."

"But Jason said my Indian family were killers."

"Then he'd have to say the same about his family. You see, Takoda, in a war, people fight each other and both sides kill each other. The winner is the one who's still standing at the end. Do you understand?"

Takoda's face showed he didn't understand.

"Okay, let me say it like this. Do you remember last week when we heard that sad story about two dogs fighting? Remember, one died at the end? Who do you think won that fight?"

"Oh, I guess it was the dog that was still alive."

"Yeah, in a way. But when people fight, not everyone dies, and yet, nobody really wins. In the fight between the Indians and the settlers, the Indians lost and the government took their land and their homes. But both sides killed people."

"But the Indians were here first, right?"

"Yeah, they were."

"That doesn't seem right, does it?"

"No, it doesn't, and a lot of people don't think the Indians were treated fairly. But let's get back to Jason. You see, some of our history books make it sound like the Indians were the only bad ones. But you know, Takoda, both sides were bad, and both sides were good."

"Well, I don't like it when they make fun of me. But I don't want to change my name."

"Your name is beautiful. What does it mean?"

Oh, my name Takoda means friend to everyone."

Finally, Jeff saw some pride on his little face.

"That's a nice name. You'll learn some people make fun of things they don't understand. That's what people do. Maybe someone in Jason's family doesn't like Indians because of some stories he heard. People do that, you know. It's not the right thing to do, but they do it. You know a lot of people don't like other people for silly reasons."

"Yeah, I know." Takoda was thinking. Then he said, "I remember when Jackson Dudley lived here. Some kids didn't like him because he was black. I thought he was a lot of fun."

"He almost became my roommate, but then he got adopted. Takoda, you're smart for a seven-year-old, you know that?"

"Really, you think I'm smart? Why?"

"You're smart enough to know you have to give every person a chance. You have to like or dislike each person because of them alone. You know what I mean?"

Takoda nodded.

"I liked Jackson, too. Those who never took the time to get to know him, but disliked him only because he was black, well, that was their loss. You have to give every person a chance. If not, you may have lost an opportunity of having a good friend."

"But what should I do about Jason?"

"What do you think you should do about Jason?" Jeff wanted Takoda to think of an answer.

"My teacher said he was going to talk to them and their parents. I don't want to hate him. But what do I do if he starts being nasty again?"

"What do you think you should do?"

Takoda was thinking hard. "Well, I could walk away and talk to other kids. I do have some friends who don't care if I'm Indian or not. I could tell him I think I'm okay, but he'd laugh. I don't want him to laugh at me. Maybe I should stay away from him for a while."

"There are always going to be some people who'll laugh. That's okay. Everyone isn't always going to like you. That's okay, too."

"Really?"

"Sure it is, and your ideas seem good to me. And you could think of other ideas later, too."

"What other ideas?"

"I don't know. What do you think?"

Jeff saw Takoda look at him with a smile. Suddenly there was a knock on the door. Mr. Edmond peeked in to remind them dinner was almost ready.

"I was thinking, Jeff. How come you always answer my question with another question?"

"I don't know. Why do you think I do that?"

This sent Takoda into little giggles for the first time.

"You're funny, Jeff."

"Thank you. I'll take that as a compliment."

"I think you're kind of sneaky. You are, aren't you?"

"Oh, is that a question?"

Takoda laughed out loud. He was doing better.

"I think you want me to figure out what I should do."

"Bingo, and you know why? Never mind, I'll answer this one. Because I think you're smart. You know as well as anyone what you should do. Do you want to know what I think?"

Takoda laughed, but nodded as he looked at Jeff with a much happier face.

"Well, I think today you were caught off guard. You know what I mean? Sure, well, that happens to all of us. There are a lot of times people are mean. And you know what? Sometimes it has nothing to do with you. Maybe they're in a bad mood because someone else was mean to them. So they want to hurt someone else. Does that make sense?"

Takoda nodded again.

"Of course it does. We all do it. We're all mean to each other sometimes and other times we can be real nice. Maybe tomorrow Jason will be nice again. You've told me you've had fun with him before. Maybe somebody hurt him, and he took it out on you. You understand that, right?"

"Yeah, but it hurt so much."

"Life does hurt sometimes, but other times it feels good. I think you're feeling better now. Right?"

"I always feel better when I talk to you."

"You can talk to me anytime. And other times, I may need to talk to you, okay?"

"Really?"

"Yeah, really."

"I can think of one thing that would make me feel real good." Jeff saw an anxious face looking at him.

"Name it, Takoda. What can I do?"

"You could let me sit next to you at dinner."

"Oh great, I'd like that too. We'd better get in there before Mr. Edmond comes back for us."

They both started walking toward the kitchen. Jeff remembered times in the past when bullies had been after him and Steve had helped. He figured Steve must have felt as good as he felt right now.

***

Shortly after dinner, Jeff was called again to Mr. Edmond's office. It seemed that Takoda's teacher was on the phone asking how he was doing. Jeff was invited to take the call. They talked, and Mr. Edmond left the room. When he returned, Jeff had a question.

"Mr. Carson has invited me to come to the school. It seems he wants to give an awareness class for his group and wants a presentation on Native Americans. I guess Takoda's talked about me, and he'd like me to help." Jeff saw a look of pride on Mr. Edmond's face.

"You'd be great at this. This would certainly help Takoda, but it could also help the other children really understand what happened in our country. That's great."

It was obvious to Jeff that Mr. Edmond was excited. So he finished by adding, "I was going to ask for permission to be part of this presentation, but I can tell you like the idea. Then it's okay?"

"I think it'd be great. Wouldn't that help these kids to understand?"

"Yeah, I'd like to be part of that." Mr. Edmond added, "And you're the perfect person for the job."

***

Jeff felt pride as he went back to his room. He was excited to tell Steve. Anything good that happened brought Steve to mind. After settling back on his bed, he continued with his project. Relaxing was welcomed, and then the thoughts resumed.

I know that, by myself, I can do nothing. Something much bigger does all the creating, and I can be an instrument if I submit and cooperate. A quick thought flashes across my mind. Jesus said, "The Father in Me, He does all the work." Yeah, I remember that from religion class and wasn't sure what that meant back then. Now I think I know. The Supreme Being is the One who does all of the creating, but he does it through instruments or people who are willing to be useful in the creation of the world. I myself create nothing, never have and never will. The Supreme Being, with his spirit commingling throughout our world, does it all.

The world has never stopped being creative and never will. More is created every day, and more instruments that are willing are needed. The willing ones grow and relinquish their will to the Supreme Will, and they become part of the pulse of the universe. That doesn't mean that they get everything they want, but they're in a more positive flow of goodness, and the beauty of it is they don't have to worry about the results. They perform their tasks as they're guided and leave the results up to the All-knowing One. And when people seem to complete unbelievable tasks, it's really the Supreme Being who does the work.

Now I just sit and wait. Who am I? What am I? Who and where is my family? The universe says it doesn't matter. I am who I want to be. I create myself every day with the thoughts, ideas, and efforts that I put into my existence. I can only live one day at a time, and living in one-day compartments is enough. I create what I can for one day and then I must rest. I see the results of my mental creation every day by looking around and seeing the circumstances I live in. Anything can be changed, and I do that with my thoughts.

Jeff heard someone at the door, and was jolted out of his meditation. He had reached an unbelievable area of acceptance with the universe with information coming to him from all directions. He'd learned to simply relax, accept, and learn. That was all he had to do. The interruption was almost painful, and Jeff's usually good-natured personality felt a tremendous irritation at being disturbed. Yet he leapt up to attention, which took his mind completely out of its comfortable visit with the great intelligence and accepted the disruption.

Opening the door, he discovered another student was sent up to tell him that he had a phone call. Feeling embarrassed about his bad mood, he thanked his friend and headed downstairs, reminding himself as he skipped down the staircase there are never any accidents or coincidences in life. The universe would probably always have guidance and messages whenever he took the time to cooperate with it.

As he approached the foyer, entrance another student mentioned that he thought the phone call might be long distance, and Jeff's heart skipped a beat thinking it couldn't be possible for Steve to call him; or could it? It most likely was someone else far away.

"Hello, this is Jeff Barnes," he answered, holding his breath in anticipation of what would come next.

On a static-filled line that was mostly cutting in and out, Jeff heard an excited yet familiar voice that thrilled him.

"Hi, Jeff, it's Steve, Steve Johnson. Everything's okay, but I needed to hear your voice. I'm leaving sometime before Saturday, and wanted to talk to you. How are you doing, little brother?"

At this point, Jeff could have cried. Instead, he quickly allowed himself to get caught up in the same excitement that he felt coming from the other end of the line.

"Oh, my God, Steve. It's so fantastic to hear your voice. Is everything okay? You haven't called in a long time. Are you okay?"

"Yes, I'm fine. My buddy George let me use his phone today. Lots of static, for some reason. I tried to call a few months ago, but you weren't home. Things are okay here. We've been working hard and getting in good shape. How are you doing?"

"I'm just fine. You're leaving Saturday? That means you'll get home sometimes in 2007, right?"

"Yep, three years from now. I'm not sure if I'll make it home for your high school graduation, but if not, it'll be shortly after. And I'm heading directly to Scranton, Pennsylvania to spend time with you. Can't wait to see you, little brother."

Jeff loved the excitement in Steve's voice. "Wow, I can't wait. Are things bad where you're going?"

"Well, they're bad all over Afghanistan, but we'll be on a base and only get off in guarded convoys, I'm told. I'm sure we'll have our scary times, but others do it and I can, too. George, here has to stay about two months longer than me." Jeff heard some noises in the background. "And he's mad. I told him I refuse to reenlist. Actually when he gets out I've asked him to come to Scranton, and we can all spend some time together."

"We're going to have one big party when you get here, I can guarantee that."

"Yes, and guess what? I'm going to finish high school and the army will help me with college. And I'm going. Me, Steve Johnson, is going to college. Can you believe that? I'll be in a war zone area, but they've opened an Education Center right on base. I can take online courses from there. Can you believe it?"

"Yes, Yes," answered Jeff emphatically. "That's great news. You can email me if you need help and I'll get Ross involved, too."

"I only have another minute or two, but I want to let you know that I love you, little brother, and you're still my family."

Jeff loved hearing that. "Me, too. Guess what?"

"Hope it's good news."

"Yes, it is. We have an Indian kid here named Takoda Lightfoot. He's been here about six months. He's only about seven years old, and lately, kids have been mean to him at school because he's Indian."

"Here we go again. What's wrong with people?"

"They're kids, too, and they don't understand. Anyway, I've been asked by his teacher to help him out with a presentation, in History class. We're going to talk about the Indians and their contribution to this country. It has to start somewhere."

"God, you're the perfect person."

"I know, and one other thing. The other day he asked if I'd be his big brother. That brought back memories. So by the time you get home, you'll find out our family is growing."

"That's great. I know that George and I are quite connected, too. Funny, huh? We're supposed be orphans and alone, yet we've made such good connections."

"Yeah, it's great, isn't it?"

"Yeah. George says hi, and he can't wait to meet you. I've told him what a terrific kid you are."

"Well, I hope he isn't too disappointed. I still remember our last night together."

"Me, too. I think about it sometimes. I hate to do this, Jeff, but I've got to go. This five minute call went so fast. Try to behave yourself, okay? Just kidding, if I remember right, you always did behave yourself. Keep those good thoughts, and I'll see you soon. Keep writing. I love getting your letters."

"Me, too. Love you Steve. See you soon."

"Bye, Jeff."

"Bye, Steve."

And with that last comment, the phone line went dead quickly. It happened so fast Jeff actually felt shocked. Their five-minute phone call seemed short. In his mind when he heard Steve's voice, no time had passed at all. Steve was his brother, and the feelings inside for him never changed. Part of Jeff was numb and still frozen, so he sat there in the chair next to the phone and didn't move.

Then slowly and mechanically he started back upstairs. He felt he couldn't possibly regain the momentum he'd had in his meditation, nor did he want to. He'd been jolted to the present moment in his current life, and didn't want to change that fact. Instead, he wished to relive this precious phone call a few times and let all of the words and feelings etch into his memory to be relived over and over.

Jeff took a quick shower to settle down and shake off the impending feeling of dark shadows. These forebodings still occasionally came and could be frightening. It was probably because he missed Steve, he thought. They were both growing up physically, mentally and philosophically and totally without their daily discussions. He hoped they wouldn't ever be out of sync with the other.

To totally unwind from his contact with Steve, which was proving more difficult than he thought, he decided he'd write him a letter. He'd save it until he got his address. He included his latest contact with the universe and some amazing information he'd received. Being sensitive to the fact Steve would be in a war zone and in daily danger, as was his friend George, Jeff wished to relay encouragement and lofty thoughts that might help. Steve was a brave person who usually hid his fears entirely. Yet, he'd hinted of scary and intimidating times ahead. This spoke volumes to Jeff. So he ended his letter with an Emily Dickinson poem that said perfectly what was on his mind:

> We never know how high we are,
> Till we are called to rise,
> And then, if we are true to plan,
> Our statures touch the skies.

Jeff fell asleep that night remembering the feeling of belonging he'd shared with Steve. The scene crossed his mind when Steve first told him he'd love to have a little brother like him. They decided they'd be brothers. And so they were. They were family in the truest sense of the word. He couldn't wait to see Steve again and hoped he could make it home for his high school graduation. It would be so great to have him there in the audience. Hopefully, it could happen. And his last thought that night was to bless his brother Steve and his friend George.

# CHAPTER XIII

Steve noticed John accepted his fate nobly, packed his belongings and was ready to go on command, just like the other soldiers. It was a fateful Saturday morning about 11:00 a.m. They were told to pick up their gear and follow their sergeant to buses that would take them to the airport. Steve hoisted his belongings, looked around for one last time, and prepared to leave the barracks with the others. It was at this exact moment George took a big backward step in his new model of thinking and stopped, frozen in his tracks, unable to move.

"What's wrong, George? You knew we were leaving today. What's wrong?" asked Steve. He recognized immediately the expression of terror on George's face. Although it was obvious George was trying to fight his fear, he still couldn't manage to gather his equipment and move his feet toward the barrack door.

"We've got to go now, George. We've only got a few minutes. Tell me what's happening," asked Steve again in growing concern. "What exactly are you thinking?"

"It's not going to Afghanistan. That's not it," answered George, with obvious tremor in his voice.

"Well, gees, what is it then? George, put a definition on your fear."

"I'm ... I'm afraid to fly. I have to get on an airplane to get to Kabul. I've always thought I wanted to fly one day, but I never have. I can't get on that plane."

"Oh, my God," said John disgustingly. "I can't believe what I'm hearing. We're all going to Kabul, Afghanistan to be put in the middle of a lot of danger. Our lives will be on the line every day, fighting here and there and who knows what else, and you're afraid to get on a stable safe airplane? I can't believe this. Come on, Steve, let the sergeant handle this."

"I'll catch up to you John, we both will," Steve said as he waved at John to leave.

As he left, Steve heard John growl over his shoulder. "This kid has to grow up and find out that life has a lot of tough times. Anyway, George doesn't have a choice. He has to fly on this plane today. End of story."

Watching John shaking his head and totally irritated as he grabbed his duffel bag and walked out of the barracks, Steve knew he was facing his own demons. He turned to George, whom he understood better than most.

"Okay, George, what are you feeling? What are you telling yourself right now?"

"I don't know. I know I just can't do it."

"Okay, you're telling yourself you can't do it. Did you hear yourself? That's what you're mentally telling yourself inside. Got it? You're saying, George, you just can't do this."

"Yeah, I guess that's what I'm saying," repeated George as a tear slipped down his right cheek unnoticed by him.

"But you physically can do it, and you know that. But you don't want to do it, and why is that?" asked Steve.

"I don't know."

"Yes, you do know, in fact you're the only person in this world who does know the reason why. It's okay to be afraid, George, but it's not okay to let fear overtake you completely and freeze up your mind like this. You know you can mentally switch your thoughts. That's your choice. So why aren't you doing that?" With this last statement, Steve sat and waited for an answer, giving George a moment or so, while noticing the change in his facial expression as his body language relaxed ever so slightly.

Taking a deep breath that came out slowly and shakily, George admitted something first to himself, and then to Steve.

"When I was little I thought I'd like to take a plane ride. I told my dad, my mom and my grandmother. Then my dad said the only way any plane would take on a little wimp like me was to tie me to the wing of the plane, and I'd have to hold on with all my might. I remember how scared I was, and I cried for weeks. When the sergeant said we were to head for the plane I got a quick flash of that memory, and I felt frozen to the floor."

"Your father was unstable. You'll be sitting inside the airplane in a seat right next to me if we can manage it. I'm sure we all have hundreds of petrifying thoughts in our memory banks that cause us problems. But once we learn to face our fears, well, then we can conquer them. Try concentrating on enjoying the plane ride. Remember, you do have a choice of thoughts. You might really enjoy it. After all, you've never flown. I have to tell you honestly, George, I've never flown either, and I'm a little nervous, too."

"No, not you! You're not nervous; are you really?"

"Yes, of course I am," said Steve as he slowly started to pick up his equipment and noticed George was involuntarily following his lead. "Oh yes, and just like you, I've always wanted to fly, but never had the chance. I wonder how I'd have felt if I ever had the chance before now. I'll never know. But I have to fly now, so that's probably good. Right, George?"

"Probably. I'm scared, but I've got to do it. Right? I can do it. I can do it." George was talking to himself, ignoring Steve for the moment. "Actually I'm going to be okay. So let's go. Let's go right now." George's hands were still shaking quite a bit, and his voice didn't sound very convincing, but he picked up his bag and forced his body toward the door.

George managed to have a slight smile on his face as they walked out to the buses. Steve caught the surprised look on John's face as they walked toward him. He had obvious questions and even opened his lips to speak, but apparently thought better of it. Another time might be better. There had previously been talk about a pattern of thoughts and ideas in

John's presence. Steve was quite sure sometime in the near future he might be adding another recruit to his philosophy.

Sitting in the seat next to Steve, George kept taking deep breaths, but like Steve kept reminding him, you're on the inside of the plane. As luck would have it, John was seated on the other side of him. Since he'd flown several times already, he prepared George for take off, which although exciting, could be a little frightening. It was like being on a roller coaster he said. Steve heard John mention that after take off, it was rather beautiful once you got high into the sky.

George thought better than telling John he'd never had the guts to get on a roller coaster either. And as promised, take off was loud and disconcerting, but soon they were up in the air and could look down at the cities and make friends with approaching clouds. They all realized at this exact moment their troubles and futures looked small from their heightened view in the sky. It did seem all in life was relative.

The first stop was Shannon, Ireland. Then it was back on the plane to Adana, Turkey for re-fueling. Then after more hours in the air, there was a landing in Manas, Kyrgyzstan. After an overnight rest and recoup, most flew on to Kabul. Luckily, all three remained together. Steve felt he certainly had gotten used to flying, as did George.

From thousands of feet in the air, Kabul could have been any city. Steve realized that from the universal standpoint the people of the world were more alike than different. Cultures and customs would prove different, but people in this part of the world were trying to exist and take care of their families and grow in terms of love and maturity like any other place. Realizing when he reached ground level there would be many differences to observe and acknowledge, Steve knew the outside of the person was the most studied, and the inside of each was the most neglected.

After landing, it was onto armored, escort buses for a ride through parts of Kabul. One of the first memories Steve had was seeing the U.S. Embassy in Afghanistan, which was in

Kabul on the Great Masoud Road. George remarked seeing something with the words U.S. helped him feel he was still connected to America.

"At least the streets are paved. I wasn't sure about that," remarked John who was beginning to recognize the fact he'd be here just like the rest of the recruits.

"I don't think all the streets are paved; only the main ones," Steve said seriously.

"Don't seem too clean, but they're paved. Imagine that?" John commented in surprise.

"Looks pretty dirty and there's a funny smell in the air," George mentioned, looking in many directions and trying to take in every experience he could.

"We'll all have enough time to figure this out, I'm sure," mentioned Steve, who noticed some men on the streets. They wore a turban, a hat and long loose pants clasped close at the ankles. Most also wore coats. There was every combination of colors. With darkness closing in, not much else could be seen.

Planning to make a comment to George, Steve realized he'd nodded off. After all the plane rides he'd recently experienced, Steve was happy to see him relax enough to sleep. He knew they'd all have a lot to learn and not all of it was in the compound. Fighting sleep himself, Steve finally gave in and was only awakened much later by what seemed like a commotion outside the bus. There seemed to be some yelling, loud conversation, and everyone was startled to attention. They calmly waited to find out what was happening.

"Hey, Rambo, we're okay. Here are the papers you need." The driver waived and handed a folder to the security guard.

Rambo quickly walked toward the bus from his security position at the admissions gate of Camp Phoenix and relaxed only slightly as he recognized the bus driver. He took the papers out of his hands and read them.

Steve noticed a short, stocky man who carried a big red pipe as he approached their vehicle. A sergeant on the bus told them that Rambo, as he'd been nicknamed, was known throughout the camp. He was considered a legend and the primary gatekeeper since 2003 when the U.S. forces first rolled up to the front gate. The story is told Rambo was waiting, and he hasn't ever left. "As long as the Americans want me to stay, I will stay."

"Have a good day, Rambo," yelled the bus driver, who had become his friend.

"You, too, my friend. Be careful." That was the last message Rambo gave to the driver as he let them through his gate.

The feeling of camaraderie permeated the air as the bus continued on. Steve looked around surprised to see many soldiers waking up. Although it was dark, he strained to see his new home. Barracks were everywhere, and soon the bus stopped. Looking around outside, Steve was surprised at the tranquil and unruffled atmosphere that surrounded the compound. Being shown to his quarters was all he needed. It didn't take twenty minutes for him to be in a dream state.

* * *

After breakfast, it was orientation. Steve wanted to know what he'd have to do and how much danger he'd face. He was told all would be multi-tasking and everyone took turns on patrols and convoys. No one was given all the dangerous tasks, and no one was given all the easy functions. Everyone shared. Also, no one was allowed off the base, except on a mission. There would be no shopping or walks around the city. There was too much danger. Okay, he realized, this was the army.

As they left the meeting room, Steve looked at George and John. They felt a mixture of fear and excitement. Nobody wanted to be here, but there was a certain strength of heart that would gather the perseverance needed to get the job done. They each had to carry their load as those ahead had done and leave the path secure for those who'd follow. In that fact alone, they were all in agreement.

"Gees," John said as the first one to react out loud, "I wish I knew the routine right now. It's not knowing that's getting to me."

"I'm sure by tomorrow we'll start our routines, then we'll take the mission one day at a time. That's all we can do," Steve answered seriously.

"But aren't you afraid, Steve? Don't you ever get scared?" asked John anxiously.

"Oh, my God, yes," answered Steve, and then with a sneaky smile inclusive to George added, "I was scared on the plane. That was the first time I'd ever flown, too. It was okay later, but at take off, I thought I was going to puke."

"You'd never flown either? You were scared?" said John laughing, throwing a sympathetic glance at George.

"Why not? It's only human," Steve said uneasily. "Everyone gets afraid. We all have a skeleton or two in the closet. I wouldn't trust someone who said he was never afraid."

\* \* \*

Sure, thought John, everyone gets afraid at some point. He was afraid, too, and felt abandoned by his family who hadn't even called him. They knew the date of his departure and never bothered to call back. He felt some of his fears were possibly of a different kind, but so what? Fear was fear, and life would go on. Right now, he needed a positive thought. George had gone for a walk and luckily, Steve was available.

"I know you have your own personal philosophy, which is one reason everyone at Camp Shelby used to latch onto you. Where do you get your ideas?"

John saw Steve get quiet for a moment. It was as if he was waiting for inspiration. Then he began.

"Mostly, they're not my ideas. I mean there aren't any new ideas in life anyway. Still a few years ago, after screwing up my life royally, I began to study the masters, you know like Socrates and Aristotle, but honestly, they were pretty much beyond me. Then I discovered Emerson and Thoreau and some other poets who also had universal ideas I could use and apply today, right now in my daily life. It's worked quite well for me."

Thoughtfully, John remembered, "You know, I had a chance to study some of them at the beginning of my college years. I was too cocky back then and felt I knew everything. Now, listening to you, I wish I had. It wasn't that I thought I knew everything exactly; it was that I wanted other people to agree with me."

John paused before he continued. "You know, I didn't graduate from college," he admitted sadly, "after two years, I flunked out." He felt embarrassed.

"I thought I knew all the answers, too, when I was younger," Steve said honestly, "but even now I believe I'm only beginning to build a philosophy for myself that'll create for me the kind of life I want."

"I like the sound of that. So, in your new philosophy, what would you say about our situation that I could hang onto right now?"

John saw Steve take a moment before he said, "I was reading Emerson on the way over here, and I ran across a great statement. It says, 'Trust yourself. Accept the place that divine providence has found for you.' Isn't that a great idea, really? There's a place for everyone, and right now we're here, and that's got to be okay. We need to find the lesson involved here. After all, life is just one lesson after another anyway."

"Accept the place divine providence has found for you. I'm not sure I'd have gotten to your answer. But I do like it." John watched Steve as he repeated it. Steve looked satisfied.

Steve said, "Everyone's answer is different for themselves; that's the greatest part of this."

"I'll have to think about that, but I do like that expression. Who did you say said it?"

"It was Emerson in his Essay on Self-Reliance. But there are many authors who can give you one thought, and from that you can expand into new ideas."

John now had his opportunity. He'd been wanting to ask Steve about George. "Is this the type of stuff you talk to George about?"

"Yep, it's been great to have someone to talk to. I'm only beginning to see possibilities in the world of thought and--"

"I've seen improvements in George. He's become more self-assured and actually--I don't know--like stronger rather than timid all of the time. I like him better now because before, he used to drive me crazy."

"Do you know one reason why you like him better?" Steve asked.

"What would that be?"

"Because George doesn't care if you like him or not. Do you know what I mean?"

John knew he showed uncertainty.

Steve continued. "Before, George was so wanting and felt so inadequate he always looked to everyone else for a guarantee that he was okay. Now, he looks to himself for validation, and because he accepts himself, others accept him, too."

John saw Steve look directly into his eyes for confirmation. "Oh, I see what you mean. Hey, Steve, are you sure that you're not a psychologist or an old philosopher just masquerading as a private here? You sure do make sense."

Steve laughed. "I like to think of myself as a kindergarten philosopher hoping to graduate from college someday. I needed to make changes in my life. It was like, find a way to change or end up in the gutter someday. I was lost. I soon learned everything starts with thought and how I think about life and the world around me. I, myself, created my life, no one else. I always blamed everyone else, except me. Now I take responsibility for where my life is and where it's heading. And right now it's in the army at Camp Phoenix, and I'm going to make the most out of it."

"Here I am older than you and you seem so much more mature. You know--." John looked thoughtfully at Steve, envious of his confidence and belief.

Just then they were called out for another orientation around the complex, and John vowed to continue their conversation another time. Yet, he already had a lot to think about.

# CHAPTER XIV

The first few weeks in Camp Phoenix left no doubt to Steve that they were in the middle of a war zone. The seriousness of every single maneuver, instruction, explanation, and plan cautioned him this was the real thing. He could hear bombs in the distance--luckily, the far distance. He was told an attack on the compound was always possible. God, he'd have to be ready on a second's notice. His gun always had to be near and in ready condition. His armored vest had to be nearby. He knew what they meant--sometimes there'd be no time to think, just react and do.

There were soldiers stationed in towers around the camp and others had foot patrol duty outside the camp, which gave him some feeling of protection. However, this feeling of protection only provided warning, hopefully, before an attack. Attacks on the compound didn't occur too often, as it was known they were able to defend themselves. But nothing was taken for granted.

On the way to the dining facility, all three started swatting flies. They were everywhere.

"Damn, have you ever seen so many flies? What the hell," complained John, who was revolted at the idea. Steve saw him close to choking.

"Hey, you'll have to get used to them. They don't go away," yelled one soldier passing by.

"This is common?" John said in a disgusted tone of voice.

"Oh, yes, they love Camp Phoenix."

"It seems that flies flourish around Kabul since it's not one of the cleanest cities. The sewer system isn't usually functioning." That explanation came from a more seasoned soldier.

"That's probably why it smelled so bad on the bus ride in here," remembered George.

"Look at it this way," said another soldier. "It's not that the stench ever goes away, but you do get used to it. You don't like it, but your senses will adjust."

Steve said to himself and out loud, "That's a cheerful thought." He hoped the dining area at least blocked part of the smell so he could eat.

Entering the facility, Steve was hit with a heavy plastic covering that hung from the top of the door frame to the floor. The blowers above the door attempted to stop the flies from getting in. And it did make it tough for the flies to get in and a bit challenging for humans, too. Fortunately, it did smell better inside. And the food was unexpectedly decent.

"I'm surprised this base is so small," said John, "only about a square mile. There's about 2,500 of us here, soldiers and civilians."

Steve watched John rummaging through some paperwork bringing up details.

John continued. "There's also a PX where you can shop and hope something you want isn't out of stock." They all laughed at that.

George commented, "I've heard there's a bazaar of Afghan merchants every Friday night. And they sell everything from sunglasses to Persian rugs."

"Who told you that?" John asked.

George was happy to tell what he knew. "Amanda Sanderson. Remember that Sergeant who gave part of the orientation speech? She said she'd bought some good stuff at a cheap price."

"Better start saving all my money so I can bring home some presents," teased Steve as he watched John and George attempt to adapt to their new surroundings. He knew it'd become home soon, just not yet.

John twisted his face and said, "And to think I thought Camp Shelby was bad. Looking back, it seems like a palace."

"I told you guys." Steve laughed as he watched John scowl again. "Everything in life is relative."

By the beginning of the second week, Steve was beginning to breathe a little better. Kabul was 5,700 feet above sea level, he was told, so the air was quite thin. He'd heard it could take up to a month to adjust to the elevation.

Then on the second Saturday after they'd arrived, all three were assigned to more seasoned soldiers and were preparing for their first mission outside the gates. They'd had a lot of orientation and classes as to what to expect. But now, the real tour of duty was beginning.

* * *

Steve went out first, early on Sunday. He'd learned they worked seven-day weeks since attacks didn't have any priority on the day of the week. As he put on his body armor, he gave George and John a smile. No words were needed.

He was on foot patrol around the outside of Camp Phoenix. His partner was Sergeant Joel Rodrigez from Colorado, who'd been here over a year. Steve felt comforted.

"Well, Private Johnson, this is all in a day's work. We must evaluate suspicious people; others are searched, and still others are reprimanded."

"Just the two of us?" Steve felt more soldiers were needed.

"Oh, no, usually we have several soldiers in a few units. Lately, even more have been assigned. The word coming on the silent communication is to stay together. So we'll be covered."

"What do I do?"

"Every time it's different. We protect Camp Phoenix, of course, first and foremost. But we also provide aid. Lots of kids play around here. There are wild dogs that pose a threat, and we discover drug needles all the time. Just keep your eyes peeled and stay close to me. Be ready at all times. Inform me of anything unusual you find. Okay?"

"Okay," Steve said as they moved out.

Steve saw Joel pause for a second to say, "The first time's the hardest and scariest, I know. I've been there, too."

Steve put his personal safety out of his mind and concentrated on the job at hand. Looking around the dirty, smelly area and keeping a roving eye, were small groups of soldiers. He looked for anything out of the ordinary, ignoring the smell, disregarding the dirt and sand causing his eyes to water. He could hear the gravel crack under his army boots and within a few minutes felt sweat rolling down his back.

In other areas were puddles that wouldn't dry, and he trenched through mud halfway up his leg. The buildings he checked were old and slum-like. None were occupied and presented dangerous possibilities. He saw only a few children come close. They only waved and moved on. God, he thought, this is unreal, like something out of a movie. It seems like a dream. What am I doing here? Yeah, what is anybody doing here?

Shaking off his thoughts Steve couldn't help realize how different life was here from back home. At home, there were muggers and robbers, usually at night. Here it was a constant. In the middle of the day on this patrol, his chances were as bad as at night on a convoy into Taliban country. There was no escape from danger. His body was tense and shaken. He swallowed hard several times. He couldn't allow fear to take over. Others were in the same peril and they performed. He would, too. It was a different life. Little kids lived with this all the time. Gees, he thought, one world, but so many different parts to it.

"All clear here," came the sound from one sergeant.

"All clear here," from another. This task was finished.

Then they were asked to check along the Kabul River. It took them past a few small villages close to Camp Phoenix.

Everyone was to keep an open eye--at all times. After about thirty minutes, Steve spotted something unusual. He yelled immediately to Sergeant Rodrigez.

"What Private Johnson?"

"It looks like a mine. Am I crazy or what? Is that a mine?"

"Gees, you're right," said the Sergeant. "Stay right where you are. Don't move. Good catch."

He remained in place, and quickly a soldier from the explosive ordnance disposal team came on the scene. There were tense moments. The mine was brought over to a nearby vehicle and placed in a small wooden box in the back of a truck. Steve and the Sergeant rode back to Camp Phoenix with this anti-tank mine right behind them. The roads were bumpy. Steve thought it was the longest two miles he'd ever traveled in his life.

Later, walking back to his barrack, he had images of being blown up. Sergeant Rodrigez had told him being in constant danger was real here. It wasn't that you ever got blasé about it, but the tension did get common, and you functioned the way you must. Gees, he thought, I can't ever remember being so scared. I remembered every second there was an explosive device right next to me. But I didn't panic. A few times I think my mind was numb. I wasn't even thinking. But I remember being happy when we reached Camp Phoenix. We got out at Rambo's gate, and some other explosive experts took over from there. I'd done my job. And I made it.

"Steve, how are you feeling?"

It was Sergeant Rodrigez. He'd stopped him for encouragement and praise.

"I think I'm doing okay. I was really scared, though," replied Steve as he looked into a more seasoned face that understood.

"Of course you were scared. So was I. We're all scared, every day, but you functioned. And that's all this army can ask of any one of us. Good job."

"Thanks, Sergeant. I appreciate that."

"Actually, today was more intense than walking around the compound usually is. You had a hell of a first assignment. And being scared is just part of a day's work."

As he walked away Steve thought, Gees, that's what I used to tell George. It's okay to be afraid, but it's not okay to let fear stop you. Funny how things come around.

* * *

As time passed, Steve found it strange when both George and John were out on patrols. He was used to one of them being around and they worried about each other. They had all experienced difficult convoys, some with attacks and some with tragedies. He'd already lost a few new friends who were involved in fatal attacks. He wondered about life more and more. Why was he still here? He knew there must be something higher that governed this.

He felt older. He'd developed some close friendships that were teaching him how life could be creative and productive but also tragic and hurtful. By his nineteenth birthday, Steve had reached Private First Class (E-3). He'd accomplished something in his life. And he'd finally graduated from high school.

He was especially thrilled when he began college classes at the Kabul Army Education Center right inside the camp. Since no one was allowed outside of the base except on a mission, there were occasions he had time on his hands. He used the opportunity to get some extra credits that would help him later. It was almost funny, he thought. Although he was a soldier fighting a war on terrorism, he still had an opportunity to further his education, right in the middle of a combat zone.

As he sat on his cot taking a much-needed break, his thoughts were on Scranton, PA and his hope of getting back home. He still felt homesick at times. Yet, except for Jeff Barnes, he had no family. He occasionally heard from his mother, but she was still being cared for by the state. Her weakness of mind and body wasn't an improvement he waited for anymore. It was hard to entirely erase hope in his heart, but it wasn't at the top of his list anymore. The reality of the situation was evident with each of the two letters he'd received from her. His thoughts were interrupted by George calling him.

"Steve, get out here right away. There's an important announcement coming over the loudspeakers."

That information came from a George, who was visibly upset and agitated. Steve jumped up immediately since these announcements were seldom good news, and this time it proved to be alarming.

"Attention, Attention. This is to let you know the convoy returning from Khorog is under attack at this moment. We have extra convoys in the area on their way, and one for sure is no more than fifteen minutes away. We have no known casualties at this time, and our soldiers are well prepared. We were warned more than an hour ago of this possibility. We're in a good position. There are no further details at this time, and we'll update you as soon as more data comes in. That's all for now."

With that information, the loudspeaker went dead, and everyone on the ground stood still. George was shocked to silence, and no one was moving nor had the appearance of breathing. Steve realized there hadn't been an attack for a few weeks. These alarms were felt with awe whenever these announcements came. The soldiers knew anytime it could be them, and their hearts went out to their fellow soldiers.

"John's in that convoy, you know," added Steve as George locked arms with him, feeling the same emotion travel through their bodies. They stood still for a few more moments before even turning around. Steve never got used to this. Each time was like the first time. Then, in a trance-like silent state, they slowly made their way back to their barrack.

"Is John in that convoy?" asked a passing soldier, knowing they were friends.

"Yeah, he is," answered Steve, more mechanically than not.

"Help is close by. They should be okay."

"Sure hope so."

Steve couldn't quite get over the shock. Death was a real possibility when you were stationed in Afghanistan, as the soldiers were particularly sought after targets from the terrorists. Knowing this still didn't prepare you. He wondered how John was handling it all. Entering their barrack neither Steve nor George had spoken a word to each other and had no desire to now. They just sat quietly on their own beds lost in a multitude of thoughts that always rush your mind at times like these.

Within fifteen minutes there was another announcement. It was encouraging.

"Two other convoys have reached the area, and we have control of the situation. All three convoys will remain together and head back to Camp Phoenix, arrival time expected within the next three hours. That's all for now."

A huge relief was felt by all. Steve would still worry until John returned.

Steve went back to his studying, although his concentration was disturbed. He couldn't get it back on track as his wandering thoughts took over. Times like these let you know for sure that life is temporary at best and how little control we have against outside evil influences. Yet we can't escape life, even if we try. We can only control our little corner of the world to a degree. Then Steve remembered his own most frightening convoy attack. It would live on more lively than any of the others in his memory.

He'd been in a rather large convoy moving through an area near Ghazni. The last few hours had been calm, strangely so, and Steve drove with caution, keeping his eyes moving. Suddenly the tranquility dissolved as explosive devices detonated near the end of the convoy, several yards ahead of Steve. He managed to bring his twisted fiery truck to an abrupt stop. By then the convoy was the target of insurgents carrying out a surprise attack. Bruised and shocked for a moment, Steve had to be pulled from his vehicle. But he regained his wits within a moment. He soon discovered his superior had been killed. He took control. Realizing another soldier in his vehicle hadn't made it out, he went after him and managed to haul his body half-way out before help came. They got this unconscious soldier out just before the ammunition caught fire and began exploding in all directions.

All was not over. At this point they'd been separated a bit from the rest of the convoy and were being attacked again. Grabbing hold of a nearby M-16, Steve fired until reinforcements arrived. Then he performed first-aid on the unconscious soldier. Even as other help came Steve continued to ignore his own injuries and aided many of the other wounded.

Steve's injuries had proved minor, and he was back on duty within a week. But he'd always remember what he'd been able to do under pressure, under attack and under life-threatening circumstances. Some things in life were more important than living, he thought. In that situation, he'd completely forgot about himself, living or dying, and just performed. He'd been proud of himself and yet realized the pride wasn't his at all. He'd only reacted, and something bigger than he had taken over.

* * *

Later, Steve was awakened out of a sound sleep by soldiers cheering as John walked back into the tent almost five hours later. He looked good, and was laughing in a careful manner. To those who didn't know him, he seemed self-assured, making light of his involvement in the attack. All the soldiers did that, and John had good answers to the excited questions thrown at him.

"Hey, buddy, good to see you back. How many were out there?"

"We didn't know for sure," John said, "but they seemed to come from all sides, and quickly. It was almost dark, and it's hard to get a feel for anything. The first we knew they were firing at us, and it seemed to come from everywhere. The amazing part was everyone seemed to be so focused on their jobs. The commander immediately called in our problem and reported help was near, and we started firing back knowing we could hold out for quite a while."

"Another of the hundreds experiences to enter into your journal," joked one soldier.

"Right. I know I'll never forget this one," answered John seriously.

It was obvious John was almost sleep walking in exhaustion, and if they didn't let him find his bed, he'd probably grab anyone's bed to rejuvenate his body. All respected his need for sleep and avoided his area of the room. Steve stood for a moment and looked down at his peaceful expression as he entered into his dream world. John continued to perform well and could now look inside and realize he'd mastered himself in one area of fear. It was of no concern whether the moment of truth was forced upon him or not.

* * *

The next few days gave earned recuperation to the soldiers caught in this latest convoy attack. As they continued with their duties, each soldier carried away some effect knowing if one of them was attacked, they were all attacked. And if one of them made it home safely after escaping a terrorist attack, they all were safe, at least for now.

Steve realized John had been spending more time alone than usual. One night after sundown, Steve crossed his path quite by chance. He hadn't even seen John standing near the last barrack until his lone low voice beckoned for his company and comfort.

"How's it going, Steve? This is one lovely night, isn't it? The dust has cleared enough to see a few stars, and that's unusual."

"Yeah, I guess it doesn't matter where you're standing on this earth, stars are beautiful."

Some relaxed silence ensued. Then John began in earnest talking about his feelings during his latest experience.

"Thanks for not asking me too many questions about the last attack. This one was tough."

"It always is," Steve said knowingly.

"I've talked to the chaplain a few times and of course to the commander, and it does help, but you and I shared other things. I'd like to talk about it with you."

"Okay, go ahead," said Steve as he found a spot in the dirt that held an old blanket where they could be comfortable and out of sight from others. John sat next to him willingly.

"To say I was scared wouldn't even come close," John began. "Those first couple of seconds were jolting. I've been through this plenty of times, but I reacted like an inexperienced rookie. Everything inside of me cried. I wasn't a brave soldier, but a frightened little coward. Yet, as I looked around quickly, I knew the others were scared, too. Then I remembered you saying we don't have control over our first reaction, but what we do after is what counts."

John paused for a moment. Steve didn't comment, but watched the labored look on his face.

"Then all of us took action. The convoy leader called in our position. We fired back at random because it was tough to see anything, yet we needed to let them know quickly that we weren't defenseless. My heart was pounding, but it wasn't totally out of fear. It was as if the adrenalin finally started kicking in, you know?" John paused as he relived his experience. "My mind was totally focused on what I had to do, and that pushed the fear into the background. I was part lookout, and I took turns with Dave. You know him, David Brokert from Tennessee, and we double-checked with each other on procedure and on every detail. Their fire slowed, but they still occasionally let out some shots so we'd know they were still there."

Steve noticed John pause occasionally in different parts of his story. His emotions were still strong.

"It seemed like a long time, but I understand it was only fifteen minutes before the first convoy met up with us and the second was five minutes later. The terrorists evaporated heading out to their territory. We'd already delivered the supplies and were on our way back. I thought I'd been pretty well seasoned. God, Steve, what happened to me? Why did I react that way?"

"What's wrong with being scared John? God, you could've been killed out there. Remember Sergeant Rodrigez? I went out on my first patrol with him. He told me everyone's scared. But as long as we perform, that's all the army can expect of us. I hope I continue to perform okay."

"I know you will; hell, you're the one who taught me."

"No, I didn't," said Steve, laughing at John's approving look. "I may have given you a couple of ideas you chose to use, but you're the one who did it."

John continued in a serious tone. "Somehow I don't think you'd have gotten all tied up being angry at your reaction. I'm still having trouble with it."

"You've got to lower your standards, John. You're human. We all get scared. God, we can't always be calm in these terrifying circumstances. These wars are damn scary. What I think will be hard is getting back to normal after living here."

"That's a point. Hadn't thought that far ahead. I like what you said. These are scary times. It's okay not to be perfect."

Steve liked watching John when he was considering a new thought. He was very willing to learn.

"We're not perfect. We're human, remember? How did you like delivering those supplies. Isn't that an eye opener?" Steve noticed John's mood change.

"Yeah, right. Makes me wonder sometimes what's really important in life. If you could have seen the people in that village just clamoring after us for food and clothing, well, it's something. But, oh wait. You've made that trip, too."

"And I agree with you. It's really something, isn't it? Made me realize some deeper things inside of me, too."

Steve thought those charity missions had given him a lot to think about, too. His goals in life had changed because of some of the lessons learned here.

John added, "My family does charity work, but usually only if it gets them publicity. I'm not blaming them, but they do think money and social position is the most important thing in the world. I'm sure it's because of how they were raised. I always hated that part and I guess that's why I never totally connected with them."

"Do you sometimes wonder why people end up in certain families?" Steve asked casually. "Of course, I have very little family and I've told you about my mom. She struggles with herself every day. I've decided when I get home I'm going to visit her. I want to see if I can be of some help to her. It's by helping someone else we grow, John. We only see in the world what we've become."

"You know, Steve, I understand what you're saying. It'd be hard to understand something we haven't experienced. I could never see anything from my parents' point of view. Yet, I never experienced their young life. Now, I can at least give them a chance."

John retreated into himself for a few minutes. He was finally seeing his parents in a different way, as human beings, trying to do the best they could.

Steve continued. "We all seem to judge people knowing very little about them. We all walk around judging and we don't know each other at all. We humans are such complicated creatures, don't you think?"

"Yep, but you're one of a kind, Steve."

"We're all one of a kind, aren't we? And that's exactly what makes life so interesting."

"I'm beginning to understand you more and more each day, and believe me, Steve, that can be scary," joked John.

"I'm a scary person, aren't I?"

"Really, you are. And I mean that in the nicest way. You make me face myself, and you force me to think. Oh, you don't really do it, I know, but you throw out these thoughts that reel me in and won't leave my mind until I study them. Now I want to start reading some of those same books you've read."

"Sure. Anytime, and there are many other great masters I haven't even begun to read. So much to learn and only one lifetime to do it in."

"Some people believe in reincarnation, you know? What do you think about that?"

"It's interesting, and when I say I don't care, it's because I believe I should study and work and live the best life for Steve Johnson this time around. That's all I can do, and if I'm reincarnated someday then, that'll be okay."

John seemed like a changed person to Steve. Some of his old traits were still there and shot through occasionally. He still wanted to be the first in line for dinner. And sitting in the front row in the best seat at the movies was still important. Yet, slowly even that changed, and Steve noticed John hanging back occasionally and purposely letting someone else beat him in line. When Steve experienced an episode one day he accidentally caught John's eyes, and they spoke volumes. He looked satisfied, and that was a new feeling for him.

Another growth Steve noticed was John taking the time to listen to people, something he'd rarely done before. He paid attention to George, letting him know his thoughts and words were important. And like George, he wanted Steve to tell him more of his philosophy. Steve resorted to referring them both to the masters.

# CHAPTER XV

Jeff Barnes thought that eating in the high school cafeteria reminded him of being in the middle of a beehive. The buzz of conversation had to be ignored by a conscious effort on his part. He much preferred quiet surroundings. As Ross approached his table on the first day of Grade 11, he noticed an enthusiasm in him.

"Ross, what's up with you? You seem excited."

"I am, Jeff. I'm starting my Advanced Physics class today. I've been so looking forward to it." Noticing Jeff's reaction, he said, "What?"

Jeff smiled. "Sorry, Ross, I can't help it. Not too many students would be excited about that class, not even the gifted ones."

Jeff knew Ross was amused. He'd get a certain look on his face when he felt satisfied. He always took a moment or two to chuckle in his young voice. But being only thirteen years old in Grade 11, Jeff felt he should be allowed.

"I know, and you're right," said Ross as he tempered his humor. "But to me, I've been looking forward to this class for a long time. Do you want to know why?"

"Will I understand it, you think? I'm taking my first basic Physics class this semester. So, keep it simple."

"I won't get too technical because this class is Grade 12 Advanced, but I'm allowed to take it. Dave Patterson is back. He's my favorite teacher."

"Oh yeah, he's good?"

"He's great, Jeff. You'd like him, too. He wasn't here last year. He's funny, kind of relaxed, and usually relates Physics to life situations and stuff. You know how you and I talk about thought waves and vibrations and how our thoughts get into the atmosphere, well, he always finds a way to discuss that in class. He said he'd love to get a class on thoughts and their practical use. Maybe he will before we graduate."

"That sounds great. But you know what?" Jeff took a quick look at his syllabus. "I've got a Mr. Delaney for my basic Physics class, but I'm also taking Science/Philosophy and I've got Dave Patterson."

"Halleluah, you're going to love him. I took that class. He's right where we are, you know?"

"Where do you know him from, another class?"

"No, I met him through NAGC."

"NAG? What's that?" asked Jeff.

"NAGC (National Association for Gifted Children); I call it NAG for short to irritate my mom. Anyway, Mr. Patterson has been a speaker there a few times. He's good. Listen, I got to run. See you later."

"Right. Now you've got me excited too."

Ross gave Jeff a big smile as he left. As Jeff watched him hurry away, he thought he seemed too little to be carrying all those books. After all, he wouldn't be fourteen for a few months yet. Jeff remembered a conversation he'd had with Ross last year.

"Thanks for your help in trigonometry and statistics, Ross. I was barely making it, even with my tutor. How can you understand all this stuff?"

Jeff only meant to make a casual comment, yet it started a discussion that changed their relationship to a bonding beyond ordinary friendship.

"Somehow I seem to hone in on answers. They come from somewhere. People have tested me and I try to tell them I don't do it, not alone. It just comes to me without any effort. They don't accept that. You know, Jeff, I could say the alphabet in four languages around three years old. Now come on, it wasn't me personally, but something outside of me, yet inside of me at the same time. It's like a feeling and a position of mind."

"Wow, that's something." Jeff's interest perked up quickly. "I like what you said, a position of mind. It's like you know how to line up with something, but it's automatic to you."

"That's what I think. I know people say I have a super I.Q., but I'm not stupid enough to believe I know all this stuff by myself. Do you know what I mean?"

Jeff sat back speechless listening to Ross talk about things in line with his thinking. Ross was in tune with the universe. Okay, he didn't have all of the answers yet, but who did? Even knowledgeable people of the world were still trying to figure them out. In this particular area of study, Ross was at the same point as everyone else. He was able to get information, but wasn't sure how he did it.

Jeff said, "I think I do know what you mean, Ross. Sometimes I dream things, and other times I get strong feelings about things, and they come true. I've been trying to figure out how this happens."

"Oh, you dream things and they come true?"

"They don't always come true, but sometimes they do. I used to think of it as a message from the universe, you know? Even the dreams I don't understand might have a clue for me to work out and try to understand."

"That's a thought. And--"

Just then the bell rang, bringing Jeff out of his reminiscing and back to the present, reminding him he had exactly five minutes to get himself to the other side of the school for his class. He grabbed his books and ran.

* * *

Later that day, with classes finished, Jeff met Ross for a drink. They both tried to relax after finishing the first intense day of school.

"How did you like Mr. Patterson?"

Jeff said, "He's cool, and funny. He told us not think too hard today, because tomorrow our thoughts would still be in the atmosphere in our classroom."

Ross laughed. "See, he works that stuff in all the time. He told me it's just part of who he is."

"I think I'm going to like this class. I'd say taking it was an accident, but I don't believe in accidents."

"You needed another science credit, right?"

"Right, but this is my elective. Go figure. I'm interested in why things happen, Ross, and how much we can attribute to coincidence. How much do we bring on ourselves by the thoughts we entertain, and allow to stay on our minds? I believe thoughts make a lot of difference. Do you agree or not?"

"Absolutely. It's like you'll attract into your life what you concentrate on all day long, whether you want it or not. Whatever you focus your energy on, you'll attract. We all give off vibrations of energy whenever we think or feel. Vibrations are picked up by other people. Vibrations are picked up by the universe, good or bad. There is a Law of Attraction that states whatever vibrations you give off, the universe will respond to."

"You seem to know a lot about attractions and vibrations." Jeff was impressed and always forgot Ross' age when they discussed things. Talking to Ross was almost like talking to Steve, except Ross had taken some impressive classes.

"The credit isn't all mine. Remember, I've had classes in philosophy, creative thinking, universal laws, and a lot of other things."

"I didn't even think about all these possibilities in terms of universal laws," said Jeff. "I knew there were certain laws in math that everyone accepts, like one and one equals two and of course in English grammar and other things like that. I didn't think about laws of thoughts and mental activities. But sure, the universe is disciplined and orderly."

"Remember, Jeff, all is relative. One and one doesn't always have to equal two. If you're multiplying, one times one still equals one. But if you're adding plus one and minus one, then you get zero. I'm not trying to be ridiculous, but just like the world of thought; it depends exactly on what you're doing."

Jeff looked at Ross thinking, He's always so exact, but that's a good thing. Your thinking must be exact when working with the universe.

"You're right, Ross. This is the type of stuff Steve and I are always thinking about. You want to include yourself in our little group?"

"Sure." Jeff could tell Ross was excited. "I love this stuff. In most of the sciences of learning, the answer is what it is. But in the world of psychology, philosophy, or anything mental, it's still a wide open field to discuss. Even the so-called geniuses have a lot to learn because that field hasn't been half-discovered yet."

Just then Tim and two other boys from their algebra class wandered by and stopped for a moment. They knew from the syllabus they'd need help, and Jeff usually got a tutor.

"What do you think, Jeff?" asked Tim, who seldom included Ross in his conversation.

"Sure, I could probably help you to a certain point, but Ross here could get you all the way to home plate. Why not ask him?" Jeff saw Tim look over at Ross, almost unpleasantly at first. He resented Ross since he'd beat him last year in Science. But he needed help with algebra, so he relented.

"Sure, if you're willing, Ross, I'd appreciate help from anyone who could get this stuff through my head. I'm great in biology and statistics, but algebra is getting to me. I made it through last year, but only barely. My parents were a little irritated. But I don't even know where I'm confused."

Jeff saw a thankful look on Ross' face. It was nice to be included, not only in the casual conversation, but also to be recognized for someone who could give help.

"Sure, I'd be willing. Jeff, you wanted a review, too, didn't you? We usually meet after school. We're planning a preliminary preview tonight. Join us if you want."

Teasingly, Jeff added, "And for my benefit especially, I try to get Ross not to double talk, so I have a chance to understand him. With effort and patience, he can get it down to my level, about grade 4 or 5."

Ross and Jeff both laughed. Then Tim laughed with them, as did two of his friends. Jeff could tell they were surprised to find out Ross had a sense of humor. Another point realized was Ross didn't lord it over anyone. Jeff hoped this could be a beginning for some of them to realize Ross was a real person. They might start to know him for the first time.

"Okay, then we'll meet you where?"

"We usually go to the back part of the library in one of the private rooms. Then we can discuss things aloud when we need to. Sometimes I need Ross to go over things a few times." Jeff added, "especially in this algebra stuff. It got real complicated for me last year."

"Okay, I'll join you," Tim said, "in about half an hour or so?"

"Yeah, that's about right."

And his friends added, "Yeah, we'd like to join you guys too. Thanks Jeff, Ross. Later."

It was obvious Ross was delighted. So was Jeff. Finally, some of these guys would appreciate Ross for who he was, an average human being who just happened to have a high I.Q. Maybe this could be a new beginning for all of them.

* * *

Before they left for the library, Jeff wanted to finish a few points in their recent conversation. He needed to explain his point of view.

"You know Ross, my situation was a little bit different because I certainly don't have your I.Q, but when I was younger, about ten years old, and I met Steve, we often talked about the mysteries of life. In our situations, both orphans, we knew there must be answers out there--something to connect with that would guide us. It was a feeling we both had. We just knew, you know? I know I'm stumbling here but some things can't be put into words. That's why we started searching, trying to find whatever it was."

"I understand. The enormity of everything can certainly be overwhelming."

Jeff was quiet for a moment. "Did I tell you that Steve is in the army in Afghanistan?"

Ross nodded.

"He's out there reading Emerson and Thoreau and he recently finished high school. Funny how life turns out."

"Sounds like he's on his way."

"Yeah, he's doing good. And I pass on our discussions about attraction and energy. He loves it."

"Well, this is an open field, and my I.Q. means nothing here. We're talking about intuition, premonition, and simply knowing. It's about connecting with something out there that I call the Universal Intelligence or Supreme Being. But whether you call it God or whatever, there's something out there to connect with that has all the answers we need."

"Speaking of connecting, we'd better get to the library. Some guys want to connect with us right now, well, really you."

"I wonder if they'll respond to what I explain," said Ross, not thoroughly convinced.

"They will if they're smart." He saw Ross smile. "But I think they will. They're seeing you in a new light now. Besides, they know you're the one who knows."

"But I think they still resent me."

"They probably do. It's hard for them to accept your intellect. Don't get all shy with me. I know you're smart and I don't mind, but I'm not one of the gifted ones. Some are still having a tough time with you. But now, they need you," Jeff laughed. "Sorry Ross, but this is fun to see. I always need help, so I'm different. But they need to find out it's okay to need help sometimes."

"I need help, too in certain things. Maybe it hasn't shown up in these classes, but I need it too."

"Yeah, we all do. But it's neat to hear you say it."

\* \* \*

Back in his room at the orphanage, Jeff was satisfied. The study session had gone quite well. All received help from Ross. Yet what pleased Jeff was these other students finally realized Ross was not a snob. He was a sensible, no-nonsense person who didn't lord it over them. By the end of the session, everyone was comfortable and Ross had received genuine appreciation from the others.

Jeff looked over at Steve's side of the room. It was still empty. He'd only had one roommate since Steve left. And he'd been adopted quickly. It bothered Jeff a little, but he remembered there were no coincidences. Would he have begun such a vivid philosophy and desire for growth if he'd lived with his original family? Maybe, but with his fears, and pains, and hesitancy derived directly from being snatched, he'd depended more on feelings, and intuitions while learning to develop a belief in himself. And he was happy here. This had been his home now for over ten years. And he didn't mind calling this orphanage home. Best of all, he'd met Steve.

He took a deep breath, realizing he was pleased with himself. Even though he was an orphan, he'd become a Junior Advisor, and that was a paid position. There was a big satisfaction, in helping the little ones over the same rough spots he'd walked. His little friend, Takoda looked up to him every day, and depended on him for support. Jeff was always there to congratulate him on passing a math test, or to coach him on the rules of proper behavior. Jeffrey Barnes had a few others who depended on him every day as well. And to him, that's what a family was all about. Maybe his life was a little different, but that could be good.

# CHAPTER XVI

The 12th Grade was another turning point in Jeff's life. He felt something was always happening to point him in a certain direction, and it happened again. He'd loved Dave Patterson's Science/Philosophy class. He'd struggled a little with the Science portion, but with Ross's help, and a lot of hard work he actually got a B in the class.

The exciting part was Dave Patterson did manage to start a class called, Thoughts and Their Effects On Your Life. Jeff and Ross hurried to sign up, since Mr. Patterson was a popular teacher and his classes filled up quickly. Luckily, they were both accepted, and even better, they managed to get into the same session. Jeff had told Ross that even though Steve was many miles away, he'd make sure he was part of the group. Jeff would send him reports on their discussions, and had permission to tape the class for that purpose. He knew Steve was doing helpful work with his new knowledge.

\* \* \*

The first day of class confirmed Dave Patterson's sense of humor.

"I asked Ross Inglewood to help me out up here in front, but he declined."

The students chuckled. No one wanted the center spot here. Jeff always said that he would rather merge into the woodwork and absorb from there.

"However, Ross, Jeff Barnes and I, had some first-rate conversations last semester. We began discussing our relationship with the universal power, what it is and what we can control through thoughts and choices. I really was prepared to talk about some atmospheric links to our universe--" He paused purposefully as mixed vocal reactions of groans and moans from his students caught his attention. Then, he slowly continued.

"Okay, okay, I get it. I can see you're not thrilled about that topic, so I'll save it for another time."

"Save it for another semester," yelled one student. Everyone thought that was a good idea.

"Let me begin by quoting a paragraph from author Charles Swindoll on Attitude. Charles said, 'The longer I live, the more I realize the impact of attitude on life. Attitude to me is more important than facts. It's more important than the past, than education, than money, than circumstances, than failures, than successes, than what other people think or say or do. It's more important than appearance, giftedness or skill. It will make or break a company--a church--a home. The remarkable thing is we have a choice every day regarding the attitude we'll embrace for that day. We cannot change our past--we cannot change the fact people will act in a certain way. We cannot change the inevitable. I'm convinced life is ten percent what happens to me and ninety percent how I react to it. And so, it is with you--we are in charge of our attitudes."

"Okay, let me ask each one of you. Do you believe we are in charge of our attitudes?"

"Yes, I think we are," answered one student.

"And why is that?" asked Dave.

"Because we have the power to change our mind."

"Good, that's right. We can change our mind. And how do we do that?"

"We think differently about something," offered another student.

"Sure, we think differently. So we all have the power to think. What a gift, right? We can all think. And we can change a thought, right?"

Jeff noticed most students nodded.

"Okay, let me ask you a few more questions. How do you think or react when people make fun of you, hurt you, embarrass you and constantly irritate you? Do you let yourself get caught up in these upsets? Do you relive the facts over and over and plan revenge? Can you eventually go beyond the hurt? Our society tells us retaliation brings satisfaction inside, especially in the form of confrontation. Do you believe this?"

"Sometimes it helps if you confront people. You'll usually argue and yell, but then it's over," said one student.

Another said, "Yelling and arguing doesn't always help. Sometimes it makes it worse, and people are still mad."

A third student offered, "But you get the satisfaction of having told a person to their face you won't be their punching bag, so to speak."

"Okay, Jeff and Ross, you two are mighty quiet and I find that highly unusual." Some chuckles were heard around the room. "What about it, Jeff?"

Jeff responded, "Well, I think if you confront someone in a downbeat way, you're putting too many negative thoughts into the atmosphere that don't just disappear. It's like adding more fuel to the fire. I don't see how it could accomplish anything good."

Ross nodded.

A few other students said, "Huh? I don't understand."

"Okay, I don't want to get ahead of ourselves here, so let me explain a few things and give you some future reading, and we can start a hot discussion tomorrow. I don't like to be the one always preaching or lecturing, whatever you want to call it. I really enjoy discussions because then I can learn, too. But I need to give you some basic facts and then in the next few weeks we'll have a lot to talk about, fair enough?"

"Sure," said one of the guys, "you can preach today and we'll all take turns preaching in the future."

"I like that idea," said Dave, "I'll be able to sit back and you students can teach me a few things."

Everyone laughed.

"Okay, bad things happen to all of us at different times in this world, but this is where our attitudes come in. We choose what we think about all day long. We could choose to concentrate on the good things. I know people who tell me hardly anything good ever happens to them. Okay, if only one good thing has happened to you in the past month and twenty bad things have happened, choose to concentrate most of the day on the one good thing. Did you hear what I said? Concentrate on the one good thing that happened to you. Why? Because what you concentrate on most of the day is what you'll bring into your life. You want more bad things to happen? Then by all means, concentrate on bad things in the your life. You want more good to come into your life, then concentrate on the good things."

Jeff thought Dave had a tone in his voice and a personal mannerism that gushed not only self-confidence, but an enthusiasm for living and life that was hard to match.

"Are you saying we attract into our lives what we concentrate on?"

"Absolutely. I'm talking now about universal laws and the basic one that everyone should commit to memory is 'the Law of Attraction'. Did you hear that? There is a universal Law of Attraction. We attract into our lives what we think on all day long."

Some students looked at each other and shifted in their chairs. He was kidding, right?

"I've never thought about that. It works that way, really?"

"Really, look, some of you made it through my other science classes. There are other universal laws we accept easily enough such as gravitation. I remember one of my students asked me, if the world really is round, how come the water doesn't drip out at the bottom and end up in other galaxies?" There was a ripple of laughter throughout the room. "You laugh, but when you think about it, that's a very good question. That's your Law of Gravitation, which keeps the water in our lakes, seas and oceans. The Law of Attraction has its rules, too. It works somewhat like two magnets. One side of the magnet attracts, and the other side of the magnet repels. It's very much the same with you. At any given time, you're either attracting people, places and things to you; or you're repelling them. This is based on the energy vibrations you're sending as a request to the universe in the form of thoughts, feelings and actions."

Jeff noticed some of the students looked confused. They didn't know this class would be about universal laws and formulas. They'd had enough of that. Dave must have picked up on the vibes quickly as he continued.

"I know, I know," said Dave, "more laws to learn, but listen to me. This class is only about a few universal laws. And one of the most important laws is ignored, or at least not taught or talked about in everyday life. What law? It's the law of Thought Force which brings to us that which we desire or that which we fear. Take a moment and think about it. What you concentrate on you attract. If you want to spend your life studying the most important thing you'll ever want to know, then study the law of Thought Force. Study how energy and vibrations work and how you can connect and use them in a positive manner. Of course, I'm assuming you want good things to come into your life, right?"

One student asked, "There's a law out there that says like attracts like. Is that what you're talking about?"

"I sure am and much more. And we'll talk about more next time. But I want you to see your list of required reading. Emerson's Essay on Self-Reliance is well known to most of you. And the Law of Attraction has suddenly got popular again. But this stuff has been out there and studied for hundreds of years. I've added some older readings that should fascinate many of you from Wattles to Atkinson to modern day. And, of course, people like Napoleon, Hitler, Gandhi, leaders of countries all used the power of thought and were aware of it."

"There's a lot to this stuff, right?"

"Exactly, and you won't learn it all in one semester. Look, guys and gals, I'm still learning after many years, but I want you to all be aware of the possibilities within your own mind. You'll all come up with your own individualized method for yourself. Okay, that's it for today. See you next time."

Less than a moment later the bell rang and most were sad to leave this class.

Jeff and Ross immediately began discussing the new theories of thought. They decided that each would begin reading a different author and compare notes. Jeff had the added task to transcribe some notes for Steve. Ross offered to help.

\* \* \*

Immediately Jeff used a few ideas he'd learned on the younger children at the home. He wanted to teach them good thinking habits early. He'd kept it simple, but was surprised how quickly the little ones learned and improved themselves. He loved how the innocence and purity of their minds had the ability to believe easily. How sad, he thought, that we allowed our mind to be warped as we matured. It didn't have to be that way.

Mr. Edmond noticed and overheard some of Jeff's comments. He, too, became interested and began reading and studying some of Jeff's lessons. Imagine that, Jeff thought, even my director is interested. It's amazing how many people want to learn after they realize that life has a system, he thought. God provided everything. It's up to us to learn.

\* \* \*

Toward the end of the semester, Dave knew he had to get more technical, but also needed to personalize the information so he didn't lose his students.

"Now you know it takes power and energy to think. Okay, so when you go home after a hard day at school and you want to relax, please, don't think. It takes too much energy." Dave paused for the length of the laughter. "Your thought power sends out vibrations into the outer world and there it looks for a like pattern of vibrations. You know vibrations have different speeds and if you send out a slow vibration, you cannot expect it to attract a fast vibration. The luck of the draw doesn't apply here. The important thing to remember is when Like attracts Like, it doesn't care if it's positive vibrations or negative vibrations."

"So if you send out a negative thought, it can't connect with a positive thought, right?"

"That's true. Exactly why is mysterious. Many think negative and positive vibes have different energy and vibration levels. I tend to think so as well, but that hasn't been totally proven to my satisfaction yet."

Dave was pleased with this class. They're getting the idea, he thought. He wanted to get these minds going in the right direction.

"Can you erase a thought, once you thought it? It gets complicated out there in the universe," was one question.

"Yes, it is complicated, but luckily, the universe knows what to do and all you have to do is control your thoughts. Although we can't exactly go out there into the thought atmosphere and erase a thought like chalk on a blackboard, we can alleviate the effects of an angry thought. We can pour positive energy on it or bless any tough situation and let the positive vibes do their job. So many of us get angry and send out bad vibes. This is characteristically human, but then we feel guilty for having done so. Now we have angry vibes out there in the atmosphere, and we follow up by sending guilty vibes. Eh Gads. We humans are so tough on us humans."

"So we can send good thoughts out and help to soften a situation?"

"Right, and remember back when we talked about arguments, you could send out good thoughts to the person or situation instead of getting more negative stuff out there. Just a thought."

"I like that idea. Beats fighting all the time."

"Here's another thing. Do you really think the atmosphere in this room is empty? I'm sure you realize by now there are millions of thoughts and ideas and feelings and emotions being held in abeyance in this environment. And not only from today but also from people who aren't even with us anymore. Whew! That's a rather scary thought, isn't it? Actually our atmosphere has more living elements to it than the eye could ever hold, even if we were able to see it. Doesn't that make you wonder why we can't see a thought? I think God planned it that way. We couldn't handle all that information."

"Holy cow," said Jerome, one of the more vocal students in the class.

"Thanks for keeping your comments decent. I appreciate that," Dave said.

And Jerome, known for his spicy language, laughed so hard he got everyone into hysterics for a few minutes.

"Seriously, Jerome, you've talked real nice in my class. I prefer this to your outdoor conversations."

"I'm going to have to watch it from now on. Not sure what some of those words do out there in the atmosphere."

Dave was pleased. Jerome joked a lot and he was a tough personality, but he understood what was going on here.

"Okay, Jerome, with your permission, I'm going to pick on you a little."

"You've got my permission, teach, but keep it positive."

"Okay, thanks Jerome. We know thoughts are things and they don't immediately disappear. They're sent into the atmosphere to join other like thoughts and avoid unlike thoughts. Ideas from others will join yours if they are like your thoughts. If they are not like your thoughts, they will move on to other people with whom they have a connection. Okay, now Jerome, if there's a nice, sweet girl whom you're trying to date and can't get anywhere, maybe your thoughts are the reason.

Think about it. Haven't you ever had an immediate like or dislike of a person? Remember, we all carry around an atmosphere of our life stories."

"Mr. Patterson, I think you may have struck gold in my thought arena."

Dave knew Jerome enjoyed the attention.

"Somehow I knew you'd pay attention to that one. But we have another obstacle to overcome. All of us are also under the dictates of the race mind. That's the thoughts of all those around us, near us, or those who've been here before us, who still have thoughts and feelings in the atmosphere. Cheerful thought, right? We not only have to fight the here and now, but the yesterday and years before. It may seem like a giant battle and it is, but let me give you some encouraging data. For those of you who want to change your thinking, the method is actually quite simple, though it does require some patience. However, I'm saving that for next week, the last day of class."

There were moans and groans heard, but Dave reminded them to keep positive thoughts and study what they'd been taught. Then, they'd be ready for the last dose of work.

It had been a fun class, and to Jeff it had been another 'grace along the way.' Steve was so excited he even managed to send Jeff some emails from Afghanistan. Jeff had showed them to the teacher. Some of his fellow soldiers were enjoying a much-needed boost due to this philosophy. Steve wanted Jeff to thank Mr. Patterson for allowing him to tape the class. Jeff was reminded again that we never know how far and wide we affect each other.

***

There had been a noticeable improvement at the orphanage. Both Jeff and Mr. Edmond worked in unison and others were getting on board. Mr. Edmond had mentioned to Jeff it might have been one reason he remained here all those years; he was needed. That statement brought a lump to Jeff's throat.

Entering the last day of class, Jeff felt sadness as was his usual reaction when something good was ending. But he was reminded when the old went out the door, it gave room for something new to enter. Another positive thought from Dave.

"Okay, I promised all of you a new method to help you become more positive and in control of your thoughts. It's not complicated at all. It's simply this. Whenever you notice yourself entertaining a negative thought or pattern in your mind, you immediately change it to a positive thought. Some just bless the negative thought, let it go, and immediately go on to a new positive pattern. Simple, right? I see the look on your faces. Disappointed? You think it should be more complicated. Well, then I should prepare you because in practice, it's not easy."

Gees, Jeff thought, Steve used to talk about something like this. He was more basic, but the idea was the same.

"Okay," Dave continued, "so you jump in and start wherever you are and the amazing fact is after a while, it does get easier. However, I want to warn you of something. For a little while, especially at the beginning, it seems everything goes wrong. Errors come out of the woodwork, and negativity will come at you from every side. You just have to dig in your heels and hold on."

"For how long?" asked Jerome.

"Just a short time, really, but it will seem like a long time. The vice-hold on you will ease up, and you will see the intelligence of staying on the positive side of the universe. Don't be thinking if you stay positive for one day the next day will be terrific for you. No, no, that's not how it works. Challenges will continue to make their way to your doorstep. You have years of negative patterns in your immediate atmosphere to eradicate and destroy, but you have to start somewhere, and you don't want to continue to add destruction to your atmosphere. Hang in there, and new strength will come to you. Then, in the not too distant future, you'll begin to reach upper areas of dreams and successes that were impossible for you before."

Sure, thought Jeff, I get this.

"Thoughts, attitudes, and beliefs are all interconnected. Keep them linked in your mind on the constructive side, and you'll be on your way. I want to read a letter I got from Jeff's friend, Steve Johnson. He's the soldier in Afghanistan who was interested in this class. He was somewhat familiar with the power of thought so I let Jeff tape the class and send him a copy. Here's what he had to say.

Dear Mr. Patterson:

I want to thank you for allowing Jeff to tape this class for me. Copies have been passed around Camp Phoenix where I'm stationed. Many have reacted positively to these ideas. It gave them hope and something to hold onto. You never know what a little kindness can do for someone, as Jeff and I have learned. We thank you and want you to know that we soldiers are sending you positive vibes from Afghanistan.

Hope to meet you when I return, God bless,


Steve Johnson


You can tell Steve that dinner's on me when he returns. And thank him for those positive vibes."

"Thanks, I will," said Jeff, feeling proud.

"Okay, we're almost done here, but I want you to know I'm a person who has always remembered good lines I've read from anywhere that are positive and help me out. I'd like to share two of them with you. First, Richard Lovelace wrote in "To Althea from Prison,

Two men looked out from prison bars,
One saw mud, the other saw stars."

See students, it's a choice. And the last one I didn't find in any philosophy book, but, believe it or not I noticed it on the wall of a donut shop."

The students roared at that one.

"I'm not kidding. Some of the best lines come from the most unusual places. My donut shop poem goes like this,

As you travel on through life brother
Whatever be your goal,
Keep your eye upon the Donut
And Not upon the hole."

"Teach, I'm going to remember that one," said Jerome. And many others agreed with him.

"Glad you liked that one. There's a lot of fun in thinking positive. I know this school has many gifted children here. When I first met Jeff Barnes, he was quick to tell me that he wasn't one of the gifted children. I'm so happy you said that to me, Jeff, so I can say back to you, and to all of you great students, YES, you are. We're all gifted, each and every one of us, just not in the same way. The trick to life for you is finding your particular gift and using it to improve yourself, society, and the world.

"This has been a great class and you students made it special for me. Thank you."

All of the students gave Dave a standing ovation. That seldom happened in a classroom, but special thoughts were in this atmosphere.

\* \* \*

Arriving home, somewhat tired, but happy to be alone in his room, Jeff relaxed in his favorite position on his comfortable firm bed and remembered again there were no coincidences. Of course not, and he realized that he was meant to take this class with Ross. It was no accident that he'd met Ross and became friends with him. It was meant to be that

Steve Johnson had been moved into his room at the orphanage and they became brothers. But that would also mean it was meant to be that he'd be snatched at four years old and his life would be altered permanently. That happening still confused him.

Okay, he had to accept all parts of this life. He couldn't say he agreed with the pleasant stuff and not with the bad. Either you believed in coincidences or you didn't. And Jeff didn't. He might never know why he wasn't destined to live with the family he'd been born into, but he knew there was a reason. Life always had a reason.

Ross had mentioned something interesting to him. Later in life, when school was over and Steve had come home, he'd asked Jeff if they could form a club and share all of the information they had learned. Maybe they could teach a class together, and the possibilities continued.

# CHAPTER XVII

On his way to the Task Force Commander's office, Steve was in deep thought. He barely noticed George coming out of their barrack.

"Why are you going to see him?" asked George.

"I have no idea. I was simply told to report to his office. He's asked to meet with me, and that's all I know."

Walking into the office, Steve noticed this was the largest office in the complex, and rightfully so. After all, he was the Task Force Commander of the entire base. Commander John Bertinand had been here only a few months longer than Steve. He had lots of books and papers on his long sturdy desk, but they were in reliable order, with place markers of odd colors adorning certain pages. Large pictures on the wall dominated the room, mostly showing certain areas of Kabul, first in black and white, then in some variance of color. This was the first time Steve had been in his office and quietly accepted the seat he was offered.

"I want you to relax, Specialist Johnson, as I want this meeting to be informal. I have no problem with you, and my decision to meet with you is of another matter."

Steve sat all the way back in his chair at that comment, took an involuntary deep sigh of relief, and allowed a semi-smile to cross his face. The commander was about fifty, had brown hair, speckled with grey, and a friendly smile that disarmed you.

His voice was even tone as he began. "In the past few years, I've had to put in six-month progress reports on you. I know you expected it since you joined the army to avoid jail time, but I have to make these reports until you're twenty-one years old, and you haven't quite reached that age yet. Now, don't worry, you've done well; extremely well, actually, so I usually just send these reports in as a matter of protocol. I realize this may be one of the last reports I have to do for you since you're approaching twenty-one. Then you can leave the service or reenlist. Any preferences yet?"

"No, Sir. I'm not sure yet what I want to do," answered Steve.

"You're a good soldier, Steve. When I read the first admittance report, I can't imagine you're the same person I see before me today. Whatever was going on in your young life seems to be in the past. You've become a respectable and model soldier. I'd like to hear your story."

Steve looked at the Commander's strong yet caring face as he began. "I appreciate the kind thoughts, Commander," began Steve hesitantly, "but I did deserve to go to jail." Steve found it difficult to discuss his early life. He shifted uneasily in his chair. "I was an extremely angry kid. I'm sure you know that I was in an orphanage because of a deceased father and an alcoholic mother. I was always angry and did some stupid things getting myself in a lot of trouble. When I joined the army I realized this was my last chance."

"Well, that was a pretty tough young life for you."

"Yes, Sir, but others had rough times, too. My roommate at the orphanage had a story even tougher than mine, but he did okay. Anyway, when I got into the service I knew if I screwed up here, I was definitely going to jail. My roommate, Jeff, and I had created a partnership on learning to think in better ways. It's like a system of thought we worked out. So I thought I'd better apply it seriously."

"Sounds like a lucky coincidence you met this Jeff, right?"

"Actually, Sir, neither of us believes in coincidences. You see, life is just a series of choices you make every day. It sounds funny to say that here at Camp Phoenix where we're constantly in dangerous situations, but we can choose how we think about these situations, too. Folks are killed at home every day, too. We're all in hazardous situations every moment of our lives. We must all accept the fact that some situations are such that we have no control over them. Gosh, sorry, Sir, I could go on and on about this stuff all day long."

"No, no, this is one of the reasons I called you in at this time. You see, word has come to me from around the base that there was this one young soldier many talk to when they're down. He always has something uplifting to say. I was told this soldier helps you sort out your thoughts and leads you to think about life in a better way. You've done a lot to lift the morale around here. Are you aware of that?"

"Well, no, not really," said Steve, feeling surprised. "I just listen to the guys, and when they need support or some new ideas, I feed them what I've learned and what's worked for me. That's all."

"You've developed a good philosophy. Where did you get it?"

"I feel I'm just beginning. I read a lot of the masters, Emerson, Thoreau, even poets on occasion, and certainly the Bible, and other philosophers. Some of their lofty ideas are still beyond me, but many ideas that I didn't understand at first are easier now. And what I learn, I try to pass on."

Steve felt uncomfortable for a moment. Who would have thought the Commander would call him into his office to talk about his philosophy of thought? Wouldn't Jeff be surprised.

"That's a tremendous amount, especially around here. You think and talk like it's just a little thing, but I want to tell about one soldier, Hank Emerist, remember him?"

"Sure. He got discharged a few months ago." Steve liked Hank, a rather shy yet congenial personality.

"Yes, well, do you remember when he got that 'Dear John' letter from his fiancé?" Steve nodded. "The chaplain helped him some, but he had a rough time for quite a while. I was worried about him and had some people watching him so he didn't do anything drastic. After a while, he seemed to slowly change for the better, and I thought it was because time had elapsed. I always believed time would help him begin to heal."

The Commander offered Steve some coffee, and then continued. "One day the chaplain came to talk to me. He spoke to Hank regularly and realized he was finally improving. Of course, the chaplain hoped it was his talks and the Bible. Yet Hank said that was only a small part of it. He mentioned you, Steve. He said Hank told him he used to sit and talk to you regularly, and you helped him immensely. He saw life differently, full of possibilities and challenges to be overcome. He said you thought we could only see life from the way we were inside, and none of us saw it all. Therefore, he started looking inside of himself and made improvements. Then he looked for miracles, love, hope, and great things in life on the outside. By the time he left, eight months later, he was a changed man."

Steve sat listening in disbelief. He felt a lump developing in his throat. He knew a lot of guys talked to him, but they talked to everybody. One big family was the environment on this base, and everyone helped each other. Yet he knew some soldiers were quite negative and couldn't see any possibilities in life. That's when Steve would jump in and tell them what he knew and then, of course, it was up to them.

"You seem speechless, Steve. I didn't want to throw this at you except to let you know you've been a positive influence on many soldiers here. You have good leadership skills. And I'm recommending you for Officer's training. A leader with a positive philosophy like yours would be an asset to the army."

"Oh gees," Steve said in total shock. He just shook his head before he continued. "I don't know what to say. I don't. I'm not doing anything special. It'd be nice if I helped some, but--"

"It doesn't sound to me that you truly realize how many guys you've helped revise their thinking, and therefore the direction of their lives. We've all noticed the difference in

George Holland. I'm told he walks around quoting you." Steve noticed the Commander laugh. "John Freeland is another and I'm sure you're aware of him. I hope you're putting some thought into remaining in the service as a career."

"No, I haven't. I haven't thought far ahead at all. But being an officer in the army would be a good career. I just don't know yet. It certainly is an opportunity I'll consider."

"You could be utilized in many areas. You're good with people, and that means a lot."

"Thank you, Sir. I appreciate that."

"In the meantime, I wanted you to know about the recommendation to Officer's training. You'll not have any prison time on your record, but some of the earlier mischief may show up. I'm sure your good performance will offset any negative influence. Good luck in your future and continue to pass on your philosophy here. The morale on this base is quite good considering where we are. The entire operation of the base wants to thank you for your part. That's all."

Steve stood slowly, saluted, and left the Commander's office feeling he was somehow a little taller than when he'd first entered. He was being recommended for Officer's training. Jeff would be delighted. Steve noticed for some reason that the base didn't seem as dusty or smelly as it usually did.

* * *

Arriving in his barracks, Steve found they were heading out with another convoy. This one was taking personnel and supplies to Qalat, a long trip, and then returning possibly with more personnel. He took a quick minute to send Jeff an email. This was an army free-time mission and George and John would be with him. These convoys always brought back memories of the volunteer convoys all had taken.

As they packed getting ready to begin their journey, Steve was happy they'd be together again.

Steve said, "It's been a while since we had a mission together."

"Yeah, it'll be a long one. I'm glad we're together again." George said smiling.

"And we may even get in a little sightseeing this time." John seemed hopeful about that. "Sergeant said if we have time, we might visit that castle--you know, the one to do with Alexander the Great."

"Oh, yeah," George added. "I'd better be sure to take my camera."

"We're going to have a picture party when we get home," Steve commented. "And then, George you can show us all the pictures you've taken. Deal?"

"Deal. I'd like that," George said smiling at him.

Steve realized this long trip up a two lane, blacktop road would take them through sections of southern Afghanistan where the Taliban operated. He knew you always had to be watchful for anything unexpected. Running a convoy through open country was much different from operating one in a crowded city such as Kabul. Steve was familiar with the spacing of the vehicles, which would be farther apart. That always concerned him. In congested urban areas, convoy vehicles were closer together.

On this trip, Steve was gunner, as was John, but they'd be far apart as this convoy had at least thirty vehicles in it. George was somewhere in the middle as a driver. Although Steve smiled at the thought of being together with his closest buddies, in truth they'd probably never see each other, except for the end journey stop. Steve kept his eyes peeled right from the beginning because in rural areas such as the road to Qalat, the convoys drove right down the middle of the road. Keeping a lookout from the position in the middle of the road offered the best chance of avoiding and surviving roadside bombs and suicide bombers.

Steve knew the Afghan civilians were cautioned and told repeatedly they must give the right of way to military vehicles.

All of them knew that fact. He'd been told part of his job was to make sure the Afghan drivers obeyed the rules, parking their cars, trucks or buses on the shoulder of the road as the convoy passed by. Most of them did, but Steve had to watch for those who didn't. If this occurred, Humvee drivers would drive right at them, eliminating any doubt as to what the civilians should do. If that didn't work, Steve's job as gunner was to start firing warning shots.

Being his first trip to Qalat, Steve noticed signs marking the small towns along the way, Sangar, Aghajan, Bakirzai. He also saw police checkpoints distinguished by the red, green, and black national flag flying in front. Ten miles past the third checkpoint, there were two explosions in quick succession. Immediately the scouts were out. Steve was the nearest gunner. He waited. Nothing else occurred, and he realized those two explosives had misfired from an earlier attack. The convoy moved on slowly toward their goal.

When the convoy reached Qalat in fully armed vehicles, they were right in the heart of Taliban-controlled country. They passed the Bata Haizar or Castle, a 3000-year-old ruin originally built by Alexander the Great. George was heard to ask over the communications system, "Can I walk up the street and take a photo of the fortress?"

"NO WAY," was the loud and agitated reply from the sergeant. "This is a dangerous part of town here, know what I'm saying? Inside our vehicles, we're relatively safe right now, especially because we're close to the Governor's mansion. To kill someone here is considered a bad idea. We'll deliver the cargo, have lunch at the base, then drive back inside of the castle. That's the only safe way."

True to his word, after an on-base lunch that Steve thought was relatively good considering the heat, the sergeant drove up into the fortress and into history. Entering the castle walls felt strange. Steve saw the entire Qalat valley from its peak defensive position that had been held by the Ancient Greeks, the Afghans, the British, the Soviet Russians, the Taliban, and now the Americans. Steve and George walked around the area braving 120 degree heat, mosquitoes, and flies to view the ancient columns and archways and ascending the peak. He laughed seeing George in photographic glory with his little Kodak instant camera that he managed to keep with him. If there were two inches of room somewhere on George's person, the camera got that space.

"Wow, this is fantastic. My grandma will be so excited with these pictures. She loves the old countries, you know? Isn't this amazing?"

Steve loved to see George enthusiastic. It was nice he could enjoy something out here in the middle of danger.

"Yeah," Steve said, "there's a special feeling when you think you're in the same place some of the greats in history have been. I mean, I've put my own feet on the same stone steps Alexander the Great climbed. That's really something to me."

"When I get home I'm going to make a huge photo album about all my time here in Afghanistan. I've already sent the other cameras home, and grandma says most of them turned out. I love pictures. I know these aren't the best with my little Kodak, but I might get a better one when I get home."

"Hey, that could be a good profession for you. You're always talking about photo angles and the best light. Ever consider being a photographer?"

George agreed. "Maybe a wildlife one, and also I like still life. I wouldn't like to do weddings or stuff like that."

"That sounds like you, George. Still life. I can see you doing that." Steve saw George nod approvingly.

"Really, Steve? I'd like that. I'll have to think about that."

Just then, everyone was ordered to get their equipment ready and enter their armored vehicles for the trip back to Camp Phoenix. This was done quickly, and as they were about to leave, a last-minute request was made to escort one American civilian back to the U.S. Embassy in Kabul. Soon they were on their way home with one added passenger.

Everyone was diligent on the way back. There was never time to relax anywhere in Afghanistan unless you were on your own base and someone else was in the tower watching the area.

\* \* \*

About an hour out of Qalat, three roadside bombs in quick succession halted the last half of the convoy. No direct hit was made. Awaiting further action proved futile. All was quiet. Proceeding slowly seemed to be the best course of action. No shots were fired. Again, Steve was the closest gunner. His body grew tense, but he was calm. His hands were sweating on the gun, but he remained ready. All was quiet. Everyone was listening for more action, an attack or a suicide bomber, but there was nothing. No other movement was seen, so the convoy slowly continued.

Then about two more miles down the road, a crowd of about eight men crossed the road in the middle of the convoy. They stopped in the center and proceeded to walk directly toward Steve's vehicle. They were yelling and screaming and waving their hands in the air. The driver immediately drove directly at them. They continued yelling and screaming. The men seemed oblivious to the danger. Steve fired three warning shots, which seemed to wake them up. These men moved out of the way quickly. Actually, Steve thought, they moved as quickly as could be expected for totally drunk guys who seemed to be partying.

The remainder of the trip, though long and tiring, was uneventful. Five vehicles were detouring to the U.S. Embassy in Kabul. Steve, George, and John were among them. Being in the city had the vehicles positioned closer to each other, which comforted Steve. What unnerved him was the crowd of people gathered in front of the Embassy. His mind flashed an uneasy signal. The feeling in the air was unsettling. Something isn't right, Steve thought. Communication between the five vehicles ended in a unified decision that the drop off was safe; it was a go. Steve felt more nervous than usual, even as the guards at the door of the Embassy nodded their agreement. After escorting the personnel to safety inside the Embassy, George, Steve and John headed back to their armored vehicle immediately.

All of a sudden, gunshots came out of nowhere from all directions. Steve didn't think. He simply reacted. He fired back. George and John did the same. There was immediate chaos.

"What the hell?" was all Steve got out of his mouth.

"Shit," echoed John.

Steve saw people dressed in long garb pulling guns from under their cloaks shiftily. They'd all been blindsided. He looked to his left and saw the guards out on the steps firing alongside of them, but there was no cover. All three soldiers continued firing almost aimlessly. Steve didn't even feel the first shot in the shoulder, but he heard John scream in pain as he saw him go down next to him. George kept firing, and then suddenly more soldiers were running toward him. In front, people were coming directly at them. One more shot to the shoulder and Steve went down, almost fainting. George kept firing. The next thing Steve knew, George was on top of them, bleeding. At this exact moment, many U.S. soldiers came on the scene, and the gunmen were killed instantly. Everything happened in less than twenty seconds, but it seemed much longer.

After the dust cleared and the situation was secure again, soldiers tended to the wounded. John had passed out and was unconscious. Steve recovered only to find George still on top of them both.

"Hey, buddy, we're okay now. It's over," Steve said shakily.

But he got no response from George.

Again he tried and said, "Hey, George, George. It's okay now."

There was only a prophetic groan. Then Steve looked at George's face. He felt fury and plausible rage entering his body. He shook off his own pain to move and get a better look at him. George had been shot twice in the back. Steve screamed for help, and the guards were immediately screaming for the medics.

"He's not going to make it," they yelled louder and louder. "Medic, Medic, over here, over here. WE NEED YOU NOW."

"Look, Look," one guard noticed. "He's trying to say something."

Then they screamed aloud, "WHO'S STEVE? WHO'S STEVE? This soldier is asking for Steve."

"THAT'S ME," yelled Steve, as best he could with tremor and pain in his voice.

"You've got to know throwing his body over you like that probably saved your life and your other buddy here. He was shot in the hand and couldn't fire anymore. That's all he could do to help you."

They all helped move his body so George could see Steve's face.

"Steve ... Steve," said George, stuttering his name slowly and unevenly.

Steve held his head firmly and looked into the bravest face he'd ever known.

"Love you brother, Steve." His breathing was uneasy, and his voice shaky and labored.

"Love you, too, George. Hang in there, buddy, the medics are coming."

"No, no. Won't...make...it." George hesitated between his words. Yet he seemed calm and peaceful to Steve. "But...tell them. Okay?"

"Tell them what, George?" For Steve, time was standing still. "What do you want me to tell?"

"Everybody...About...the Excellence. Okay? Tell them... excellence."

"Oh my God, George," Steve said, crying himself, shaking and sobbing.

"I'm...not scared...Steve. There's... out there. You taught me." George's voice was getting weaker and weaker, and his breathing wasn't good. Steve couldn't understand all of his words.

"What'll I do without you?"

"I'll...always...be...around you somewhere. Just...don't forget...me."

"I could never forget you, George. You're the bravest."

And with a satisfied smile on his face, George took his last breath and left Steve as well as an awakened John speechless, in shock and disbelief. The medics took his body off Steve while he still held onto his hand. Steve found it hard to let go. Both of them were being taken inside the Embassy on makeshift cots for stabilization.

# CHAPTER XVIII

Jeff fought gloomy feelings most of the morning. Darn, he thought, this was his special time to study. He was close to mid-terms and wanted good grades. He laughed as he remembered how his friends teased him about being a fanatic about his grades and his job as Junior Advisor. They didn't get it. How could they, he thought? They hadn't been there.

"Psst, Jeff, Mr. Edmond wants to see you in his office."

"Oh, okay, I'll be right there."

Jeff shrugged off this request as routine. His concentration wasn't at its best, anyway.

Entering the director's office, Jeff immediately noticed an unusually troubled expression on his face. He immediately remembered the worrisome thoughts clouding his mind earlier.

Mr. Edmond got right to the point. "Sit down, Jeff. I want to tell you straight out Steve Johnson is okay, but he was in a bad situation at the U.S. Embassy in Kabul. A few of the soldiers were shot and Steve was one of them. They assured me he'll be okay." Jeff saw Mr. Edmond flinch with the obvious distressing news. He continued, "He received two gunshots to the left side, one in the shoulder and one further down. Although this is not to be taken lightly, he's expected to recover totally."

Jeff sat there staring in space, feeling numb. It was never totally unexpected that Steve could get hurt. He'd told Jeff he hoped it wouldn't happen. But if it did, he didn't want to be maimed for life.

"He's going to be okay, right?" Jeff asked. "Will he get use of his arm and shoulder again?" He shifted forward in his chair and his body automatically took on normal tenseness.

"I don't know more than I've told you. From what they said, he should make a full recovery in time. He had two gunshot wounds. One was fairly close to his lung. But his lung wasn't hit, so the prognosis is good."

"Wow, I don't know how I feel right now, but I'm glad he'll be okay. Where's he now?"

"He's being taken to a U.S. Military Hospital in Germany for immediate surgery and treatment--it's called Landstuhl Regional. When asked who they should contact for him, he said his brother and named you."

Even in dire times such as these that comment brought a big grin along with some unrelenting tears to Jeff's face. Feeling a little embarrassed, he quickly wiped them away and looked down at the floor in an awkward moment.

"I shed some tears, too, Jeff. Steve's a great guy."

"I know, Mr. Edmond. I'm so glad he'll be okay."

"Okay, good. He'll be allowed to call you later on, and he left a message for you." Mr. Edmond looked down at the paper that contained his notes. "Jeff. Don't you dare worry. It'll send out the wrong vibrations. I'll be fine. I'll call as soon as I can. Love, Steve."

Jeff had to laugh. He acknowledged good vibrations were definitely in order.

"I'm not going to pretend I understand that entire message, but some of it I do. You seem to be okay. Are you? I know you've got a lot of studying this weekend with mid-terms soon, but I felt I shouldn't delay telling you."

"Of course not. You couldn't delay this message. I'll be okay. In fact, I'll always be okay. And so will Steve."

"I think you boys are onto something. I'd noticed things about you and Steve even before he left here. Although Steve took a winding detour to somewhere, he's been back on track since he joined the army. I've gotten reports, and the army is proud of his service record and also of how he helps his fellow soldiers."

"He recently got recommended for Officer's Training. Did you hear about that?"

"No, I hadn't heard." Mr. Edmond leaned back in his chair with a look of satisfaction. "Well, isn't that something? That boy is going to be okay. He certainly is going to be okay," said Mr. Edmond reflectively and thoughtfully, yet obviously proud.

Back in his room, Jeff knew some great feeling was trying to come through to reassure him. He felt it. He was anxious to talk to Steve and be reassured his friend would be okay. Yet he knew his job was to send out positive vibrations into the atmosphere. This he could do easily now. Knowing Steve was on his way to Germany was a comfort. He'd be in a good hospital, and that helped anchor his feelings. He wished he could be there. He lay back on his firm bed, stretching out his legs that had become longer in the last year, and tried to remember everything about Steve.

* * *

Steve remained in Germany for over a month. His intensive care was longer than expected since the two bullets from his wounds had proved more complex in removing than anticipated. The bullet close to his lung area caused him trouble breathing on occasion. He felt scared at times. Improvement was slow and he was impatient.

Yet Steve knew he was lucky. He often thought of George. That was one fact he still had trouble accepting. The phrase, "Greater love hath no man--" kept crossing his mind. Someday he'd see George again. It was as George had said, "I'll always be around," and sometimes Steve could genuinely feel George's presence next to him. It was mystifying and disconcerting when it first began, but later it felt more comfortable.

Steve heard John ended up at Landstuhl Regional Medical Center too, although in a completely different area. John had received a gunshot wound to his left leg, directly in the tibia, but also affecting the fibula bone below his knee. Both bones had shattered and fractured most of the way down his leg, causing even his ankle to encounter weakness and infirmity. He had several surgeries in his future.

After three weeks, Steve surprised John by wheeling into his room unexpectedly.

"God, it's great to see you. How're you doing?" asked John.

"By the looks of it, probably better than you," said Steve. "At least I don't have nearly as many contraptions in my room." Steve heard John laughing as he looked at all of the traction and mobile apparatus needed for him to mend.

"Yeah, they keep me pretty tied down most of the time. Finally they believe my leg has a good chance for complete recovery. Still, I've got at least five more surgeries in the next few years."

"Wow, no kidding. At least you're going to be okay."

"Yeah, I am."

There was a silence in the room as if a door had shut insulating them from the outside. Both looked at each other as their bodies reflected their memories.

"You know, Steve, I think back and can't believe we used to call him Nervous George. I mean, he ended up being the bravest of us all. I mean--" and his voice trailed off, leaving the end of his tearful thoughts somewhere in the air.

"I know. I agree. Who'd have known? I wish the guys from boot camp would know about George and how he turned out. You never know about a person."

"Yeah. I've written off a lot of people in the first five minutes. Actually, George was one of them, I'm ashamed to say."

"Listen, John, we all have. We've all come short of the glory."

Steve saw agreement in John's face.

"God, don't we have a lot to learn?" said Steve. "Most of the time I feel like I don't know anything."

"I feel you know a lot, Steve. You got me thinking in a better way."

"The potential inside every one of us is in the realm of unbelievable, but we don't believe in ourselves enough. Back in my young school days when I was forced to read the Bible," said Steve, stopping and smirking for effect, "I liked a passage in Mark that said, 'Anything you ask, believing you have received it, you shall receive it."

"Sure, I've heard that one, but it seemed superficial to me." John replied.

"Not really. I thought so, too, for years. Then I paid attention to the tenses of the verbs. Look what Jesus said, believe you receive it and you shall receive it."

"Yeah, so?"

"Well the point is you must believe first. I think most people, me included, are in 'hope' and not in 'belief,' if you know what I mean."

"Not sure I understand, Steve."

"Okay, Jesus says first you believe, and then you receive. Most people want to see it first, and then they'll believe. Then where's the faith? Faith is believing something before it happens. Like if you ask for rain, and you really believe and have faith it'll rain, then when you leave the house you'd better take your umbrella. And that's true, even, and especially if there's absolutely no sign of rain. Get it?"

"Oh, yeah," said John,

Steve noticed John looking at him for more clues.

"I think I know what you mean. Otherwise you're only hoping it'll rain. Yeah, I think I usually just hope when I ask for things."

"Most of us do, John. Hope is good, too, but faith gets results. To what I understand, the universal intelligence has no preference. What you believe and put into it, is what you'll get back."

"Hmmm. That does leave a question for me. Did George want to die saving us like that?"

"I don't think he had time to think; he just reacted."

At that moment, a quite attractive young blonde nurse with appealing attributes walked in carrying a tray in her hand.

"Hi, John. It's your needle time. Which side do you want it in this time?"

Steve saw John blush a little. "I don't care. By now, they're both sore."

"I could leave," said Steve. Then attempting to shock the nurse added, "but we've taken showers together."

Not to be outdone, the nurse added, "You must be Steve, the one with the quick wit and great philosophy."

"Gees, I guess that's me." Steve was showing embarrassment. Then he asked both of them. "Do you want me to roll out for a minute?"

"That's up to John. Do you want a private session or can your friend stay?"

Both were laughing. She's a great nurse, thought Steve.

"Okay, you two, I hurt when I laugh." Steve said, trying to hold it in.

John got his shot.

"Gees, John, you didn't even cry. Good for you."

"That's enough, Steve, or I have a very funny story to tell you."

"Okay, I give up."

"Well I think you guys are doing quite well. Glad to see that. Have a good day."

As she left, both of the guys were watching her. She turned at the door and said, "Not too bad, right?"

"Pretty good, pretty good," they answered together, laughing.

Steve said, "Gees, you've got a cool nurse there."

"Yeah, she is," admitted John. "The others aren't bad either. How are yours?"

"I must admit, they're really good. But not quite as cute." Steve said, "I'd better roll on home or they'll come looking. I'll probably stop by again tomorrow. I miss seeing you every day."

* * *

It was several days later when Steve managed to return.

"You could tell time better in the army," John teased.

Steve laughingly replied, "Yeah, but here my time's not my own. They put me in therapy already for my shoulder. It was supposed to be tender and mild. Just a light beginning. they said. Eh Gads. It was tough. And I was exhausted. I slept forever."

"How's that shoulder, Steve?"

Steve appreciated John's concern.

"It's going to be okay in time. That's the good news, but I have a lot of therapy ahead, and possibly more surgery. They're trying to keep my muscles supple. That's how they can tell what they need to add to my muscle tissues."

John said, "The body is so complicated, isn't it? But it does sound like you'll be okay."

"Yep," said Steve, "they all say it'll be good as new. I couldn't ask for more."

A new nurse came in asking about snacks and juices. Steve was offered some, too. As she left Steve said, "Gees, John, you've got all the good looking nurses. That one's a cutie. When you're alone, do they get more personal?"

Steve was definitely interested.

"No, they're usually professional, but sometimes they stay and talk for a few minutes. Most are pretty caring and interested in what we went through."

"Yeah, mine have asked a few questions, too. Not too many, but enough to show concern."

"So you've got a few nice ones, too."

Steve noticed John looked eager for his response.

"Yeah, you don't have a monopoly," he joked. Steve suddenly felt downhearted. "You know John, I'm glad we all got close at Camp Phoenix. George was glad he finally had friends. He once told me he was happy there. Imagine that. Here's a soldier stationed in Afghanistan on a dirty and stinky base, in constant danger, thousands of miles away from home and everything he knows, and he's okay with that. He's enduring 120 degree heat on most days and cold winters, and he tells me this was one of the happiest times of his life. Go figure that. Can you?"

"Yeah, well, after we talked some, I was beginning to like Camp Phoenix, too. I thought you did, too, Steve."

"I did, and that's what I mean. George had a tough childhood, too. Yet life is just a learning process, something like a school, and you have to pass one grade to get to the next. He'd finally gotten comfortable with people. For him, that was major. Another thing is that George was willing to learn. Some aren't, you know? But hadn't he changed remarkably already? I used to love to watch him interact with the other soldiers; he sure could hold his own. He had a kind and empathic heart. I don't think he'd ever have lost that."

"I'll never forget George. I wish I'd been conscious. When I was hit and went down, I apparently hit my head on those cement steps, and I was out. You told me he said he wasn't afraid."

Steve nodded. "Can you believe it? I kept telling him to hang on because the medics were coming, and he calmed me down and said, 'It's okay, I know I'm not going to make it.'" Steve had tears.

"At least, he had a friend nearby when he passed. I'm sure that helped. I know you were his favorite person in this entire world."

"I feel now that it's a burden in a way, but a wonderful burden. The last thing he said to me was, 'Don't forget me,' as if I ever could. I told him I could never forget him and I didn't know what I'd do without him. He said, 'I'll always be around.' I'm going to make sure he's never forgotten."

Silence overtook them. After a few moments, John was the first to speak. "I talked to my dad a few days ago. I heard he tried to call a few times, but I was always sedated after surgery." John seemed hurt. "Honestly, I thought at least my dad or maybe my mom, too, would come over to Germany to be with me. They've both been to Germany before, but they aren't coming. Dad said mom is too emotional right now, and dad's schedule is just frantic."

"That's too bad," said Steve.

John continued. "Maybe it's not too bad. Once, I'd have been furious with them. Other times I'd have gone into a tantrum about poor me and why didn't they act like good parents. Now I feel differently. I've learned from you and now I think maybe they're doing the best they can. Just because other parents might have rushed to the bedside of some of the soldiers here, it doesn't mean it's best for everyone. I look at you, and you're not only satisfied, but looking to the future. You don't seem to take yourself too seriously, and you don't have anyone who's rushed here for you."

"I guess I'm more used to it than some."

"Maybe some like me get too dependent on people. Anyway, I talked nice to my dad, who ended up telling me he thought I'd be angry. See how funny life is? He told me they'd see me the first chance they got. That was a surprise. Now I'm standing more on my own, not needing them, and then they start coming around. That's not why I did it, but I do see a connection."

"Remember George? He finally realized he didn't need anyone else because he was a total and complete system himself. Then people started coming around. Everyone needs to know how to be alone and not lonely, how to be one and be enough."

"I'm glad we became friends, Steve, and I'm thankful for what I've learned from you. I have a way to go, but like you always say, you can't reach the top of the mountain unless you start to climb."

Steve laughed. "I keep getting more of those little pearls every day."

"You should write them down. I'll bet a lot of people would profit. I did."

"That's what George said. He said I should tell everyone about the excellence. He didn't get his entire statement out, but I knew what he meant. Remember, whenever I said something to him that helped, he'd say to me, 'that's excellent, Steve.'"

"Yeah, I do. He was always saying that. And maybe that's what you should do."

"Maybe I will. Maybe I will." Steve felt in his own world for a minute. Then, he remembered something. "Oh, I finally got my letter back."

"Huh? What letter?" asked John, confused.

"Remember, I always carried around that letter from the little kid back at the orphanage? Well, my shirt was all bloody so they threw it away, and I bugged everyone to find it and get my letter." Steve said, laughing.

"Oh Yeah, I remember that little note you carried around. And they found it?"

"They sure did. And guess what? There's a bullet hole in the top corner of it. One of my prized possessions is just a little more significant now."

"It sure is. That's great."

# CHAPTER XIX

Less than three months and two operations after Steve had arrived in Germany, he  headed for Walter Reed Medical Center in Washington, D. C. This was a hospital he'd only heard about and never thought would be his home. But this was where his final recuperation would take place. He felt grateful.

Within two weeks, Steve was able to put through a call to Jeff.

"Are you okay? Are you really doing alright?" was Jeff's first demanding question.

Steve felt thankful for a caring brother. "I'm doing fine and improving every day. I had another surgery last week because they keep trying to attach some extra something to the muscles of my left shoulder. It's supposed to help it gain strength. I think all surgeries are finally behind me, but I've got lots of therapy ahead. And how are you? You must be getting close to graduating from high school. I don't think I'm going to make it."

Steve loved the enthusiasm he heard from Jeff.

"You're healing, and that's the greatest present. As far as graduation, it's a few months away. Ross Inglewood will get the top honor student award. I'm getting an award, too. Guess in what subject?"

"History. It's got to be history," said Steve, who heard himself laughing.

"Of course. I got the best grade on my term paper. I wrote about Thomas Jefferson from a unique perspective, and the teachers liked it. Can you believe that? I'm getting an award. And I beat Ross. History's the only place I'd even have a chance. Hey, I suppose no Officer's training now, but won't you get an medal for being wounded in battle?"

"Yeah, I will--later. But there'll be mention of the recommendation in my discharge papers. Imagine you and me getting recognition awards. Who'd have thought?" Steve could feel Jeff's agreement.

"Actually we would have thought, wouldn't we? We always knew what we could do."

"Well, you always knew, Jeff. I found out a bit later."

"I don't think so, Steve. You always knew inside, where it counts."

"Maybe so. Too bad I had to take some detours. But that was my method of learning."

"How are you handling the loss of George?"

Steve was silent for a moment, then said, "It's hard. John and I talked a lot in Germany. He said he couldn't believe we'd ever called him Nervous George. You can never tell about people. Only God knows what's in their hearts and all the potential that's there."

Jeff said something that surprised Steve. "I've never heard you refer to God so much. You always preferred the Universal Intelligence or the Supreme Being, and I know it's all the same thing. But you never said God very much."

"It's all the same thing, but you're right. I think the word God had bad memories for me. Now I could shout it from the rooftops because whatever you want to call Him, He's everything." Steve joked, "But I still use a lot of His nicknames."

Jeff said, "That's great. I've been working with Ross because he catches ideas differently. He loves the mystery of the mind, and one of the reasons is he's on even par with everyone else. "

"I can't wait to meet him. The three of us should have great meetings of the mind. Hopefully, John will join us, when his leg heals."

There was an interruption at Steve's end of the line. Jeff thought they'd been disconnected. But then Steve returned.

"I've only got a few more minutes. Then I've got more shoulder therapy, but the therapist is quite cute."

He heard Jeff laugh.

"That should make everything easier," Jeff offered.

"It does help" answered Steve. "You know in time I'm going to be leaving here and heading for Pennsylvania."

"When? When do you think you'll come here?"

"Not sure when. But I have a choice of getting medically discharged now or hanging in there until I'm twenty-one. I'm staying in until twenty-one because that was the deal. I mean to finish my term of service. I can't do a lot of hard work but they're going to get me some kind of desk job at the Tobyhanna Army Depot. Can you believe it? Have you ever seen it? It's at the edge of the Pocono Mountains. I'll only be about twenty minutes from Scranton."

"That's great. We'll be close then."

"By fall, I want to start some college work." Steve heard Jeff laugh. "I knew you'd like that."

"I hope you go to University of Scranton with me."

"Well, not yet. I'll have to do classes online at first. I can't carry backpacks or sit for too long. Maybe by next year, who knows? It'll depend on my health."

"If you need help, we've got Ross. Got any ideas for your major?"

"No, I keep changing my mind. I think when I start in classes I'll get some ideas. I wanted to do some coaching, but now I can't. I think I'd like to do some counseling though. Hopefully my life has given me some insight. What about you?"

"I'm thinking of going into teaching."

"History, right?" Steve waited for the confirmation from Jeff.

"Absolutely. But maybe research, too. I was thinking of doing some counseling, too, on the side. Go figure about us."

Steve felt they might end up as a team again. Maybe a counseling clinic. "What about Ross? I'm sure he has many choices."

"He vacillates but some big companies have been scouting around him for over two years now. Imagine, he's not even officially in college until September. They wanted him to skip Grade 12 but he said he wanted to stay back with some of his friends. That was more important than moving quickly through universities, because that'll definitely come in time."

"Yeah, I'm sure he'll move fast when he officially starts."

* * *

Jeff was quiet for a few minutes. Steve heard him stutter before he began talking again. His friend was trying to find the right words.

"I've got something important to tell you, Steve. But I want you to know first that I'm not huffing and puffing on this, but it's just a thought. I've told Ross about my life, you know, about being snatched and all. I wanted his perspective because he's so connected."

"Yes, good idea. What'd he say?"

"He listened. I told him I knew it wasn't possible to find my parents. Yet, I had always dreamed that it would be nice if I could let them know that I turned out okay, and I could find out where I got my brown hair and why I'm six foot one."

"Six foot one? You're six foot one, and you haven't even stopped growing." Steve heard himself sounding envious. "I'm only five foot eleven."

"No kidding. I've always looked up to you, Steve, and I promise I still will."

Steve laughed and loved the memories.

"Anyway, Ross looked at me and said, 'What do you mean, it's impossible to find them?'"

Jeff continued, "I mentioned to him the police had tried at the time with pictures of me on TV, commercials, and posters, but there were no clues. I told him it was just a dream of mine anyway. And do you know what? Ross said one word to me that changed everything."

"God, don't keep me in suspense. What was the word?"

"DNA."

"DNA? Oh, Yeah. But isn't that just for criminals and if you happen to be arrested, you'd be on record?"

"Yes, right now, that's true. But Ross said he has an idea for a project in his first year of college. He wants to do some background work now ... yet he's thinking of starting a database for missing children and their parents. It gets complicated. I'm heading up to Yale with him this weekend. He's got a few helpers and one Professor on board. They're hoping to get a Federal grant, so everything has to be done by the book. I'm to give my DNA sample. They want to use me as a test case." Jeff was laughing.

"Wow, that's exciting," said Steve.

"Yeah. They have to get the police involved and other agencies. Law enforcement will know which parents lost children and how to contact them for their DNA. Then I give my sample DNA and they create this database and start searching. It'll be a long process, but some agencies have already okayed it. They believe most parents would jump at this kind of chance. I'm willing, and I love Ross' enthusiasm, but I can't put my heart and soul into it. I must remain somewhat detached. If nothing happens for me, I can't let it destroy me.

"Yeah. But you never know Jeff. We'll both start putting positive vibes out there. A lot of others could benefit, too."

Jeff sounded encouraged. Steve picked that up right away. He couldn't imagine what being snatched must feel like.

Steve had one more thing to mention. "Remember I told you that George asked me to pass on the Excellence? I think there must be a way for that, too. I'm hoping we could all work on it together. After all, it's our philosophy, not just mine. What do you think?"

"Sure, and maybe Ross and John could help, too."

"Gees Jeff, I think I've used up my phone minutes for the next month," joked Steve. "I'll probably be emailing you from now on. I'll let you know the moment I find out when I'm coming back. After all, we only have one lifetime and we have a lot of work to do."

"Love you, little brother."

"Bye, Big brother."

* * *

Yale was impressive and Jeff had never been to this part of the country. Ross had visited several times and since he'd chosen to attend Yale, the professors were happy to assist him. Ross showed Jeff, Woolsey Hall, and the Harkness Tower. The scenic tour was short, but fun.

Arriving inside the lab building, Ross and Steve had to be buzzed into the lab area. Much confidential work was being done and some of it was under lock and key. Jeff felt impressed. Within minutes, an older man in a white lab coat came toward them.

"Hi Ross. Was hoping you'd make it today. I'm anxious to get started, how about you?"

"Me, too, Professor Hargrove. And this is our test case, Jeffrey Barnes. Sorry, Jeff, but everyone will call you the test case, probably more than your name."

Jeff internalized that agenda quickly. It seemed like a small price to pay for a chance to discover his past. He nodded agreeably.

Professor Hargrove added, "Ross is right. Don't take it personal, okay? Some of the language used in here is very formal. Are you into this forensic study?"

"No, I'm not," answered Jeff. "But I sure am interested. Ross has taken me into some areas of study I'd never thought of and understand even less. I don't want to show my ignorance but I'm not a high I.Q. like Ross."

"Few are like Ross," said the professor, smiling. "He's very special to all of us, but doesn't like to hear that. Don't worry about feeling ignorant, I've got to tell you some of my students confuse me a lot, Ross, more than most. But it's wonderful to be around these brains. Amazing, actually."

"I'm going to let Ross show you around this lab and explain a few things and then we'll get to work. We'll only need a DNA sample and ask you some questions for the record. You're okay discussing this part of your life?"

"Yes, I am. I kept it a secret for years, but now I realize there are others out there. If I can be a type of pioneer in this study, I'd love that."

"Okay, see you later. I'm sure Penny is due soon and other students are excited about this work but just won't be here today."

"Right, thanks Professor Hargrove," said Ross

"Nice to meet you," added Jeff

"Good to meet you, too. Life has no guarantees, Jeff. But science has come a long way. We all believe we can create a great system here."

Jeff followed Ross around the lab and found out where and how they'd keep the DNA samples. And they'd be under lock and key. Only those working on the project would have access. After a quick tour, Jeff had another question.

"Who's this Penny? I think you got a sparkle in your eye," teased Jeff.

"Yeah, we really click. She's almost eighteen and she'll be starting in the fall, too. Her specialty is Forensic Science. That's how I met her. She's smart and her life's been a lot like mine so we can relate."

"You mean she has a high I.Q. like you?" asked Jeff, feeling amazed.

"Oh yeah, She's competition for me anytime in a lot of subjects. It's great to know someone like her. She understands where I'm coming from and where I've been. Do you know what I mean?"

Jeanne Drouillard

"I think I do. The two of you can see the world from similar viewpoints. Not that the rest of us are stupid, but you two would see a very sophisticated viewpoint of life."

"That's one of the things I've always admired about you, Jeff. You're not jealous; you're willing to learn. And you realize we're all at different points in our lives. Some are higher; some lower and you're okay with that. I'm only talking about I.Q. here. You're great with our thought project."

"You're always so careful not to offend me," said Jeff admiringly. "I understand and I'm okay."

"Here comes the professor, I think we can take your DNA sample now. We need to work in teams so everything can be documented and have a back up. Federal grants are very complicated."

Then the DNA samples were taken. Just a cotton swab inside Jeff's mouth. They proceeded to complete the test when the phone rang. Ross took it. It was Penny and she needed to be buzzed in.

"Jeff, can you go get her? Neither one of us can leave."

"How will I know her?" asked Jeff.

Ross was about to answer and then he looked at the professor and they both grinned.

"Jeff, I've got to tell you. You'll know her immediately."

Jeff left the lab feeling a little frustrated. Why couldn't they say more? He heard his own grumbling. How was he supposed to be sure who she was? He'd have to walk up to people and ask, 'are you Penny?' He knew he was going to feel stupid.

Getting down to the entrance, he realized there were several people waiting to enter. Gees, he thought, this is embarrassing. Then in a flash, he saw this girl standing there and Jeff knew immediately. He had to fight hard not to laugh out loud. This was hilarious, he thought. Ross was right, he knew her right away. In front of him stood this attractive girl with bright red hair and horn-rimmed glasses--the female version of Ross.

"Hi Penny, I'm Jeffrey Barnes. It's good to meet you."

"Good to meet you, too. I can tell you want to laugh and it's okay. I get the idea Ross didn't tell you how much we look alike."

"No, he didn't. Neither did Professor Hargrove. They just said, Go down and get her. Don't worry, you'll know her."

He saw Penny laugh and then he joined the laughter. "Ross is so hysterical at times. I don't think people realize his great sense of humor."

"I always have and today, more than ever."

"Well, Jeff, Ross has told me some wonderful things about you. It meant a lot to him when you befriended him in high school. I can appreciate his dilemma. I've had my critics, too. He's told me about your thought project. That's so interesting. Ross keeps me up to date."

"I'm glad you're interested, too. We want to do something with all this later, after we're finished with school. I'm sure you'd be welcome."

"That's a thought. I'll certainly keep my hand in."

By this time they reentered the lab. The professor and Ross waited for Jeff's comment.

"You were both right. I knew her immediately."

They all laughed and paused in their work.

Jeff answered more questions than he thought they'd ask. They delved into his background in great detail, all necessary for the experiment. After they were finished, Penny, Ross and Jeff went out for dinner.

Ross was excited. "I'm glad we've finally got this started. It'll take a while, at least a couple of months to get things organized, right Penny?"

"At least. Then, the way I see it, we'll start getting samples from all over the country. Most snatched kids are taken a distance away so you could be from anywhere and I'd add Canada, too. But you don't seem European, although we can't rule that out yet. With the age of the man who had you,

I'd guess he probably didn't have any elaborate plan. So I'm guessing you're not from Europe or South America."

Jeff sat there listening with interest to the suggestions and possibilities discussed. More came up every few minutes.

"This is a new science so the probabilities aren't all in the place yet," said Ross. "But Penny and I've decided it would make the most sense to start with United States. Even crossing the border from Canada could have presented difficulties. The lower forty-eight states will be our first priority."

"That's why you're considered a test case, Jeff," Penny added thoughtfully. "Later we'll discover patterns people take when they snatch children. There are always exceptions, of course, but a basic pattern will emerge. For now, we'll be heading in a lot of directions trying to discover this pattern."

Jeff felt Penny was quite detached, professional and proficient. She had helped him to realize emotions didn't have any place in this experiment. Your thoughts had to remain focused and persistent. These two will make a good duo. Jeff felt confident in their abilities.

* * *

Arriving home later that evening, Ross needed to make a few things clear to Jeff.

"This isn't going to be a short experiment. This will be a long, on-going, continuous project. We don't expect it to end. I guess what I need to say is later, when we start adding others, it could get tricky. Others may get matched first. You're not to get discouraged, understand? A DNA match could come at any time. We don't know when; no one does."

"Oh, someone knows, Ross. That universal intelligence knows it all. I've got to start putting in positive vibes."

"Gees, Jeff, you're right. See, I need you to remind me. Sometimes, when I get too scientific, I forget the God factor. You know many scientists don't even believe. Imagine working with all these scientific facts and not believing. Crazy to me. You're good for me. Don't ever let me get too scientific, okay?"

"Okay, and you know I don't believe in coincidences. But there will be a time for me, Ross, I feel sure of that."

"I'll bet you're right, Jeff. Your time will come."

# CHAPTER XX

Noticing Jeff looking out the window from the entrance of the restaurant, Steve approached him.

"Hi Jeff, I thought I might find you over here."

"Steve, you're looking good. How're you feeling?"

"Pretty good. My shoulder's still healing, but it feels good."

"That's great."

Steve looked at Jeff who was looking down at him. He got a perplexed feeling, thinking the situation should be reversed.

"You know, Jeff, I can't get used to looking up to you. How tall are you now?"

"I'm now 6'2", and I haven't grown in almost a year. I think this is it for me."

"I stopped at 5'11" and since I'm 22, I know it's over for me. Somehow I never thought you'd be taller than me."

"But I'm still your little brother." said Jeff in a teasing way.

Steve laughed.

"Is Ross here yet?"

"No, he told me he might be a little late. Want to grab a table now?"

"Sure."

They'd only received the menus when they heard a familiar voice.

"Hi guys. I see you haven't started eating yet, so I'm not too late. I was caught up in talking to this professor at Scranton on theories of why electricity works. You know how I get caught up in things. Steve, you're looking great. Shoulder okay?"

"Yep, it's fine. How are you, Ross? You're looking pretty cool these days."

Steve noticed a surprisingly shy yet appreciative smile cross Ross's face. He'd always been teased about his bright red hair and horn-rimmed glasses, but as he grew older his hair color finally toned down to a more acceptable darker auburn shade. And he wore contacts most of time. Steve liked his satisfied look and had to admit Ross was now one good looking boy.

"How do you like your contacts?" asked Jeff.

"I'm getting used to them. It's been about two months. But for all the work I do during the day at school, I still use my old trustworthy horn-rimmed glasses, which still seem to be part of my persona."

"Ross, what are you, sophomore, junior, senior? I don't understand how they keep track of you at Yale?" asked Steve.

"It's a little different," answered Ross, smiling. "I'm on a special path. They pull me in where they think I'll grow best. I get units of credit for all I do. Remember, I was taking college classes in high school. I'll be adding everything up at the end of this year, so then I'll know exactly where I'm at. Everything will fall into place at that time."

"Do you like it that way?" asked Steve.

"Actually, I do. At least I'm not bored. Sometimes I think they pull me out of one area when they think I'm too close to knowing enough to bore me and put me somewhere else. That's good for me. These are all suggestions on their part as I have the final word. But they present me with many opportunities. How about you, Steve, have you decided on a major yet?"

"Well, I'm thinking of counseling," Steve said, "but I'd like to do work with the power of thoughts. If I can put those two things into a way to earn a living, I'm in."

"Aren't you a Junior at Scranton?" asked Ross.

"No, no, I'm only starting. I have a few credits to my name, but that's all. Jeff here is one year ahead of me, aren't you?" Steve saw Jeff nod in agreement. "But you know, this has been good for me. I still needed to get my thoughts and ideas together, and as my body was healing, so was the inner part of me. I must admit there was a certain amount of mental healing needed from being in the war. That does something to you."

"You've learned to trust that Divine Spark within yourself," Jeff said, "so there's no way you'll fail."

"Failure is relative anyway," Steve said. "The world may look at someone as a failure and yet he may be where he's best suited. We don't all need to be the richest or smartest or best looking or most knowledgeable in the eyes of the world. The outside world doesn't see what's inside anyway. God's my only judge. Gees," Steve laughed, "since the war, I'm so philosophical." He saw Jeff smile.

"One of my major breakthroughs was when I first realized I wasn't limited," said Jeff. "When I was younger I used to get so stuck in my own problems. I had no one to help me, so I tried to imagine myself overcoming my problems and getting beyond them. I know I came across this idea quite by chance, possibly as a gift to a child desperately needing help. But I realized when I concentrated on the solutions, instead of the problems, I got help. Ideas just came to me."

Steve added, "What some people don't realize is they have this power within them. And we do, everyone of us. We've heard it, and we've talked about it. We've been lectured and bored with it, but seldom told what it is or how to contact it. The fact is we're always in contact with it. We need to believe. I was thinking we need to believe like the little ones."

"Yeah," Jeff agreed. "The little ones really have the connection."

"Which reminds me," Steve interjected a quick thought. "I'd like to try and get in touch with Michael Mason--oh, that's right, he has a new last name, right? Bouchard, isn't it?"

"Yeah, I think that's right," offered Jeff.

"Yeah. I'm going to ask Mr. Edmond if he'd get in touch with his parents to find out if I could see him. What are my chances, Jeff?"

"I don't know. You can try. Why? What's up?"

"Well, you know I told you about the letter--the one that got a bullet hole through it. Well, little Michael had said he'd pray for me every night for the rest of my life, and I feel that he must have. Anyway, I'd like him to know I carried his letter around with me. I want him to know how important it was to me. And I want to show him the letter with the bullet hole. I'm hoping it would be important to him, you know? Maybe make a good and lasting impression. I can't imagine his parents would mind. What do you think?"

"I think that's a great idea. I talk to Mr. Edmond regularly. I stay there occasionally between semesters. And I'm still a Junior Advisor. Let's meet with him together."

"Good, let's set it up for next week."

"That was quite a story. Jeff told me," said Ross.

"Yeah, quite a miracle, I'd say. How old would Michael be, about fourteen, right?"

"Umm--Yeah, about that." Jeff said as he nodded.

Steve asked, "How's that DNA project going?"

"We're progressing. No match yet. But it's only been a year. We don't even have a quarter of the country on board. It takes time. We've got about ten missing children in the data base now."

\* \* \*

Steve brought up another subject. "I wanted to mention I'm planning to get to Arkansas and visit with George's grandmother. I've been corresponding with her, and she's invited me to come. I'd met her at the boot camp graduation. I have a need to learn more about George's childhood, and I think his grandma would enjoy it. What's more I have some interesting tales to tell her about George."

"If you need company, I'll go," Jeff said immediately.

"Me, too," Ross agreed.

"I think I'd like to be down there alone this time. But later, I'd like his grandmother to get to know the two of you too. Did I tell you he got the Purple Heart and the Good Conduct Medal and is being considered for the Congressional Medal of Honor." Steve saw the proud look on their faces.

"That's so impressive. Isn't it?" said Jeff considerately.

"This time I want to spend time at George's gravesite alone. Everything happened so fast after the shooting. They took George away in one direction and I went in another. I never got to see him again. Imagine, we were the three musketeers for such a long time, then, suddenly, George was gone and John and I were separated for almost a month. That was just as painful as the other wounds."

"We'll come whenever you want us. I'd like to meet his grandma, too." Jeff said. "Where exactly is he from?"

"He's from a little place called Conway, Arkansas, which is just north of Little Rock in the center of the state. Not a big place really. George talked about some of the places he used to hang out, and I'd like to see them. I think it might help me bring some closure on the one hand and also reconnect with him."

Jeff seemed empathetic as he said, "That'd probably do you good."

"His grandma said both of you were mentioned in his letters. He was looking forward to getting together in Scranton, so I'm sure she'd like to meet you both."

"Funny how we all affect each others' lives. I didn't even know he'd even heard about me. Imagine that," reflected Ross.

"I keep remembering those last words of George. I'll never forget the peaceful look on his face. I know he must have been in tremendous pain or maybe he was in shock, but it was like he was in half a trance. He looked at me, and I'm sure he saw me but ... I don't know. Yet the last words he said was, Tell them all--tell them all. He repeated it to emphasize what he was saying. And when I asked him, tell them all about what? He kept repeating. Tell them about the excellence ... the excellence." Steve shivered at the memory. God, he thought, I could still cry. It's like I'm back there all over again.

"That must have been something," Jeff said.

"I think back when Jeff and I would talk about this stuff at the beginning. Never would I ever have imagined the last words on someone's dying breath would be to tell someone about our philosophy. Isn't that amazing?" Steve saw Jeff smile.

"Yeah, it must have affected him a great deal for that to be the last words he'd speak--spread the word," mused Ross.

* * *

Steve opened a folder he'd brought with him. "I have some important notes George's grandma sent me. I remember him writing things in this little book. It was his journal, and he always wrote his thoughts there. I just received some of the pages of his personal notes recently. It's nothing more than things I talked to him about. His grandma says she has a lot more to give me later."

"You wanted to know how to honor George's request," Jeff said, "well, why don't you write down his thoughts and create an article or a book based mainly from his notes? We could all help by adding more thoughts to it. What do you think?"

Steve liked the idea. "Yeah, I had a book in mind, but you're right, Jeff. It should come mainly from his notes. Those were his impressions, and that's what helped him. I don't have a knack for writing, but wait until you read his notes. It seems to flow so smoothly."

"We could all help," said Ross.

"Remember, Ross," Jeff said carefully, "we have to keep the language and concepts simple enough for all to understand." Steve realized Jeff was trying to be delicate.

Ross replied. "You were recently talking about how important it is to remain in a positive state of mind, Jeff, at least fifty-one percent of the time. When I think something positive about a person, I know this is also related to a radiation of electro-magnetic waves. It's also dependent upon what wavelength the receiver is on, and there are also amplifiers as well as transmitters which could cause interference. Do you think this type of information would be helpful?"

Ross looked back and forth between the two of them with a curious yet eager expression on his face.

Steve felt an immediate panic. Didn't Ross get it? People wouldn't understand that kind of stuff. Hell, he didn't even understand it. He looked urgently to Jeff for help. As Steve shifted in his chair uneasily, Jeff leaned forward in an effort to clarify the situation.

"While I think your information is certainly useful, it might--," started Jeff carefully, but he was immediately interrupted by Ross.

"I can avoid using the double language, as you used to call it, Jeff. I know you told me it caused you to think about some things I'd said for days. I do understand what you're trying to do and you're trying to be sensitive to me so you don't feel you're disrespecting me. Gees, I really do appreciate the two of you."

Steve saw Ross throw out a quick yet roguish smile as he looked at them with a 'gotcha' expression on his face. Both were relieved, and Steve returned his body to a more relaxed position.

"You know, Steve," said Jeff respectfully, "our friend here from Yale is almost finished with a Masters Degree in Math and another in Physics and Philosophy. So he can and deserves to get high in his conversation whenever he chooses. But we do want to reach as many people of ordinary intelligence, like Steve and me, okay, Ross?"

"No offense taken. You know, my mom still stops me a lot and says, Get it down to my level, Ross, maybe Grade 5 or 6."

"Are you really getting degrees in both of those areas at the same time?" asked Steve.

"Yeah, but don't forget they allowed me to take college classes while I was still in high school so I wouldn't get bored. That put me ahead of the game."

Steve looked at Jeff in amazement. Ross was still unaffected by his brilliance, which made him modest and unassuming in his achievements. People could get comfortable with him, thought Steve, before they realized what he was all about.

"Okay," Steve started, "I made copies of George's notes for the two of you. There's a lot of stuff here. There are more notes coming, too, but I thought we could start with the first ones he wrote down, which are extremely basic and naïve. It's a pleasure to see him get more self-assured and sophisticated as time goes on. When I wrote in a journal, I just jotted down some little thoughts here and there. George wrote mostly in complete sentences like he was telling a story. These aren't in order so I marked them by month."

JUNE

Met a guy named Steve Johnson, and I think he may want to be friends with me. He has a wonderful way of talking about life and problems and how to make the best out of our time on earth. He's a great person to know. He has taken time to talk to me and although no one here dislikes me, most don't bother with me. That's been true most of my life and I accept it, but Steve says he wants to be my friend. I asked him and he said he thought we were friends already. I've named his philosophy "terms of excellence" since they improved Steve's life, and I plan to have them improve mine.

Idea No. 1 There seems to be a power larger than we are that we can all use to make our lives richer, more spiritual, more successful, and more content. I like that. This power isn't hard to find because it's within ourselves. Some call it the Supreme Being, Universal Mind, or God. But another way to think of it is your subconscious mind. This power has all the information any of us will ever need and it knows everything. So it seems to me Steve is telling me I have everything I need within me to become stronger and more confident and to have the courage to do and be anything I want. I do want to be a more self-assured person whom people will like. I'd like to be more like Steve--the other soldiers like him a lot. He has a confident way about him and I want to be like that.

I want my grandma to be proud of me. I know my grandma is proud of me now, but she wants me to be happier and she says, "Just know you're somebody important, too." I'm going to ask Steve how I contact this power within. Maybe I just talk to myself and my power inside will listen. Or maybe I just sit still and listen and that power will talk to me. Since Steve says it's always with me, maybe I can ask it for some help and sit still until I hear an answer. What a long way I have to go yet, but a few days ago, I didn't even know about this power. So at least, I must be at the beginning.

JULY

<u>More Ideas</u>I've gotten several more "terms of excellence" from Steve.

1) All of us live and exist in this mind. It's as if you're walking in and through a cloud; you're within and without the cloud at the same time. God is a spirit and is within and without you at the same time.

2) What you concentrate on you attract into your life. Just as a magnet attracts other magnets, similar thoughts attract similar thoughts.

3) God is no respecter of persons. In other words, God has no favorites--actually we're all His favorites. (It's good to know I'm a favorite of God.)

4) Evil is the result of man's thoughts, not of God.

5) The only activity of the Subconscious Mind is to manifest into reality any thought held by the conscious or subconscious mind as belief.

The above thoughts alone and together have given me so much to think about. I'm especially drawn to the second term of excellence. What you concentrate on in your life is what you bring into your life. I always remember the bad messages my dad and mom used to say to me like failure, wimp, loser, stupid, and many other bad things, and I can see now that was all I concentrated on. Therefore I brought a bad picture of myself into my life.

What I need to do is think of success, and like Steve told me one day, "If you can only remember a few successes in your life and a lot of failures, then, concentrate on those few successes all day long and don't even think about the failures." I know what he means but it isn't easy. I told him that this was hard to do, and I'll never forget what Steve said. He answered, "This isn't a little game we're playing here, George. This is for your life, your entire future life." And he's right, it isn't easy, and it isn't for the timid at heart. It's tough, but I can do it.

Steve said that when you start working on controlling your mind, don't be surprised if you get headaches and sweat beads on your forehead because the devil, I'll call him, doesn't want you to succeed and he'll fight you every step of the way. He doesn't want to lose his grip on you. So don't be surprised if every bad thing you've ever done crosses your mind at this time. It could be things that haven't crossed your mind in years, but just know it isn't a friend bringing up all the crap. It's the evil one not wanting to lose control of you. Just hang on, and when these failures cross your mind, just bless them and let them go and continue to remember the few successes you've had. Soon you'll have many more successes to think about." (I'm not sure if these are the exact words Steve used, but I know I did capture the meaning. I had to write them down quickly so I wouldn't forget them).

Everyone paused for a few minutes. They put down their copy of the notes and just looked at each other. Steve was the first one to speak.

"I didn't know I talked so much. But you know when I get started on this stuff, it's hard to stop."

"But this is great material Steve. It's the ideas we talked about as little kids, but didn't know for sure how to put into words. George has done a great job." Steve could tell Jeff was impressed.

Steve looked at Ross, who'd been unusually silent. "It's touching because you can feel the passion George had in his notes. Had he lived he would have been a great one to lecture, don't you think?"

"You're right. We'll have to remember he's here in spirit. Anyway, I've just about had enough for tonight. But I'd like you guys to read the last page. It's titled, November, 2005.

NOVEMBER, 2005

The next "term of excellence" is still one of my favorites.

(1) Every one of us sees the world from where we are. That's all we can do. Other people do the same thing. We're not all at the same point of maturity at the same time, so it's important to listen to other people and find common ground. I'll have to finish this later because we have another convoy, but I want to mention it makes a lot of sense to me. Just a quick final thought. Steve loves Emerson and he's always quoting him. The last quote he said I liked a lot, "The mass of men lead lives of quiet desperation." Isn't that sad? I've got to tell Steve to find a way to spread these "terms of excellence." Got to go.

\* \* \*

After the reading, Steve mentioned again a few of the pages of the journal were out of order and this final point was written the last day of his life. He never got back to finish his thoughts. He acknowledged George's grandma said there were many more pages in the middle of his journal. She'd send them later.

Steve was excited. The look from both Ross and Jeff was enthusiastic. George had brought up some wonderful points. He'd studied and picked up some important insights into their philosophy. Steve believed George's notes plus their own thoughts would go a long way to edge people into thinking in a more encouraging frame of mind.

And then with satisfaction, Steve had to mention to his colleagues. "Wouldn't George be surprised to know what he'd started?"

"Yeah, and so pleased," Jeff said caringly.

"I have a strong feeling George's father would be thoroughly surprised to know his George was a good little soldier after all. He was the best."

After that last comment they all just sat and stared. All were experiencing great feelings of satisfaction knowing George would be proud of what was being started. He would be thrilled he was a part of it. And he'd always be around.

\*\*\*

Jeff's mind suddenly thought back quickly over his life. He remembered his loneliness at the orphanage and his attempt to speak and listen to that image that he had of someone out there. He was always thankful for having Steve Johnson as a roommate and knew they were meant to be together and begin this philosophy that seemed to have helped people already. Yes, he thought, someone has been directing their lives and edging them in a certain direction. Steve, he knew, always wanted to help people get past their problems and into solutions. Yet, he wasn't able to do that until he figured out the pathway himself. They were both on to a universal purpose that they could accomplish in their little corner of the world. And Sister Margaret had put it as well as it could be said. Just watch and listen for the Grace, Along The Way.

Jeanne Drouillard

Grace Along the Way